LOVE and CHAOS

ELIZABETH POWERS

Copyright © 2013 Elizabeth Powers
All rights reserved.
ISBN-10: 1489538224:
ISBN-13: 978-7489538222

Cover design: Rinn Siegrist

 ONE

Emma leaned back into her overstuffed couch cushions, scratching her dog's ears and glaring at her sister. Her gorgeous, wild, free-spirited, irresponsible, and extremely irritating sister who at this moment was glaring right back at her with equal exasperation.

"You owe me," Jen stated, pointing a perfectly manicured finger in her direction.

Emma sighed. It was true. As one of his last acts before quitting his job and heading to Bali to 'find himself', Emma's beloved but completely useless travel agent had booked a flight for her into the Rochester airport, just before Thanksgiving. The only problem was that he flew her into Rochester, New York instead of Rochester, Minnesota – and there were no available flights out until after the holidays. So it was either miss Gran Jameson's homemade stuffing and pumpkin pie, or it was a 15-hour road trip in Thanksgiving traffic, if she could even find a car to rent. Emma got apoplexy just thinking about it, but her sister had been in Michigan at the time, and had cheerfully volunteered to head east and pick her up. The drive was long and the traffic was horrendous, but they made it home just in time to see their Dad attacking the turkey with his electric carving knife, and their grandmother hiding the box of Stove Top in the garbage can.

Gran had looked guilty, but rallied quickly, balancing her martini glass as she quickly closed the lid of the plastic container.

"I was too busy to make the real stuff this year," she said in her defense. "They added an extra bingo night at the Moose Lodge. And you can't tell the difference anyway," she muttered under her breath.

Emma leaned down to kiss her cheek. "Hello dear," Gran added. "Glad you could make it. Cutting it a little close this year, aren't you?"

Rolling her eyes, Emma sighed. "Don't change the subject. Please tell me you made real pumpkin pie. It's the only reason that I didn't just hunker down in a New York hotel with a well-stocked mini-bar until after Thanksgiving."

Her grandmother looked furtively toward the freezer, taking another swig of her martini.

Emma gasped. "No. You didn't! Frozen pie?"

"It's Mrs. Smith's," the old woman stated defensively. "It's the best. I even bought full-fat Cool Whip to go on top."

So while Emma's dog vacuumed the floor, eating all of the turkey morsels that were dropping from where Emma's father was slicing the bird, and while the Stove Top simmered on the burner, Emma had realized that, for the sake of a frozen pie and boxed stuffing, she now owed her sister big. She was such a fool.

And now her sister was collecting. But this wasn't a 'drive me to Minnesota' kind of a collection. It wasn't even a 'loan me a thousand bucks' kind of a thing. This was getting in the middle of a personal interaction - the kind of thing that Emma would normally fake a terminal illness to avoid.

Still, Emma owed Jen. And she knew it. Sighing, she pulled the couch pillow to her lap and leaned back. Chaos, her 2-year old lab mix, sniffed her hand suspiciously, hoping for food, but then settled onto his back for a belly rub. Emma obliged.

"OK. I know I owe you. I just think this is a really lame-brained way to collect."

"But you'll do it?" Jen asked, leaning forward with a combination of hope and suspicion in her expression.

Emma rolled her eyes. Her sister, her gorgeous, wild, free-spirited, irresponsible, and extremely irritating sister, also had an impulsive streak. And in this case, the impulsive streak had led to her 'engagement' to a very rich, very arrogant, and probably very socially maladapted man. Jen had met the man at a charity event, he had pitched her a story about needing a fake wife, and viola! She was getting married. Only now, she was clearly having second thoughts. Emma, always the sensible one, appreciated those thoughts, encouraged them even, but did not want to get in the middle of this arrangement. Still, there was the 15+ hour road trip to consider. In Thanksgiving traffic. So...

"Yeah. I'll do it. But tell me again why you can't just tell him yourself. And don't give me any crap about being scared of the man. If that were the case, you wouldn't have agreed to something so crazy to begin with."

Jen gave her a half smile. "Look. He's going to be mad. Not violently mad, but mad. And I just don't want to be there to witness it."

Emma looked over at her, sensing that something was off, but not able to put her finger on it. "Why not?" she asked shrewdly, tossing the pillow aside and leaning forward, temporarily abandoning Chaos, who rolled over and looked up at her questioningly. Sensing Emma's distraction, he skulked off to the kitchen to vacuum up any crumbs that might have magically dropped to the floor since his last investigation ten minutes earlier.

"Because. I'm happy. I want to just go be happy," Jen proclaimed, a big happy stupid grin on her face. Emma rolled her eyes again.

"And, like I said, you owe me," Jen said again, the goofy smile gone, and an intent look on her face. Again, Emma got the sense that there was something Jen wasn't telling her. But really, what could go wrong? She'd deliver the message, pass on her sympathies, and quickly leave. This wasn't an emotional thing, Emma reminded herself. It was a business deal. So how hard could this be? She sighed.

"Look, I'll do this for you. But more because I feel sorry for this guy than for any other reason," she added under her breath.

Jen looked up at her, alarmed. "Do not feel sorry for him, Emma. He will take advantage of your weakness and pounce. Why do you think I'm running the other way?" she asked.

Emma snorted. "Because you met a guy in a bar and decided you liked him better. Enough to back out on a monumentally crazy deal you made. I'm actually glad you're not going through with this, Jen, but wow. What a way to renege on a commitment. How much of a financial investment are we talking about here? Caterers, plane tickets, what?"

Jen wouldn't meet her eyes. Suddenly intensely interested in the coaster on Emma's side table, she mumbled, "He can afford it."

"Pardon?" Emma asked, only having heard mutterings that sounded like Charlie Brown's teacher.

"I said that he can afford it. Em, he's richer than Croesus! This is like pocket change to him."

"But it's the principle of the thing."

Jen shook her head. "I can't afford to have those principles, Emma. Look. He'll be fine. His whole family will be relieved beyond measure. They all hated me. His horrid mother will probably bequeath him even more money, now that his gold-digging girlfriend is out of the picture. So stop feeling sorry for him. Just tell him that I backed out, and grab my things. That's all you need to do," she added, still looking everywhere but at Emma.

"And if he refuses to even let me into his house?" she asked softly.

Jen looked up then. "He'll let you in," she said with assurance. "Believe me, he's nothing if not polite."

"What do I say if he asks where you are?"

Jen smiled tightly. "You don't know. That's why I'm not telling you. He'd get it out of you somehow. So it's better if you honestly don't have any idea. He'll believe you. Eventually," she added.

Emma shook her head. "OK. I'll go over there tomorrow morning before I go to work. I assume you'll be gone by then?"

"Oh yeah. My car is packed. I'm taking off as soon as I run a few errands and stop by to see Gran. But listen, Em. Mason goes to work really early. Better to go tomorrow evening."

Emma tossed a pillow at her sister. "Fine. I'll go tomorrow night. I'll take Chaos with me," she added, looking around for her dog, who was suspiciously quiet at the moment. She stood up and looked around the corner of her kitchen island. The dog was splayed on his back in the middle of the floor, looking longingly up at the countertop, ever hopeful. When he saw Emma, his tail began wagging, sweeping the kitchen floor in the process. Emma noted the need to get her dust mop out - Chaos was shedding again.

Jen's voice came from the living room where Emma had left her. "Don't. He hates dogs."

Oh, now that was a serious red flag, Emma thought. In fact, she wasn't sure she'd heard right. What man didn't like dogs?

Jen was still talking. "They slobber. And shed. He's kind of a perfectionist. Or neat freak. Or..."

"Oh for the love of God. So no great love for cats either, I presume."

"Nope. Part of our deal was no animals. See? No need to feel sorry for him. You can't possibly feel bad for a guy who would hate Chaos."

Emma laughed as Jen stood up and gathered up her coat and purse. "OK. So call me. Let me know you're safe and when you're coming home. I still love you, even though I think you're a nutcase."

"Right back at you," Jen grinned. "And don't worry. I wouldn't miss Thanksgiving and Gran's 'homemade' stuffing for all the world."

Emma snorted. "Ha. Funny. At least the potatoes are still real. If they switch to boxed potato flakes, I'm boycotting dinner."

Jen laughed as she headed for the door. "On the bright side, if dinner becomes inedible, there's always Chaos. We can feed him under the table like we fed Jasper when we were kids," she said. "And then go get hamburgers at Joe's."

Emma grinned, remembering many a meal when they were kids when they did exactly that. When their parents weren't looking, they would feed the parts of their dinner that they didn't want to their very large mastiff who used to lay under the table, his head facing toward their chairs. Some nights, Jasper ate two full dinners, plus his own bowl of dog food, while Emma and Jen found excuses to go outside for a while, then raced down to Joe's diner on their bikes. Ah, those were the days, she thought. Chaos should be so lucky.

Watching her sister drive away, Emma again gave thanks for the close relationship that they had. She loved Jen, crazy impulsive nature and all. She was fun. She was loving. And most of all, she was Emma's best friend, and had been since they were kids. As different as they were growing up, they were probably even more different now. Jen moved from job to job, from man to man, and just lived life to its fullest. Emma was the opposite - she had worked in only two different jobs since she graduated from law school, and dated only occasionally. And even though Emma was the younger sister, she often felt older. Considerably older. Ancient. She sighed. Ah well. Truth was, she'd miss Jen, wherever the heck she was going, and for however long she was gone.

Stepping inside and closing the door, she bent down to scritch Chaos on the head.

"It's you and me again, sweetie, at least until your Auntie Jen comes to her senses and comes home again."

Chaos looked up at her mournfully.

"I know. We love her," she said softly. "Even if she is crazy. Come on. Let's find you a treat."

The next evening, after leaving Chaos at home and in his crate with a now-empty bowl of dog-food, a now-licked-out Kong of peanut butter, and a soon-to-be-destroyed squeaky toy, Emma headed out the door.

"Momma will be back soon, sweetie. I've gotta go break a man's heart for your Auntie Jen. Sorry about the crate," she added remorsefully. "But until you stop chewing like a puppy, you're grounded."

Chaos looked up at her disdainfully, then resumed chewing on his toy. Emma let herself out. Plugging the address Jen gave her into her GPS, she noted that she was headed for the *other* side of town. The part of town where a one-bedroom efficiency apartment cost more than her 2-bedroom house. And while Emma made decent money and could have afforded something small in the other neighborhood, she had different priorities. Plus, she didn't want to have to worry about Chaos doing his business on the perfectly manicured lawns that made up the ritzy area. No, she and her dog were better off where they were. Besides, she liked living with her sister. And she liked being close to her parents and her grandmother. She always knew where she could get a good martini.

Pulling up in front of the address that Jen had given her, Emma looked up in a combination of awe and chagrin. It was a beautiful home. Correction. It was a beautiful mansion. But it looked cold and imposing. No flowers, no decorative pots, no steel dog made of engine parts sitting on the front stoop…. it just looked cold.

Well, it didn't matter. She was here for one thing, and by God she was going to do it. Climbing out of the driver's seat, she smoothed down her short black skirt and pulled her dark purple cardigan tighter around her middle. Fluffing her curly brown hair, she caught a quick glimpse of her reflection in the car window and sighed. She was intimidated, she realized. And it quite honestly took a lot to intimidate her. She was a lawyer, for crying out loud. OK, so she wasn't tall, blonde and gorgeous like her sister, but she looked pretty good. And though she no longer practiced criminal law, she used to deal with bad guys in court all the time. So why could she do that, banter with the cops and even some of the repeat offenders that she saw all the time, but she couldn't go face some obviously crazy man who was paying her sister to marry him?

Taking a deep breath, she opened the gate, strolled up the front walk, and rang the doorbell. She heard it reverberating through the house, and fought the urge to turn around and run for the hills. Instead, she forced herself to stay in place. She heard footsteps approaching the door. For some reason, she had been expecting a butler or a servant to answer her ring, but the moment the door opened, Emma knew that she was face to face with her sister's 'fiancé', Mason Parker. A very tall, very imposing, and oh dear Lord in heaven, a *very* sexy Mason Parker.

The man stood in the doorway, looking down at her. "Yes?" he asked.

Emma took a deep breath. "Mr. Parker? My name is Emma Jameson."

For whatever reason, her last name didn't seem to register with the man, since he just repeated himself. "Yes?"

She fought the urge to roll her eyes. "I'm Jen's sister. She asked me to come see you."

His grey eyes narrowed as he finally connected her name to his fiancée. He stepped back. "Then you'd better come in."

As Emma stepped into the house, she shivered. The inside was much the same as the outside. Modern. Austere. Probably symbolic of something that made no sense to her. Surreptitiously checking her skirt for dog fur, she turned around and waited for Mason to lead the way.

"You have a lovely home," she lied.

Mason seemed accustomed to compliments about his home, and brushed it aside. "Thank you. I didn't know Jen had a sister. You don't look much alike," he said, apparently going straight for the jugular.

Emma was used to it. "You're not kidding."

Mason looked back at her as he led the way down the hallway and into a large room that he obviously used as his study. "I don't suppose this is good news you're bringing me," he said dryly.

"I guess it depends on your perspective," Emma answered. "But perhaps not."

In the study, Mason pointed to a couch, then sat down in a chair opposite her, leaning back and crossing one leg over the other. "Where is she?" he asked, almost casually.

Emma sighed. "I honestly don't know. I would suspect on a plane somewhere, but she deliberately didn't tell me."

"So she's not coming back," Mason clarified.

Shaking her head as she set her purse down next to her and straightened her skirt over her legs, Emma said quietly, "I don't think so. You never know with Jen - she could change her mind at any moment. But I don't think she will."

"Why?"

Emma knew what he was asking, and had been thinking of the best way to tell him. It wasn't that Jen's leaving was going to break his heart, but she knew that men could... well... become attached to Jen rather quickly. Given her tall, blonde, kind of buxom beauty and all. So she wanted to let this guy down easy, even though he did not seem the type to believe in love at first sight or anything. Oh hell. Maybe he had a sentimental streak. Stranger things had happened.

Mason raised his eyebrows, indicating that he was still waiting for an answer.

"I don't think she meant for this to happen, but she... well..." Emma sighed.

"She met someone else," Mason hazarded a guess.

Emma was ready to spin it a million different ways, but when she looked up into Mason's hard, but wow so incredibly sexy eyes, she just simply said, "Yes."

"Damnit," Mason clipped out. Closing his eyes momentarily, he opened them and stared up at the ceiling.

Emma was unprepared for the harshness of his response. She had expected and prepared for a few different reactions, including anger, arrogance, irrational thinking.... But not this level of obvious frustration. "You care?" she asked in surprise.

"Of course I care," he snapped.

"But, I thought..."

"That we had a relationship based on a business agreement? Yes. That's true. And you're right, of course. I don't particularly mourn the loss of Jen as a person – but I needed her." He looked at Emma shrewdly. "How much did she tell you?" he asked.

"Most of it, I think," Emma said quietly, shrugging as she did so, but then she thought for a moment and retracted that. "Actually, not really very much, come to think of it. Just that you two had agreed to marry for some reason that is beyond my understanding, and that she wasn't going to be able to fulfill her end of the deal. But she really was very sorry, Mr. Parker," she added, hoping to wrap up the conversation and head home for a run with Chaos.

Mason steepled his hands in front of him, resting his elbows on the arms of the chair he was sitting in. He was quiet for several long moments while Emma fought the urge to look at her watch. She could bolt, but he deserved a little sympathy in all of this, so she stayed seated while he worked through his thoughts. She felt his eyes on her. And while those eyes in another context might have made her stomach flutter, right now they felt almost predatory. She looked away, again reminding herself that she'd stared down drug dealers before and come out the victor.

She looked back when he spoke again. "I put this whole deception in motion for a reason, Ms. Jameson. And your sister signed a legally binding contract."

At the word 'contract', Emma started, her eyes flying back to his. Uh oh. Emma was the lawyer in the family. She was the one who understood legal ramifications of deals and what binding contracts meant. And if Jen had signed something without having her sister look at it, this could be bad. "Contract?" she managed to ask, her voice steadier than she thought it should be.

Mason smiled. If she didn't know any better, she'd swear his smile was the smile of a crocodile. A very sexy, very handsome, very intriguing crocodile, but a cold-blooded reptile nonetheless.

"She didn't mention that to you?" he asked, almost innocently.

"No," Emma stated firmly. Sighing, she added, "I believe I would have remembered that."

Mason just nodded agreeably. "Then you'll love this next part, Ms. Jameson. The contract states that if she reneges on her end of the deal, she must find me a suitable replacement within 24 hours, without breaking the confidentiality agreement within the contract, or the contract is considered broken. And I can sue her."

Emma blinked. "Suitable replacement?" she echoed.

"Yes," Mason said conversationally. "The wedding is in three days. I don't really care who the bride is, as long as she meets the qualifications laid out in the contract."

Swallowing, Emma choked out, "Qualifications?" She realized that she was repeating back everything he was saying to her, but seemed absolutely unable to stop herself.

"Yes. Educated enough to carry on a conversation. Attractive, between 28 and 38 years old, and socially well-adjusted. No drugs or other addictions, no major debt, and, of course, willing to sign a contract that precludes any and all financial support once the marriage dissolves."

Emma leaned back into the couch cushions. Holy crap, she thought. "You have got to be kidding me," she said out loud.

Mason shook his head, watching her closely. "No. You'll find that I do not kid."

Emma busied herself by fidgeting with her purse straps. She needed to end this conversation and get out of the house.

"Well, it shouldn't be too hard to find someone willing to do that, even under such short notice," she said, almost half-convincingly. "I'm sure you'll have no trouble replacing her. You're obviously wealthy, good looking, you live in a nice house, you..." Emma caught herself and blushed. She stopped babbling, even as Mason looked over at her in some combination of amusement and discomfort. Taking a deep breath, she counted to ten and then said more calmly, "Look. I'm very sorry for the inconvenience. But Jen asked me to pick up her things from your room, so may I do that? And then I'll be out of your way, and you can go about your evening."

But Mason was just looking at her oddly. "She didn't leave anything here. She never stayed here."

"Excuse me?"

"And the contract stipulates that *she* find her replacement. Not that *I* do," he added.

Emma nearly screamed in frustration, but she just gritted her teeth and answered. "But I don't even know where she is. So it might be hard to contact her and ask her to do that."

"Then you'll need to do it," Mason stated firmly.

"Me?" Emma snorted. "I don't think so. This is not my problem."

"Are any of your finances tied in with your sister?" Mason asked, his eyes shrewdly assessing her reaction.

Emma turned white. Of course they were. They were sisters. Best friends. Compadres. They owned a house together. The house that she and Emma lived in.

Mason noticed her reaction, but he just shrugged. "Then it is your business. Because by the time I'm through with your sister, all of her assets will be mine. And that includes anything that she jointly owns with you. Oh, and in addition, I'll press charges against your sister, since she disappeared with quite a large amount of my cash."

"But... " All of Emma's amazing lawyer-like skills at rebuttal had disappeared and left her with nothing. She just stared at him. "You can't be serious."

"I am dead serious," Mason replied, uncrossing his legs and leaning forward, his elbows on his knees and his eyes boring into her with that same predatory look she'd seen earlier.

"This is ridiculous," Emma said in response. "I can't find you a wife in two days!"

"One day, actually, since I need time to get the paperwork in order," Mason corrected her.

"But..."

"Unless you're prepared to stand in for Jen? You're single, I presume?" he asked, looking pointedly at her ring-less finger.

Emma shivered. "I am not marrying you," she asserted.

Mason stood then. "That's fine. You and your sister will be hearing from my lawyer, and I'll be contacting the authorities tomorrow morning."

Emma remained seated. "I want to see the contract," she demanded, looking straight at him and remembering that she had a backbone. Somewhere.

"I'll have it sent to you," Mason responded. "Leave me your FAX number or an e-mail address."

"Now. I want to see it now," she said firmly, standing up from the couch and refusing to let him intimidate her.

He looked surprised. "I presumed you'd want a lawyer to look at it."

She rolled her eyes. "I *am* a lawyer," she informed him.

Well score one for her. She had startled him. His eyebrows went up and he just looked at her.

"What?" she asked defensively.

"I'm just surprised. Jen..."

"We're different," Emma said, crossing her arms in front of her.

"I'm picking up on that," he returned mildly. "Excuse me for a moment." Walking over to his desk, he opened up the file drawer to the side of his chair and pulled out a folder. After leafing quickly through it, he moved back over to where he'd been standing and handed it to Emma.

"You can sit back down if you'd like," he said with some amusement.

But Emma was too wrapped up in the file contents to hear his offer. Leafing quickly through the pages, she found herself getting angrier and angrier. Her sister had really screwed up this time. The contract was legal, it was binding, and, as far as Emma was concerned, it was damning. At least to her. Mason was right. He could sue. And he would, Emma knew, looking briefly up at where he was leaning against the wall, his arms crossed, his gaze on her face.

She shuddered, then closed the folder and handed it back to him.

"Tell me why you need this," she said quietly. "Jen never said."

"My uncle's will stipulates that I will lose his voting rights within my company if I am not married by the time I am 40. I turn 40 next month."

"Did his will stipulate that you could pay someone to marry you?" Emma asked, with some degree of scorn.

But Mason just shrugged. "I don't really think he cared. He ordered a bride from Columbia, so he doesn't exactly have moral high ground here. And he really just wanted to be sure that I had children to pass the company on to so that it stayed in the family."

Her complexion had been white before, but now it turned green. "Wait. You never mentioned children," she said faintly.

Mason smiled his cold smile again - the smile that made Emma's stomach clench and her palms sweat. "That's my uncle's rationale, not his legal demand. The only demand was marriage."

"And how long does this marriage need to last?" she asked.

"Three years."

"Three *years*? Are you kidding me?" she asked again.

"As I said before, I do not kid."

"You want me to agree to marry you for three years," she said again, out loud, making sure that she understood what he was asking of her.

"Yes. That's what your sister agreed to," he said almost casually.

"My sister," Emma asserted. "Not me."

"It's all the same to me."

"You're a piece of work, aren't you?" she asked.

"Perhaps," he shrugged. "But you don't even need to worry about it if you find me a replacement for your sister."

Emma seethed. "You know as well as I do that I won't be able to do that. Not without breaking the damn confidentiality clause of the contract."

"Ah, such a good lawyer. You noted that clause."

"It was hard to miss, it being front and center and all."

"Then I'll see you here on Friday," Mason said agreeably.

"Your uncle was a moron," Emma said quietly, crossing her arms and sinking back down onto the couch. "People don't put stuff like that in their wills these days. That's the plot of a really bad romance novel, not real life. And it cannot possibly be legally binding."

Mason shrugged again. "My uncle was a bit of an eccentric. But a very rich, very happy, and very successful eccentric. Who am I to judge? But he used the best lawyers in town, and my own lawyer has assured me that the requirements of the will are, indeed, binding."

"I want to see his will."

"Why? Doesn't really matter, does it? The contract exists, and it isn't null and void if the rationale behind it turns out to be untrue."

"Oh hell," Emma muttered under her breath. "I don't believe this mess."

Mason just looked at her. "She's *your* sister," he pointed out.

Emma narrowed her eyes and glared at him. "You were prepared to marry her, so don't get all high and mighty with me," she ordered. "And I think I probably should point out that, if I can't figure out a way out of this... this.... oh hell. Whatever this is. Anyway, this is not going to all go your way," she finished.

"Oh? And what exactly do you mean by that?" he asked politely. Or as politely as could be expected when one is holding all the cards.

Emma closed her eyes, counted to ten, and then continued. "Look. I don't know what arrangement you had with Jen, but you and I are renegotiating. There is nothing in that contract that states what kind of a relationship the two of you would have, where you would live, how you would relate to each other...."

He smiled then. That same rather predatory crocodilian smile, but a smile nonetheless.

"So Emma. Tell me what kind of relationship you want."

Emma seethed. Now was not the time to get flirty or anything other than business-like, and the man's arrogant assumption that she wanted *anything* from him at all was unmerited. She glared at him. "I may *need* to marry you to fulfill the terms of a *contract*, Mr. Parker. A contract I did not sign, I should point out, but which I *may* choose to abide by."

"To save your home," he pointed out.

"To protect my sister," she corrected angrily. Yeah, her home was important to her. But this man would destroy Jen. And even though she, herself, was prepared to strangle the woman with whatever item she had at her fingertips when she next saw her, including dental floss, electrical cords, or strands of celery, Jen was still her sister. And she would be damned if she'd let this Neanderthal take away everything that she, or they, had worked for, or that she'd let this man have her sister arrested.

"Very noble of you, considering that she practically sold you to me," Mason pointed out.

Emma looked up quickly, her eyes narrowing suspiciously. "What do you mean?"

"Why do you think she sent you over here? She could have called. Written. Sent a singing telegram. But she sent you, under the pretense of picking up her non-existent things. So you are clearly her choice for a replacement."

Emma closed her eyes. Mason could be right, of course, and some part of her had understood that as soon as she'd seen the contract.

Opening her eyes again, she speared Mason with a sharp gaze. "What did you promise Jen for this arrangement?" she asked. It occurred to her that she had no idea what Jen had been getting out of this deal. She knew what Mason had needed, but had no clue what it meant for Jen. And Mason had mentioned Jen disappearing with his money.

"$750,000," Mason responded.

Emma was actually surprised. "That's all?" she asked.

"It worked out to $250,000 a year. *And* she was going to be married and live and travel with a very rich man. So there were bound to be perks."

"How much did you give her up front? How much did she walk away with?" Emma asked.

"$300,000. So the rest is yours. We can work out the details on Friday. It's less than I promised your sister, but you'll still end up getting a pretty good amount of money."

"I don't want the money," Emma stated firmly. "Why in the hell did you give her anything before you married her?"

"I had no reason to distrust her. And she knew as well as I did that I'd get all of it back and more if she broke the contract."

"Unless she shoved it all off on me." It was hard not to be bitter. Her sister walked away with $300,000, and she was the one who would end up in a relationship with a cold-blooded crazy man for three years. All for the sake of family, God help her.

"You could walk away any time you want to," Mason pointed out reasonably.

"She's still my sister," Emma replied. "And while I may be angry as hell at her right now…."

With a shrewd look at Emma, Mason said, "That's what she's counting on, you know."

"Yeah. I know. She knows me pretty well."

Mason crossed his arms over his chest, looking formidably down at Emma. Geez, he was big. And solid. She glared back at him, but he was unmoved.

"So, Emma. That leaves us back where we were a short while ago. Friday. Our appointment at my lawyer's office is at 1:00. We can take care of the contractual details beforehand. Meet me here at noon, and we'll go from there. Shall I send a car for you?" he asked politely.

"No thank you," she responded through gritted teeth.

"Very well. On Saturday, we can start moving your things in here."

At that, Emma visibly started. Her eyes flew to his, and she crossed her arms in front of her defensively. "Oh no," she said firmly, her eyes moving around her, again taking in the starkness of his home. "I'm not living here," she stated.

But Mason quietly responded, "You are."

"No, I'm not," she argued.

"Emma, you are," he repeated with exaggerated patience. "You will be my wife."

At that, Emma turned white as a sheet. Surely he didn't intend….

But he just shook his head in annoyance. "Oh for… Not in that sense," he assured her.

"So why do I need to live here?" she persisted.

"I have social functions, Emma, which you as my wife will be expected to attend. And we'll be hosting functions. Either way, you and I will be seen as a couple. There will certainly be expectations that a husband and his wife will share a home," he said logically.

But Emma was not moved by a logical argument. "There are no expectations," she stated firmly. "You are marrying for money. I am marrying under duress. Nobody is going to believe that we met and fell in love, and we don't need them to. If I understand correctly, all you need to do is to be legally bound to a woman for three years. And after that, we divorce and go our own way."

But Mason just sighed, looking down on Emma with some impatience. "Not exactly," he said.

 TWO

Looking over at Mason with narrowed eyes, Emma asked, "What do you mean by 'not exactly'?"

"You and I know the details of this marriage. As did Jen. As does my lawyer. But nobody else will. I have a reputation that I need to uphold. I work with many business people who value families and respect marriage – I do not expect them to understand this kind of an arrangement."

"But if you took Jen to court, or pressed charges against her for stealing, it would all be out in the open," she pointed out.

He shrugged. "It would hurt Jen more than it would hurt me. The contractual details would be buried behind the 'arrested for theft' part. And ultimately, you'd be hurt too – you're a lawyer. You can't have a thief for a sister and still retain your reputation."

Emma closed her eyes and seethed. This was a nightmare. No wonder her sister skipped town. And left her to clean this up, she thought. Only it couldn't be cleaned. She was going to be stuck, once again, dealing with a mess made by her sister. And this time, it was serious.

"So, Emma, you will live here. You will, in almost every sense of the word, be my wife. And you will play the part."

Acting as this man's wife would be the easy part, Emma thought. The hard part would be trying to figure out how to keep her own life separate from all of this, and how to keep on living it. Because she had no clue how the hell she'd inform her friends, her parents, her grandmother, her dog…. Oh my *word*, she thought. *Chaos*. That could be a deal-breaker. Maybe her dog would get her out of this! Her big, lovable, slobbering, mess of a wonderful dog!

"I will live here," she said at last, "on three conditions."

"You're not really in a position to bargain," he pointed out.

"Neither are you," she countered. "You're the one who needs a wife in less than a month's time."

"Point taken," he said dryly. "Compromise is the key to any good marriage," he added with a half smile. "What are your conditions?"

"I have a dog. He comes with me."

"A what?"

"A dog. A big lovable dog. We're a package deal. You marry me, you get my dog too."

"How big?" he asked, his eyes narrowing.

"65 pounds."

He sighed and rolled his eyes. "I'll get a dog house."

She crossed her arms. "He is not an outdoor dog. He likes couches, pillows, and beds. I crate him when I'm not home, but he does not get relegated to the back yard."

"My house is not exactly dog proof."

"Look. I'm considering marrying you and moving in here to save your damn voting stock and my sister's finances. The least you can do is put away your cherished knick-knacks and accept some fur in your life."

"I don't really like dogs."

"Too bad. I don't really like being pushed into marrying a man I don't know. So if you want to reconsider..."

Mason shrugged. "You make a fair point. OK. You can bring the dog. He stays in your room with you at night. And he gets crated during parties. And if he breaks anything, you replace it. And if..."

"Oh for the love of God. Relax. He's a dog, not an elephant. You may even like him. Eventually."

"Now I'm worried about your other two conditions," Mason said dryly.

"Was that a joke?" Emma asked, looking at him with suspicion.

"God no. I have no sense of humor. Or so I'm told."

Emma just stared at him. He waved his hand to gesture that she should continue.

"I'm keeping my job."

"Fine with me. You'd be bored sitting around here all day. You'd probably redecorate."

Narrowing her eyes at him doubtfully, she continued. "And my life."

He shrugged. "I'd expect you to do that." He paused then, as if reconsidering. "As long as your life doesn't include a man," he added. Looking her directly in the eyes, he asked, "You're not seeing anyone, are you Emma?"

"That's none of your business," she stated firmly, even as she blushed.

But Mason just looked at her steadily. "It is. Now."

"It's not. Not if I'm discreet."

"No. If you're seeing someone, you break up with him."

"And if I'm in love with him?"

His eyes narrowed. "You're not. If you were, he would have been your immediate concern, not an afterthought. So no, it's not serious. Break it off, Emma," he added mildly.

Her hands on her hips, Emma just stared at Mason. "You're a little more socially well-adapted than I expected," she said reluctantly. When he just looked at her with disbelief, she added, "I figured you'd have to be a complete recluse to be hiring a woman to marry you."

He just looked at her. "Jen didn't really tell you anything about me, did she?"

Emma shook her head, then thought of another question. "What will your friends and colleagues say when you show up married to the wrong woman?"

"You're not the wrong woman, Emma. Just a different woman. And I've told nobody about the wedding. You may be a surprise, but that's all. I never mentioned the wedding to anyone."

Emma looked surprised. "What? But…. Why not? You were going to get married this weekend. Surely your family…"

He shook his head.

"Your friends?"

He shrugged.

"Wow," Emma said softly.

"I imagine Jen did the same with her family and friends. And I imagine you will as well," he pointed out.

Emma just sighed, looking over at Mason. He was still standing against his desk, leaning back on it with his arms crossed. Physically, the man was magnificent. Even though he was dressed in his work clothes, Emma could see how fit he was. Everything about him screamed sexy. But cold. The man put distance in place between himself and others. That was clear. She felt it from the moment she walked through his door. He did not want to connect. Not with her, and not with others.

"You're a hard man," she said softly.

He nodded once. "Yes."

"You know nothing about me. But you're prepared to bring me into your home, and to legally tie yourself to me for three years. Granted, that doesn't mean a damn thing in terms of a personal relationship," she added. "But…"

He shrugged. "You came here on your sister's behalf. You show a great deal more love and concern for her than she showed for you. Seems to me that if I were willing to tie myself to Jen for three years, I'm getting a better deal with you."

"You're expecting love and concern?" she asked with disbelief.

"Not in the least. But you'll probably be liked in my social circles, and that's important. You'll be an asset."

"And your family?" Emma wasn't sure why she persisted, but she needed to know what she was up against.

"What about them?"

"Jen said they hated her."

"They didn't know her. But she's right. They weren't impressed."

"Why not?"

"They thought she was with me for my money. They weren't wrong."

"No. I guess not." Emma took a deep breath. She needed to get out of this house. Needed to get alone and think. Surely if she had a few moments to herself, she could think of a way out of this. Turning to Mason, she said simply, "I need to go. I want a copy of the contract to take with me."

He looked at her in amusement. "Looking for loopholes, Emma?"

"Of course."

"You won't find any," he assured her, moving back around his desk to locate and hand her the file he'd given her previously. The original was locked in a safe at his lawyer's office.

"I'm not optimistic, but I'll try."

"Fair enough. I'll see you on Friday. And Emma, if you don't show up, I'll file the lawsuit that afternoon. And I'll notify the authorities to pick up your sister."

She tried one last appeal. "Look, you're a nice-looking guy. Surely you know some nice young woman who would love to marry you."

He shook his head firmly. "I want no strings attached, Emma. I don't want emotion involved. That's why I did it this way."

"Why?"

"Why what?"

"Why no emotion?"

"That's not your concern."

Sighing, Emma tucked the file folder into her purse, and then turned back and looked up at Mason. "I'm going to want my own contract," she said to him.

"There's no additional financial gain here, Emma."

"Screw you. And your $450,000. I want safety nets."

She felt a glimmer of vicious humor at his surprised look. "Safety nets? What do you mean?"

"First, if you ever physically hurt me, the contract is null and void. No trial, no nothing. I go to my lawyer, who goes to your lawyer, and I'm out. Second, if you compel me to do anything I do not want to do, including forcing any physical advances on me, the contract is null and void."

"You have formed quite a high opinion of me, haven't you?" One eyebrow went up as he looked over at Emma. "First, why in God's name would I ever hurt you? And do you honestly think that I would need to force myself on a woman?"

She blushed. Actually, she imagined that most women would eagerly accept any advances this man made, but she had no illusions here - if she got sexually involved with this man, she would be left cold. He might marry her, he might sleep with her, but that would be the extent of it. The end of the road would be the same - divorce.

"What else?" he asked in amusement.

She didn't hesitate. "I want a prenup."

He looked at her with an impatient expression, as if she were a few steps behind him and he was waiting for her to catch up. "I already told you that there is no financial gain – that's already been drawn up."

Shaking her head, Emma was quick to correct him. "No. It's to protect me. I want to protect my own assets from you."

She had surprised him again, but he recovered well. "You're an interesting woman, Emma Jameson. OK. Draw it up. I'll sign."

"Good. One last thing. You cheat, I'm gone. I may not be interested in sleeping with you, but if this is going to look like a real marriage, you can't be out sleeping with other women on the side. You may have a reputation, but I have one too. Marrying you will shock the hell out of my friends and family... Oh dear God, what is Gran going to say?" she interrupted herself. "Anyway, the point is, that's already going to do some damage. So if you cheat, I'm gone. And there will be no repercussions to me."

"Very well. I agree. Draw up the necessary documents and I'll have my lawyer look them over tomorrow. But if you cheat on me, it adds two years to your commitment to me."

"What? Why would you want that?"

"I wouldn't. But neither would you. So that will keep you from running away with the first guy you meet who offers to take you away from all of this."

"Fine," she said shortly.

"Good. Now that that's all settled, we can make plans to move you in over the weekend."

Emma shook her head vehemently. "No way. I'm away on a business trip next week. I won't have time to pack."

"Emma..."

But Emma's patience was about at the breaking point. She was done, and she needed to make that clear. Her voice almost shaking with tension, she said quietly, "Do not push me. This is not my doing, and it's not anything I want."

Mason just nodded, seeming to understand that she was at the end of her rope. "I was going to say that next week is fine, Emma. I can help you pack up this weekend if you want."

Emma looked incredulously at him.

"What?" he asked, seeing her expression.

"*You* are going to help me pack?"

He looked puzzled. That's what he'd offered, so what was the misunderstanding? But Emma shook her head. "No. Thank you, but no. I'm not giving up my house, so I'm just packing my personal things. And I don't need help with that."

"Very well. When you have what you need boxed up, let me know and I'll hire some men to help move your things."

"You should meet Chaos before I move him in here," Emma said, almost reluctantly as she stood.

"Chaos?"

"My dog?" she reminded him, rolling her eyes. Honestly, she thought again, what man didn't like dogs?

"You named your dog Chaos?"

For the first time that evening, Emma smiled. "He's earned the name. You'll love him. And I'm sure he'll love you. Good night, Mr. Parker."

"Mason," he corrected. "I'll walk you to the door."

Sitting in her car, Emma leaned her head back against the headrest and sighed. This was a mess. A god-awful mess. And unless she'd missed something in that damn contract, it was iron-clad. Which meant that this was a god-awful mess that she was not going to be able to get out of.

Digging her cell out of her bag, she tried calling her sister. No response - the phone went straight to voice mail. Hanging up in frustration, she tossed the phone back onto the seat next to her and closed her eyes.

Let's examine the facts, she thought. A) - I do not want to marry that cold reptile of a man. B) - that cold reptile is probably the sexiest man I have ever laid eyes on, and in any other situation, if he showed a speck of warmth, I'd probably be tackling him to the ground. But warm is *not* a word I'd use to describe him, so no, absolutely no interest there. Well, apart from the fact that he's sexy as hell. C) - I still want to murder my sister, so it may be better to *not* try to reach her for a while until I am over this, because D) - *she's not coming back*. That was the hardest one to accept, but Emma knew her sister. She had made up her mind, and decided that she did not want to marry Mason Parker. So she had bolted. And now Emma had a choice to make. Agree to marry the hot (physically) but cold (emotionally) man, or be prepared to lose an awful lot of money. And to scramble to keep her sister from doing jail time, because even if she bought Jen out of the house, and thus kept her house separate from Jen's assets, she would not be able to just sit by and let her get skewered by Mason's lawyers. And damn, but that contract was pretty fool proof. Unless she were willing to sell out her sister, she might have to go through with this. Funny how her sister was so willing to sell *her* out, but Emma was the one who was hesitating. She sighed. Sometimes she wished she had more of a cold streak of her own.

And finally, she was going to need to tell her family. But how was she going to tell them, and what was she going to say? She was back at the beginning of her thought process. This was a mess.

Starting the car, she drove carefully out of the neighborhood with the well-manicured lawns, wondering how quickly she would become the scourge of the community. Chaos would certainly make his presence known, and that means that she'd become a pariah quickly. Could she live like that for three years? Maybe, she thought. If she spent a lot of time at Gran Jameson's house. Martinis and pie might help her to pass the days. *And* if she buried herself in her work. *And* if she and Chaos spent a lot of time at the dog park.

Oh hell, she thought. Turning onto the highway, Emma headed home.

Mason watched her for a while as she sat in her car and collected her thoughts. After she left the house, he had poured himself a double scotch, and now stood at the window of one of his guest rooms, looking out onto the street. Emma was in the driver's seat of her car, her head back against the headrest and her eyes closed. He could almost see her thought process. It would be a lot to take in, he knew.

For him, it was easy. He'd lived with the condition of his uncle's will for a long time now, and it was only in the last couple of months that he realized that he'd need to do something drastic if he wanted to retain his uncle's voting stock. When he had met Jen at a party, they had hit it off. Not in a romantic way, but more two cynical personalities coming together and enjoying each other over a drink. So when he'd eventually decided to propose a deal to Jen, it had been with an understanding that their relationship was strictly business. Neither of them was interested in the other - for two hard and cynical people, neither of them found themselves attracted to those same character traits in the other.

But Jen had gotten cold feet. That was interesting. And what was even more interesting was that she had sent her sister over to tell him about her change in plans. And her sister was clearly a completely different person from Jen. So why did she send Emma, rather than just calling him or texting him with the news? Perhaps because she was not only backing out of the deal, but she was taking a lot of his money with her. Had she sent Emma to smooth that over? Or was it because she was worried about the contract, and Emma was the one person Jen knew would feel responsible enough to fill in for Jen, thus freeing her from the conditions?

Physically, the two sisters were nothing alike. Jen was tall, blonde, beautiful, and stacked. Honestly, she was like Jessica Rabbit with blonde hair. And no bunny ears. Emma was a brunette, a bit shorter than Jen, and more petite. She was also fiercely loyal to her sister, which intrigued him, particularly since Jen was not a woman who automatically inspired loyalty.

Emma had a profession. She had opinions. She had a dog. She had a brain. And Mason was willing to bet that she was probably attracted to him. Most women were, he thought matter-of-factly. But as long as they stayed clear of each other, there shouldn't be anything major to overcome here. She was nice-looking, well-spoken, had a good job, and was obviously a kind person. So, for the next three years anyway, she'd fit well by his side. Perhaps even better than Jen would have. People would always have assumed that he'd married Jen for sex and she'd married him for money. With Emma, people wouldn't be sure. There would be gossip, questions, rumors, and lots of speculation, and Mason found that it amused him to think about that. Because nobody would ever guess the truth.

Watching as Emma at last drove away from the curb in front of his house, he tackled the one last issue that was bothering him. Emma drew him in a way that Jen hadn't. Physically, yes, but it was more than that. Something about her was attracting him - something deeper than what was on the surface. Mason took a long pull on his drink. He prided himself on his lack of emotion. So despite her appeal to him, he needed to be sure that Emma never ever got close. Because he had no intention of getting emotionally involved with anyone.

THREE

Chaos looked at Emma suspiciously. She had spent the entire night ranting and raving. And while she had remembered to feed him, and take him for his walk, and let him out to take care of business, she was distracted. So he had hopped up on the bed with her last night, put his head on her pillow, and snored into her ear. He figured it was the least he could do.

Emma woke up to a paw in her ear, dog breath on her face, and fur up her nose. Flipping over on the bed and rubbing her nose vigorously, she hugged one end of the pillow closer to her and sighed deeply. She had looked more carefully at the contract Jen had signed last night, and she saw no loopholes. Yeah, she could refuse to do anything here, and she could probably protect her own interests, but Jen would be toast. She would lose everything. And as mad as Emma was at her sister, she just couldn't bring herself to sell Jen out.

So she could either go find some stranger to marry Mason Parker, or she could go through with it herself. And given the strict confidentiality clause in the contract, she was surprised he hadn't already threatened to sue Jen for confiding in her. So she was slowly coming to terms with her fate, after a lot of venting last night at Chaos. The dog had taken it well though, she thought. But then, she had made it up to him with a handful of Snausages.

She had a busy day today. She had a full day at work, but also needed to find some sort of outfit that would suit, and then get ready for her business trip next week. She needed to draw up a contract to send to Mason's lawyer, so he could clear it before Mason signed it. This weekend, she would need to drop Chaos off with her parents, and probably explain to her family why she had gotten married to a man they had never heard of, all without implicating her sister. But today, she still needed to reschedule a couple of hours worth of work so she had time to go over to Mason's home tomorrow to sign papers and complete a legal joining of their lives. Geez, she couldn't even say the word, she thought. Marriage. She needed to make sure she had time to go and get *married* tomorrow, for heaven's sake.

She stayed in bed a few minutes longer, hoping that by refusing to get up, time would stop. But Chaos knew she was awake, and hopped off the bed, rounding the corner to plop himself down in front of her and stare. Emma opened one eye, seeing her dog sitting hopefully in front of her. Sighing, she rolled onto her back, wiped her hand across her face, and slowly got up.

"OK, OK. I'm coming. Geez, dog. You ate like a million dog treats last night. You can't be hungry."

Chaos looked up at her with a combination of impatience and adoration. Patting the dog on the head, she padded over to the sliding glass door in her bedroom and opened it up to let Chaos out into the yard.

Coffee got made, breakfast got eaten, and somehow Emma got herself ready for work. Her stomach was in knots. Her hands shook as she fixed her hair, but when she looked in the mirror on the way out the door, she was surprised to find that she looked much calmer than she felt. She dropped Chaos off at doggie day care for the day, since she wouldn't be able to make it home at noon to let him out. After kissing him on the head and scritching his ears, she told him that she loved him and that he should behave. He looked up at her with some sense of incredulity, since he believed that he always behaved, a feeling that most of the staff at the doggy day care did not share. After a friendly chat with the woman behind the desk, she headed to the office.

Work was a panacea for Emma. It took her mind off things and made her day go quickly. By the end of the workday, Emma had not only completed most of the things on her task list for the day, but she had also written the contract for Mason to sign, gone over Jen's contract one more time, and even gotten a start on some work she had planned for the next day. Funny how needing a distraction can make you that much more focused at work, she thought.

"You're a dynamo today," her secretary, Rhoda, observed as Emma dropped one more letter on her desk for mailing.

"Some days, I'm the picture of productivity. Other days, I can't put a sentence together to save my life. Fortunately, I'm having a good day today, at least as far as verbiage goes. You doing OK?"

"Fine, thanks for asking," Rhoda smiled up at her. "I managed to change most of your meetings tomorrow for either later in the day, or to reschedule them until Monday. I haven't been able to reach Ben yet to try to move your 2:00."

"If you can't reach him, I should be able to make that one, though I might be late."

"You have a hot date?" her secretary teased.

"Oh, if you only knew," Emma smiled back, thinking to herself, *no, really, if you only knew...*

"I'll keep trying. Was it time-sensitive, or can it wait until next week?"

"I think it can wait, but Ben can make the call."

"Hey, if you're free tomorrow night, a few of us are headed to that new Mexican restaurant over on Glendale. Frank wants to try their margaritas."

Emma grinned. "Any other time, I'd take you up on it, but I can't tomorrow. I've got plans, and I need to have an early night since I'm headed to San Diego this weekend. Speaking of which, do you have all of the Drellis files ready for me?"

"Most of them. I'll have everything ready to go by noon tomorrow. Is that soon enough?"

"Oh yeah. Plenty soon. Thanks, Rhoda. If the margaritas at that new place are good, I'll be wanting our next scheduled happy hour there," she warned.

"We'll let you know. Sorry you can't join us."

Me too, Emma thought. But she didn't think that scheduling a work happy hour on her wedding night seemed entirely appropriate.

Mason was pacing. It was Friday, and it was nearly noon, and yet there was no sign of Emma. He had the paperwork ready, and he had the contract that Emma had sent to his lawyer at the end of the day on Thursday. So that was a positive sign - she had taken time yesterday to put that together. But other than that, nothing. No contact, no calls, nothing. Was she coming?

If she didn't, he'd sue for breach of contract. It wasn't the money, he reasoned. It was the principle of it. People couldn't promise things and then renege. Well, Jen, anyway. Emma hadn't promised anything. He chuckled to himself. She was probably still reading through the contract on the way over here in a cab, trying to figure out how to get out of it.

He checked his watch again. Their appointment was at 1:00. They'd need to leave his home by 12:40 to ensure that they made it there in time. So that didn't leave a lot of time to work with. OK. What if she didn't come? What was the first step? Well, contact his lawyer of course. But then what? He'd have to figure out if he was going to let the voting stock go, or try to find a wife in a few weeks. He wanted no emotional attachment, of course, so that meant that approaching anyone he knew or had dated was out. He could...

The doorbell rang. Mason was surprised by the relief he felt. Straightening his tie, he headed for the door. Pulling it open, he did a double take. Emma was standing there, looking completely different from two days ago. Gone was the black skirt with sensible heels. Gone was the unruly hair and the business-like scarf around her neck. Instead, she was dressed in an ivory-colored dress suit - a lovely simple tailored jacket over a plain matching ivory sheath, that stopped above her knees. Her wavy hair was tamed, and swept up into an elegant chignon. She wore one single pearl around her neck, simple pearl earrings, and carried a teal-colored purse over one shoulder. Her legs were enclosed in silk hose, and her feet were lovingly encased in the most amazing shoes Mason had seen on a woman. Three inch heels that matched her purse made it look like her legs stretched to eternity, but the shape and height of them added to Emma's elegant appearance. She looked like a society woman, a lawyer, and a fashion model, all rolled into the same woman. And while he felt a wave of heat roll over him as he took in her appearance, he quickly hid his reaction, and just stepped back to let her in.

Emma was having a similar moment. Mason was dressed in a black suit, with an ivory-colored shirt and a blue and black striped tie. It was a normal business suit, but his appearance was giving her heart palpitations. Good lord, she thought, this man was sexy. Not a hair out of place. Not a piece of fur on him. She had needed to use the lint brush she kept at home, and the one she kept at work, to ensure that all of Chaos' fur was removed from her outfit. The suit was one she wore occasionally in the summer, so it was no big deal to wear it today - she had just thrown a scarf around her neck and used sensible shoes at work, then pulled off the scarf and changed her shoes on the way over. But Mason looked like a model from a catalog. He was gorgeous. Still, Emma noted that there was no warmth in his eyes as he pulled the door wider and stood back to let her by. So she took a deep breath, and reminded herself that this was a business transaction, and nothing more.

"You came." The relief in Mason's voice was especially surprising, given the cool way he'd looked at her when he opened the door for her.

"Of course. You really gave me no choice," she said quietly.

He smiled slightly. "True. You look lovely, Emma."

She looked at him with some suspicion. Why was he being nice? "Thanks," she finally said. "Can we get this over with please? I took a long lunch, but I'll need to get back to work as soon as we're done."

He nodded. "Of course. Did you have a chance to look everything over?"

"Yes. I signed everything this morning. And you?"

"My lawyer read over the copy you sent to him yesterday and gave me his approval. So we can countersign everything and take the forms with us. He'll take a quick look, make copies, and we'll be set."

It took less than fifteen minutes for them to deal with their paperwork, and for Emma to sign the marriage license. Emma had taken a cab over to Mason's home, so she joined him in his car on the ride over to the office of his lawyer, where a justice of the peace would be waiting. She had expected that Mason would use a driver, but she realized that this was exactly what he had told her it would be - a quiet marriage between two people. He wasn't yet ready to announce it to the world. He helped her into the passenger seat, then moved over to the driver's seat and got in next to her.

Before he started the car, he turned to her briefly. "Thank you for doing this, Emma. I know it is not what you would have chosen, and I appreciate that you are honoring your sister's commitment."

She looked over at him, her eyes boring into his, her expression serious. "I know you do, Mason. And you're welcome," she added with a slight smile.

He looked at her for a moment, then nodded. Starting his car, he focused on the road.

The ceremony was quick and formal, and before Emma could grasp that she was really going through with this, it was over. Mason bent down to kiss her lightly on the cheek, and they were husband and wife. He had thought to bring rings, which surprised Emma, since it hadn't even occurred to her to think about that. But he had bought one for himself, and had gotten a smaller and simple ring for Emma. When he placed it on her finger, she felt a small pang of conscience. Marriage was supposed to be for real, she thought. She felt some sense of guilt that they were doing this for a reason other than love.

People got married for business reasons all the time, she reminded herself, trying to work through her guilt. Royal families used to unite for political reasons. There were all sorts of reasons to marry. But this just felt odd. Probably because she never expected to marry for anything other than love. And she certainly never intended to marry a man who didn't love her. And her dog.

Shaking off the sense of discomfort she felt over what she was doing, she accepted the business-like congratulations of Mason's attorney, posed for a series of photographs with her new husband, and then finally turned to Mason.

"I've got to get back to work," she said quietly. And it was true - not because she needed to be there for any meetings, but because she needed to get out of here for a while. To be alone, yes, but also to be back in the company of people she knew well.

Before she could go, Mason gently grasped her arm and pulled her to one side of the room. "I should have asked you this sooner, but would you have dinner with me this evening?"

"Dinner?" she asked, unsure if she'd heard him right.

"Yes."

"Why?"

"I'd like to get to know you a bit, Emma. We just shared marriage vows. I'd like to know more about the woman I married."

"Because you're interested, or because there will be questions that you'll need to be able to answer?"

"Both, of course."

She thought for a moment, then nodded her acceptance. "I should be done with work by 6:00 tonight. I need to get home to let Chaos out, but that won't take long. So anytime after 7:00 would work. Tell me where to meet you and I'll be there."

"How about Alamaya at 7:30?"

"Perfect."

"Shall I send a car for you?"

Emma shook her head. "I appreciate it, but no."

"It's not a problem."

"I'm sure it's not. I'll see you at 7:30."

She gave him a quick smile, then turned to go. But Mason stopped her.

"Emma."

Turning, she asked, "Yes?"

"We can pick out a ring for you when you get back next weekend," he said softly.

Emma looked at him in surprise, then looked down at her finger. "There's nothing wrong with this one, Mason. It's lovely. Simple, which is just what I like. So no, no need to pick out anything else."

He looked startled. "I just bought a plain and inexpensive band for the wedding – I assumed that you'd want something with diamonds, and we could pick it out at our leisure."

She shrugged. "I don't much like diamonds. Besides, this is a temporary arrangement, Mason. This ring is fine."

It wasn't that Emma didn't appreciate diamonds. To her, they were brilliant and beautiful and elegant, but they just didn't fit her personality. She wore very little jewelry, and what she picked out tended to be understated. So the simple band that Mason had used in their wedding ceremony actually fit her well.

His eyes narrowed as he looked down at her. "Jen..." he started to say.

"I'm not Jen." Her words came out a bit harsher than she intended, but if Mason was going to begin comparing her to her sister, she knew that his reflections would hurt. After all, Jen was the one he had been planning to marry. She was the beautiful one, the fun-loving one, the one Emma had been compared to all her life. Emma was always the dependable one, and the dependable one was who Mason was now stuck with. Trying to soften her words, she added gently, "I'm sorry, but I'm not my sister, Mason. If you want her, please try to find her. You may be able to talk her into changing her mind. And if you do, I'm more than willing to step aside. Now I really need to get back to work. I'll see you tonight for dinner."

She moved by him and was in the elevator heading down to the street before Mason remembered that he had driven them both. By the time he had said a quick goodbye to his attorney and followed her out, she had already hailed a cab, and was climbing into the back seat, her shapely legs disappearing behind her as she closed the door. He watched as the taxi moved away, but she didn't look back.

Mason leaned against one of the pillars outside of the building. He wasn't sure where Emma's comments had come from - any comparison he would make of her and Jen would hardly be critical of Emma. Jen would have wanted a diamond, he was certain. Maybe not the largest one in the shop, but a tasteful setting with an eye-catching stone. He would have been willing to buy her that, just as he was willing to do the same for Emma. That was part of the deal. But Emma seemed to want no part of the arrangement he had struck with her sister.

For one thing, she had refused the rest of the money he had offered to Jen. She had named a few charities that she would be happy to have the money go to if he insisted, but she made enough money to be comfortable on, and had no desire to be gaining financially from this marriage. In fact, she seemed downright uncomfortable with the idea.

Pushing away from the pillar, he headed for his car, glancing down at his ring finger as he did so. He was almost surprised to see the wedding ring there, doubly so since he had been the one to purchase the ring himself. If he hadn't done so, he probably wouldn't even have needed to wear a band since Emma hadn't thought about it at all. But when he had been choosing Emma's ring, he had made a quick decision to purchase one for himself as well - if he was marrying for show, then he might as well make sure that the world knew that he'd taken the plunge. And now, looking down at the band encircling his finger, he felt like he'd made the right decision. He was married. And before long, his circle of friends and colleagues would notice. He'd need a plan to introduce Emma to them, he thought. And to his mother. That, he thought, would be interesting.

Back at work and behind the closed door of her office, Emma shifted her ring to her right hand. It fit well there, and she was not ready for the questions that a ring on her left hand would bring. She knew that news of their marriage would eventually leak out, but she had no desire at all to have that happen today. Not while she was still reeling with the consequences of her actions. Or rather, the actions of her sister.

Emma was under no delusions. Jen had disappeared. Her cell phone was off. There was no way to trace her. This was no accident. Had Jen really met someone, or had she just decided that she didn't want to be tied down to a man for three years? Mason was handsome, rich, sexy, and cold as an Antarctic winter. Did Jen decide that the money was great, but the marriage was a losing proposition?

She was sure that Mason was disappointed, though he was coping with the change fairly well. Jen was Miss America compared to Emma's girl next door. What man would prefer the latter when he had held the former in his grasp? Mason was definitely settling, though he probably had little choice given his time constraints. It appeared that he would be a gentleman about it, but it was also clear that there would be no real interaction between them. Had it been the same with Jen?

Briefly, Emma wondered if Jen had slept with him. Her guess was no, simply because she didn't see Mason as someone who would add a personal dimension to a business arrangement. Maybe once they'd been married, it would have eventually happened. But before the deal was finalized? No, probably not. Jen may have given it a shot, but Mason wanted an emotion-free relationship. And while Mason would undoubtedly be able to keep emotion out of a sexual relationship on his end, he would probably be concerned that such emotion could develop for the woman he slept with. So no, Emma didn't think they'd been together.

Emma couldn't quite picture Mason in bed. He was sexy as hell, yes. His body was a work of art, and Emma had a feeling that he would know exactly how to touch a woman. She felt a slight tingle just thinking about that, but pushed it aside. Mason was cold and hard, she thought. His lovemaking would not be passionate or out of control - it would be pleasant for the woman, to be sure, but there was no way that he would ever lose himself in a woman, unless some woman could reach him, and break through that hard outer shell. That woman would need to be someone amazing – someone way more attractive and appealing than Emma Jameson. And while she liked to think that she was a nice person, she was not anyone who could break through the kind of hard that made up Mason Parker.

FOUR

That evening, after waving Rhoda and her colleagues off to happy hour, Emma finished up some last minute paperwork and then headed over to the doggy day care facility to pick up a waggly and very happy Chaos. Back home, she let him out into the back yard, and while he scouted the perimeter for errant squirrels, Emma changed out of her ivory suit and into a black skirt paired with a short-sleeved red silk blouse. She added a pair of black heels, pulled her hair down from the chignon and simply pulled it back into a ponytail, and then fixed her makeup. As she was applying lipstick she noted her hand in the mirror, and pulled it back to look at the ring on her finger..

Nobody had noticed it today. It was a new ring, clearly, but it was on the right hand, so it called no attention. It was lovely, Emma thought as she studied it. And it signified something that still sort of terrified her. She was married. To one emotionless and kind-of-intimidating man. With some trepidation, she moved the ring back to her left hand.

Sighing, she glanced at the clock, then let Chaos back inside to feed him before re-crating him while she headed out for dinner. On days like this, she felt extremely guilty for not being home all day with him, but as long as she gave him something to gnaw on in his crate, he seemed content. Plus, doggy day care always wore him out. Doggy socializing was serious business, and Chaos was nothing if not serious about playing with other dogs. He was probably whooped.

After guilting her into giving him a frozen Kong of peanut butter, Chaos settled back into his bed and started chewing on his treat, barely looking up when Emma called good bye to him. As she headed to her car, she looked down at herself and rolled her eyes. This was why she kept a lint roller in her car. Chaos didn't seem physically capable of holding on to any fur at all when she was around.

Quickly running the lint roller over her skirt, she inspected herself carefully for any remnants of fur, then hopped into her car and started the engine. It wouldn't take her long to get to the restaurant, and if there were any justice in the world, she'd have a glass of wine in her before Mason showed up. Tonight, she badly needed Dutch courage.

For a Friday night, Emma was surprised to find that parking wasn't too difficult. Mason had chosen a restaurant that was very close to a garage, so rather than drive along the streets looking for metered parking, she just pulled into the lot, took the ticket offered by the machine, and quickly found a convenient spot. After one last look in the mirror, she headed for Alamaya.

Walking in the front door, she was immediately greeted by a friendly hostess, who asked if she were meeting anyone this evening.

Emma nodded. "I'm meeting Mason Parker. I believe he has a reservation?"

The woman smiled a warm greeting. "Yes, of course. He just called, and he asked us to let you know that he's on his way. Shall I seat you?"

Emma shook her head and said, "No, but thank you. I think I'll have a glass of wine at the bar while I'm waiting for him."

The hostess nodded. "I'll let him know where to find you."

"Emma."

Mason. She swiveled around on the bar stool and smiled up at him. Her smile faltered somewhat when she noted the glower on his face, but since she couldn't think of what she might have done that would cause a scowl she just shrugged and slid off the stool to join him for dinner. Waving her thanks to the bartender and grabbing her nearly untouched glass of wine, she turned and nearly ran into the immovable wall that was her new husband. Precariously balancing her wine, she somehow managed to not spill down his white dress shirt, or her own outfit.

"Good heavens," she exclaimed. "I didn't think you'd still be standing right there."

Reaching out, Mason gently took the glass from her hand and took a sip, his eyes on hers. Surprised, he raised his eyebrows and nodded his head at the wine. "This is quite good," he acknowledged. "What is it?"

"It's an Italian Sangiovese."

"You know your wines."

Emma grinned. "Sometimes. Sometimes I just know my bartenders. That's Leon," she added, smiling over at the young man behind the bar. "He recommended it."

Mason frowned slightly, and then motioned to the bartender that he would join her in a glass of wine before they sat down for dinner. Moving to the stool next to her, he helped her back into the seat she had just vacated. Leon placed a glass of the Sangiovese in front of Mason, then winked at Emma as he turned away to fill a drink order for a table.

"You make friends quickly," Mason observed.

"You were late. And he's a nice guy," Emma said defensively.

"You're my wife."

"Hard to forget that. Especially given the ring on my finger."

"Good." The satisfaction in his voice gave Emma pause, and she looked over at him warily.

"Why on earth do you care?" she asked suspiciously.

He just smiled cooly at her. "A man likes to think that his wife recalls that she's married to him. Particularly if she just married him that morning."

"I see."

"I assume Leon did not get your number this evening?"

Emma nearly spewed her drink out her nose. She looked up at Mason. Was he serious? He thought that she was out picking up men the same day that she'd married him? She shook her head in disbelief. "What exactly do you think I would say to the man? Sure, here's my number. Call me in three years?"

"You're an attractive woman," Mason started to say.

"With a wedding ring on her hand," she said, raising her left hand and pointing to the ring with her right index finger. "And a fairly strong moral compass. I think you can rest easy that I'm not out picking up men on the same day as our wedding." She nearly muttered 'you moron' under her breath, but decided that it might be a bad idea. Still, it looked like Mason got the unuttered message. He simply chuckled, and then raised his glass to her.

"To my wife. May our marriage bring us..." he hesitated, as if thinking of what he should toast to.

"Peace?" Emma contributed after a few seconds. "Friendship? Contentment?"

"I was going to say mutual satisfaction, but perhaps your sentiments are more suitable for a wedding day," he acknowledged dryly.

Rolling her eyes, Emma clinked her glass up against Mason's.

"To us," she sighed. "Whatever 'us' ends up being."

"You're hoping for more?" His eyebrows rose skyward as he looked over at her.

"I'd like to think that we at least might get to be friendly. But I'd settle for not killing each other." Taking a sip of her wine, she turned in her stool to look directly at him. Might as well get this out in the open, she thought. She really wasn't looking for double entendres, innuendos, or any kind of flirtation, and she probably should make that clear.

"Look, Mason. I was wrong about you. As I mentioned to you before, when Jen told me that she was marrying you, I assumed you would be some sort of crazy, reclusive, socially-maladapted man. It's clear that you're not. In fact, it occurs to me that you are probably used to women falling at your feet, for any number of reasons. But it's important that you realize that I'm not planning to do that."

Hazarding a glance at him, she realized that he was giving her his full attention.

"This is only going to work if we treat it as a business arrangement. We have a contract. Let's keep things fully professional. And perhaps friendly, if we get that far."

Mason smiled slightly as she wrapped up her argument. "Spoken like a lawyer. But I agree. I want a clean relationship, with no emotional entanglements. So your limitations work for me, and I'm happy to hear you voice them. Very well. Let's drink to a detached affiliation."

Emma laughed then. "Detached affiliation?"

"An unemotional relationship. Same thing. To us, Emma."

Emma raised her glass. "To us."

"With that settled, shall we have some dinner?" he asked.

"Yes, please. I'm starving. Leon fed me mixed nuts, but they only take a girl so far."

"Leon again?"

"Yes. I may leave you for him some day, Mason. He feeds me and places wine in front of me. He sets the bar pretty high."

Mason chuckled, then helped her off her stool. Motioning to the hostess to indicate that they were ready to be seated, he stood to the side and waited for her to lead them to their table.

"You must come here often," she observed after they were seated with menus in front of them. "They know you well."

"Fairly often. Mostly for business lunches, I'm afraid." Nodding at the wine that they were sharing, he added, "So I haven't paid much attention to their wine list."

"Too bad," Emma observed. "It's a nice mix."

"Then we'll explore it together," Mason said. "Thanks for coming this evening."

Emma nodded seriously. "I realized that I have a lot to learn about you too."

"Did you get questions at work today?"

"No. I moved the ring to my other hand and stayed in my office. But I'm sure that word will get out at some point. Particularly once I let my secretary know of my change in address," she added dryly.

"You're right. Word will get out. I'd actually like to host a reception soon, Emma. People will want to meet you once they find out that we've married."

"Same on my end. But we'll need some semblance of a story, Mason, unless you want to tell people that we met for the first time two days ago."

"Do you have a story in mind?" he asked.

"The truth is always simplest. My sister introduced us."

Mason took a sip of wine. "That works as well as anything. I first met Jen five months ago at a charity event. So you and I met shortly after that. The only person who can refute that is Jen, and she probably won't be putting in an appearance any time in the near future."

Emma twirled the stem of her wineglass between her fingers as she thought about it. "It's still a whirlwind courtship," she pointed out, looking up at Mason over the top of her glass.

He shrugged. "Five months is better than five days."

"True. But people will likely want more details."

He shrugged. "Tell them what you want to."

"Before then, we need to get a few important issues out of the way. Like Chaos. And my parents. And my grandmother. I'm not lying to them, Mason. I can cope with telling them a partial truth, but I'm not telling them that I'm madly in love with you. They know me better than that. They'll see right through it and worry."

"So what do you propose, short of telling them the truth?"

"That we met, we both see advantages to being married right now, but that it's not a real marriage. I want to leave Jen out of it."

"And that won't worry them?" he asked disbelievingly.

"It might. But less so than me covering for Jen, who seems to have disappeared off the face of the earth with $300,000 of your dollars, and some guy that nobody has met."

"Are you worried about her?" he asked quietly, realizing that while Emma was angry at her sister, she was still likely to be concerned if she didn't hear from her at some point.

"I am," she admitted. "I'm sure she's fine - she's probably just in hiding for a while longer, until she's sure that you've found another solution to your problem. But I'd like to at least hear from her. Just to know that she's OK."

"Why did Jen take the money?" Mason asked shrewdly. "Did she need it?"

Emma shook her head. "I have no idea. But if she needed money, she could have at least asked me, even if I didn't have $300,000 to give. So I'm not sure what all of this was about. Maybe she just got caught up in the idea of marriage. Maybe she liked you. Maybe she wanted more than you could give her. I don't know."

"Do you want me to try to find her?" Mason offered.

Emma looked over Mason's shoulder to some point on the other side of the room. "I don't honestly know," she said quietly. "Part of me screams yes, but another part says that she's fine. It's not like she disappeared without warning. I knew she was going."

He nodded. "So we'll leave it for a while. If you don't hear from her in a few days or weeks, I'll hire someone to find her. OK?"

Emma smiled slightly. "Yes. Thanks, Mason."

"Do you want to introduce me to your family at some point?"

"Yeah. Probably. But let me tell them about you first. Gran might have heart palpitations when I tell her that I married a guy she never had a chance to interrogate, so I want to prepare her. And that's best done after she's had a few drinks," Emma added.

"Interrogation? What kind of interrogation?"

"Mostly whether you know how to make a good martini," Emma admitted. "But then she'll want to know what you do for a living, whether you plan to give her great-grandchildren, how you feel about Chaos. My family loves Chaos. He gets more spoiled when he spends time with my father than he does when I am feeling guilty and lavishing him with treats."

"I don't like dogs," Mason reminded her.

Emma rolled her eyes. "I know. And it's one of those things that makes me question your humanity, to be honest."

He sighed. "I might as well get this over with. When do you want me to meet the dog? Tonight?"

"Not tonight. I'm leaving early tomorrow for San Diego, so I'm taking him over to my parents' house tonight. I'm back on Thursday next week. I'll pick up Chaos on Friday when I join my parents for dinner. I'll tell them about you then. So maybe Saturday next weekend?"

"To meet your dog or your parents? Which should I dread more, by the way?"

"They all need to approve of you. But Mom and Dad will approve if Chaos approves, so that's the big hurdle."

"So why do you call him Chaos?"

"Do you really need to ask?"

"Please tell me that my home will be safe."

"I'll help you dog-proof it before we move Chaos in."

"Please tell me that I won't completely alienate my neighbors."

"Can't promise you that. But any that you alienate with a dog are neighbors you probably shouldn't be hanging out with anyway."

He just looked at her. "I don't exactly 'hang out' with my neighbors."

She smiled. "I'm not surprised. Your neighborhood doesn't strike me as the kind of place that has block parties. Do you even know who lives next to you?"

"Of course. I checked into it before I bought the house."

She sighed. "Of course you did."

The waiter, who had been hovering off to the side for some time, finally approached. Mason asked Emma if she would like more wine, and she nodded, so the waiter went off to fetch a bottle while Mason and Emma glanced at the menu.

"The T-bone steak is delicious here," Mason informed her. "And it comes with the added bonus of a bone for your dog."

"Why, Mason," Emma teased. "I think you're trying to worm your way into my dog's heart. And I approve."

He smiled. "I've got some ground to gain, I think. Have you told him that I'm not a dog person?"

"Chaos won't care. He's a people dog. You'd have to seriously abuse him to get him to dislike you. And since I won't let that happen, you're safe. So why don't you like animals?"

"Never really spent much time around them, I guess. It's not really that I don't like them. I just don't know how to act with them."

"You'll be fine," Emma assured him. "And I'm not being patronizing. I just know my dog. He'll like you."

The waiter returned to bring them the wine Mason had requested, and to take their dinner orders. When Emma asked for one of their signature pasta dishes, Mason asked for the T-bone. "Medium-rare."

"Chaos will love you. We can freeze it and you can give it to him next weekend."

"Nah. We'll get him another one next week. You can give this to him tonight. Just be sure he knows it's from me."

Emma laughed. "I'll tell him."

The conversation shifted then, as Mason asked more about Emma's work, and she asked more about what Mason did. They compared childhoods, education, families, dating histories, and what they liked to do on vacations. They talked about books and movies, and even ventured slightly into politics and religion. By the time dessert arrived, they each felt like they could handle questions posed to each of them about each other. None of it was personal, but the entire conversation was designed to ensure that they could pass as husband and wife - people who had known each other for longer than a few days.

"So the next step is my family," Emma said. "And I've got to find some way of telling them about this that won't involve loud sobbing, recriminations, criminal checks, or talk of calling in Uncle Louie to have a talk with you."

"Uncle Louie?"

"Yeah. He's a car salesman who lives outside of Chicago. My family jokes that he's connected to the mob."

"Please tell me..."

"No worries. The only mob he's connected to is the flash mob that occasionally dances in the local shopping mall to old Madonna songs."

There was silence for a moment as Mason took all of this in.

"You're wondering what you married into."

"I am, rather."

Emma laughed. "Well, it's the same family as Jen, so you would have needed to deal with all of us regardless. So what about your family? Will I meet them at some point?"

Mason sobered. "Yes. I'll try to ensure that it is for short periods of time, and with others around. My mother won't be easy on you, Emma."

"I gathered that from what Jen said. They're just looking out for you, Mason."

He looked over at her and raised his eyebrows. "Maybe. But we'll deal with that when we need to." He glanced at his watch. "Are you ready to go?" he asked. "It's getting late, and I know you have an early flight."

"I do. And I am. Thank you for dinner, Mason. It was delicious, and it was nice getting to know a little about you." Pushing back away from the table, she picked up her purse from the chair next to her, and stood up.

"I'm glad you could join me," he replied politely. Standing next to her, he placed his hand gently on her back, guiding her toward the door. When they exited to the street, he asked her where she had parked. When she pointed to the garage, he offered to walk her to her vehicle.

"That's not really necessary, Mason. I appreciate it, though."

"I insist."

They strolled through the garage until they were standing in front of her car. She unlocked the doors with her key fob, then tossed her purse onto the passenger seat, locking the passenger side door as she closed it. Walking over to the driver's side, she was surprised to find that Mason was holding the door open for her.

"You're a gentleman," she observed. "Thank you."

"You're welcome," he said as he watched her settle herself behind the wheel. "Have a safe trip. I'll call you on Thursday night and we can finalize our plans for the weekend."

Closing the door for her, he stood and watched as she carefully backed out of her parking spot, and headed for the exit. When Emma looked in her rearview mirror as she turned right out of the garage, Mason was still standing where she'd left him.

FIVE

At home, Emma quickly changed into a pair of sweats and a t-shirt, then took Chaos out for a quick walk around the block. Grabbing his 'suitcase' of dog food, treats, and his favorite toys, she loaded the dog into the back of her vehicle and headed for her parents' home. When she got there, all the lights were on downstairs, and she could hear loud conversation through the door. She knocked sharply to let them know that she was there, then turned the knob to let herself in.

"Hi Mom, Hi Dad!" she called as she bent down to let Chaos off his leash. He immediately disappeared into the kitchen, knowing the best places in the house to scrounge for food. As Chaos headed into the kitchen, Emma's mother appeared from the other side of the hall.

"Hi honey," she said with a smile. "Have you eaten?"

Emma laughed. Her mom was always trying to feed her. "Yup. And I'm stuffed, so don't be pawning off any leftovers on me. I'm leaving first thing in the morning. And oh crap. I left Chaos' bone at the restaurant," she remembered. "Poor doggy..."

Her mother didn't seem to hear her ramblings. "Your father is in the kitchen, mixing up some strange concoction in the blender."

Emma looked at her suspiciously. "Strange concoction like a health food mix, or strange like a new mixed drink?"

Your grandmother is here."

"Ah. Enough said. I'll go say hello."

"What are you doing here on a Friday night?" Emma's grandmother asked her when she walked into the kitchen in search of her dog and her father.

"I can't come over and visit my loving family?" she grinned as she leaned down to kiss her grandmother's cheek. Straightening up, she located Chaos, his snout buried deeply under the counter where crumbs of food were apparently lodged.

"You should be out on a date," Gran Jameson offered. "You're young. How are you going to find a husband if you spend every Friday with your dog and your father? Your good looks won't last forever, you know," she added, waving her martini in the air.

"My sparkling personality will continue to win me attention, Gran," Emma assured her. "Look out! Chaos is going after something under your feet." The dog, on the scent of some crumb dropped centuries earlier, was nearly lifting Gran off her feet in an attempt to claim it as his own. Gran just sighed, sat down on one of the stools in the kitchen, and lifted her feet. It was impressive, really, since not a drop of martini spilled over the side.

"Hi Daddy," Emma grinned. "Thanks for watching the dog. Again."

"Oh, no problem. Gets me out of the house and getting some exercise. Besides, he cleans the floor."

"What are you making?" Emma asked, settling herself down next to Gran.

"A lemon drop martini. Ask your grandmother," he added when Emma just looked at him questioningly.

"I read about it in a magazine," Gran stated. "It sounded delicious and sophisticated, so I asked your father to make it for me."

"Well, I'm in favor. Can I taste-test?" she asked, reaching for a glass. Too late, she realized that she hadn't moved her ring back over to her right hand. And eagle-eyed Gran was looking right at it.

"Emma?"

"Yes, Granny?"

"Don't call me Granny. You know I hate it. And don't try to distract me. Is that a ring on your finger?"

Emma sighed. "Why yes, Grandmother. It is."

"Don't 'Grandmother' me either. Why is there a ring on your finger?"

"Because you're always hounding me to put one there?"

"Do not tease your Gran," she rebutted. "I'm too old and I may drop dead at any moment. Tell me why you have a ring. Have you met a gentleman?"

Looking over at her father, she realized that he was also staring at the ring. And for the love of God, so was her mother. All three of them, silent as clams, just staring at her finger.

"Mom. Dad. Dearly beloved Gran... I'm afraid that I've got some news."

Silence.

"Oh for God's sake. I'm married. There. It's out. He's a nice young man, we'll be very happy together, etc. etc. etc."

To Emma's surprise, all three of them burst out laughing.

"Ha!" her father said with delight. "Nice try, Em. Next time, leave your dog home with your 'husband' - it will be more realistic."

"Oh Em. Don't let your Grandmother make you too crazy about marriage. It will come. And she only hounds you because she loves you, you know," her mom added.

Only her grandmother looked partially skeptical. "Let me see the ring," she demanded. When Emma raised her hand in front of her face, the confusion cleared up. "Oh that's just a band. Not even a diamond. Next time, at least get a cubic zirconia ring. It will look more real."

Emma just looked at her family members in disbelief. She had managed to get the news out in a backhanded way, and nobody believed her. This was just... well... *Oh hell*, she thought. Now what? Did she sit here, the night before her flight to California, arguing her parents into believing that she'd married a man they had never met? Or did she go home, pack, get herself on a plane in the morning, and deal with this when she got back?

"Well, thanks for watching Chaos! I'd better get going. Lots of packing to do," she said, a little too brightly. "See you next weekend!"

Out the door in two minutes flat, after a quick kiss to each of her beloved family members and a scritch to Chaos (along with an admonition to be very good), she was back in her car, breathing heavily and nearly sobbing. Not sure if it was with relief or frustration, Emma turned her car toward home. What a day, she thought. What a long and absolutely insane day. She was feeling deep relief that she was hopping on a plane in the morning. She would deal with Mom and Dad and Gran Jameson soon enough.

San Diego was warm. It was sunny. It was one of the easiest trips that Emma had made in a while, since most of what she needed to do was pro forma. She ate good food, enjoyed some good company, and almost managed to forget that she had gotten married in a whirlwind ceremony the day before. Almost. The ring on her finger reminded her. She had moved it to her right hand again, but every glance at it caused her thoughts to head straight back east to Mason Parker, his huge mansion, and her family's likely reaction to the news. By the time Wednesday rolled around, Emma was toying with the idea of missing her flight and staying in California for a while, but she missed Chaos. And she knew that her dog would be about twenty pounds overweight by the end of the week if she stayed away longer. Her father was notoriously bad about slipping Chaos table scraps, and Gran just consistently dropped stuff when she was over visiting her son and daughter-in-law.

Sighing, she boarded the plane and settled into her seat, thanking God and all his angels for an aisle seat close to the front of the aircraft. She had intended on working for most of the flight home, but between the busy week and her own exhausted emotional state she actually managed to sleep for a couple of hours. When she woke up, she reached for the newspaper that she'd picked up at an airport kiosk in hopes of catching up on the news.

Ah, world news. Depressing. Local news. Depressing and not really pertinent to her. By the time she'd made it through the front section, Emma was looking forward to the lighter inserts. Book reviews. Entertainment. Anything but politics, disasters, and killing in the name of religion. An article on indoor dog parks caught her attention, and she briefly wondered how Chaos would do in that kind of situation. He would be suspiciously wondering where the squirrels were hanging out, and not pleased if he didn't smell anything to chase.

Flipping the page, she glanced at the headlines. She was just about to turn the page again when something in the middle of a column caught her eye. FINANCIAL MOGUL MARRIES. And a photo of Mason followed. And oh, dear God, there was her name. Oh no. Oh no. Closing her eyes tightly, she willed the story to disappear, but when she opened them again, the story was still there. Oh no. OK, at least there was no photo of her, she thought. So the chances of anyone back home actually reading about this were slim. Unless, of course, their local paper devoted more space to the story. Emma forced herself to breathe deeply, not wanting to upset her seat mate into thinking that she was having a heart attack, but also not wanting to actually *have* a heart attack.

OK, she thought. Mom and Dad won't see this. Gran might. People at work definitely would. So she needed a plan. First, she needed to read the rest of the article to see how bad this was. She grabbed her plastic cup of ginger ale, took a healthy swallow, then refocused on the story.

Not as bad as it could be, she thought when she finished. Her name was in there. So was her occupation, but just 'lawyer.' Most of the article was dedicated to her new husband - his business acumen, his charitable contributions, his family background. And a whole paragraph on his dating history - now *there* was some interesting reading! Wow. He'd dated a whole slew of women, Emma thought. And none of them, not one, was anything close to who she was. Wow. A supermodel. A Hollywood actress. Several society women. The daughter of a famous politician. Geez.

Emma folded the paper and leaned back in her seat. Not that she needed a reminder of how unsuited the two of them were, but this was a clear indication that she was a business decision, not a decision of the heart. Or anything lower, Emma thought with amusement. Compared to the perfect tens that these other women were, particularly when they were all glammed up, Emma figured she was about a six. Slightly above average in the looks department, but nothing like these other women. It was a wonder that Mason was willing to be associated with her in public. And she wondered again why he was.

Yeah, business. She got that. But there were other gorgeous women out there he could have married. Immediate need, and discretion. OK, she got that too. But again, not insurmountable. Maybe Mason saw her as tractable and moldable - someone who would never raise a stink down the road when they quietly ended their marriage. Someone who recognized from the start how truly incompatible they were.

By the time the plane was getting ready to land, Emma was feeling decidedly down, but determined to face her life. Tomorrow, she'd let her staff know about the wedding. Calling it an elopement would make it more romantic, and thus more acceptable. She'd talk to her parents tonight, when she went to pick up Chaos. It was a darn good plan, she thought. Until she walked out of the gate area toward baggage claim, and found her mother, father, and grandmother, waiting for her outside of security. And they did not look happy.

"I tried to tell you," Emma pointed out with frustration, any happy residual effects of the California sunshine long gone. "But then you all just talked about how I was kidding, and I figured I'd wait until I got home to deal with it! I know. It was cowardly. But..."

"Emma, this is something we would expect from Jen, not from you."

"Well that's not exactly fair."

"What do you mean?"

"You should have equally high or low standards for both your daughters," Emma argued.

"We're used to Jen acting crazy. But for you to marry this man, without informing any of us? Emma, that's just not right."

She leaned back against the seatback and closed her eyes tightly. "I know that," she said quietly. "But it seemed like the right thing to do at the time."

"How did you meet this man, anyway? And how do you know that he's any good?"

Emma laughed without humor, her eyes opening and meeting her father's in the rearview mirror. "I met him through Jen. And he's a decent man, Dad." She was surprised to hear herself defending him, a man who had essentially blackmailed her into marriage.

"Do you love him, dear?" her mother asked anxiously.

Emma never could lie to her mom. So she did the next best thing - she evaded the question. "What kind of question is that?" she asked. "Do you honestly think I'd marry him if..." she let the sentence trail off as her mother looked bemused.

"No, Emma, I guess not. But I didn't think you'd elope with a man we never met either."

"I like being unpredictable sometimes," she said with a heavy sigh. "Look, it's not a big deal. We're married. You'll like him. I'll bring him by. But for now, I've got to get Chaos and get home. I have a really long day tomorrow, and I'm tired."

"Home? Where is home now, Emma?" her grandmother asked sharply.

"For one more night, it's at my old house," Emma answered honestly. "I didn't have time to pack my things before I left for San Diego. I'm moving in with Mason this weekend."

Gran's eyes searched hers, then seemed to shutter tight. "Fine then." Looking away from her granddaughter, she crossed her arms in front of her and looked out into the night.

Emma sighed. This was going extraordinarily badly, she thought. But it wasn't like she had planned this. She had hoped to ease her family into this, not for them to hear the news by reading about it in the newspaper.

"Look everyone," she said quietly. "I'm very sorry you found out the way you did. I tried to tell you before I left, but I ran out of courage, and that's my own fault. But I didn't intentionally hurt you, and I hope you can forgive me."

She watched as her family all looked at each other, then back out into the night. Oh hell, she thought, nearly deciding to throw Jen to the wolves, but then talking herself quickly out of it. She'd made her choice. Now she needed to live with the consequences.

The reaction at work was a lot better, Emma decided. Mostly because she just lied through her teeth. She'd learned her lesson with her family - if she was going to make it through without being judged as an idiot, she needed to embellish the story so it sounded romantic and wonderful and... well, yeah, fake. But work was important, she reasoned. Her employees and colleagues needed to respect her. So she pleaded privacy, true love, whatever it took to get people to look at her with amusement and genuine caring, rather than with horror at what she'd managed to get herself into.

Rhoda was particularly enthralled. "Oh my goodness, Emma. He's absolutely gorgeous. You dark horse, you. So this is why you've been working at high speed lately - so you could get home to that man. Wow. I completely get it."

Emma just laughed. "He's something else all right. Hey, can you get me the Miller file when you have a chance?"

The only thing left was introducing Chaos to Mason. And vice versa. Mason had called the night that Emma got back into town, and they had made arrangements over the phone for Emma to move her things into his home the following weekend. Mason was cool on the phone, and very business-like, and Emma was feeling a combination of dread and stone-cold fear at the thought of moving in with him.

"Why don't I pick you up from work on Friday evening?" Mason asked. "We can grab a quick bite to eat, and then we can go by and get your dog and anything you might need for the night. And then I can have movers come and pick up the rest on Saturday."

Emma sighed. "Mason, I don't think you'll want Chaos in your car. He sheds."

She heard the hesitation coming loud and clear over the phone. "And no, he's not staying outside. That's what vacuums are for. Marry me, live with my dog," she added. "But I'll drive separately on Friday so we keep your leather clean and fur-free."

"Very well," he said with a matter-of-fact tone that, for some reason, irritated the crap out of Emma. "Shall I see you at my place then?"

"What happened to the offer of dinner?" Emma asked, half-seriously.

"I'll ask my housekeeper to leave something in the oven," Mason said after a moment of silence.

Emma laughed then. "Mason, I was joking. I'll eat before I come - I need to feed Chaos and load a few things in my car. I'll be there around 8:00. Does that suit you?"

She heard the loud sigh on the other end and grinned. She rather liked the idea that he was put out over Chaos because seriously??? Who didn't like dogs?

"I'll see you on Friday evening, Emma." As he hung up the phone, it occurred to him that he'd been outmaneuvered. He had planned to meet Emma's dog on her territory, where he could see how well or poorly behaved it was, and still influence whether the dog would be allowed in his house. But now it seemed that they'd be meeting on his territory. He only hoped that Chaos was like a well-behaved small child - seen and not heard.

On Friday night, Emma again pulled up in front of Mason's home and looked up at the imposing structure. Again, she noted the lack of anything homey about it. It was cold and fairly unwelcoming, much like the man who owned it. Her husband, she thought wryly.

"You set for this, Chaos?" she asked, looking into the back seat where her energetic dog was standing and looking out. Hmmm. He looked less energetic than normal, she thought. He looked almost... wary? With a quick pat on the dog's head, Emma climbed out of the driver's seat of her car, and went around to let Chaos out of the back. She took hold of his leash and grabbed her purse, then made her way to the large and very intimidating front door. As she had done just a little over a week ago, she rang the doorbell and waited, gripping her dog's leash nervously.

Chaos sat next to her, looking up in confusion, but wagging happily when she reached down to scritch his ears. Hearing footsteps on the other side of the door, he stood up, almost as if he were preparing himself for a formal introduction.

When Mason pulled open the door, Emma's eyes widened in surprise. He was dressed in an old pair of sweats, with an obviously well-loved t-shirt clinging to his oh-so-defined abdomen. When he just stood there, clearly amused by her staring at him, she came to her senses and asked, "What, no tie?"

He raised an eyebrow in a way that Emma envied, then looked down at the well-behaved dog at Emma's feet.

"This is Chaos?"

"This is Chaos. And I have no idea why he is being as well-behaved as he is. Not that I'm complaining."

He looked up at her, his gaze narrowing. "He's normally not this good?"

She grinned then. "He's normally not this calm. I think he's intimidated by your house. Can we come in?"

He stepped aside, still looking at the dog dubiously, as if he expected it to break off leash and go careening around his house, breaking things.

She stopped when they were in the front door and knelt down next to her dog. Chaos was shaking - that was unusual.

"Chaos," she said in a calm voice, "this is Mason. Mason is a good guy, OK?"

"You need to tell him that so he won't attack me?"

But Emma didn't really register his words or the joking way in which he said it. She was worried about her dog. Looking up at Mason, she said quietly, "He's scared. And I'm not sure why."

Mason looked down at the dog with some level of concern. The animal moved closer to Emma and was looking up at him with some trepidation.

"He might sense that I'm not completely comfortable around dogs?" Mason guessed.

Emma shrugged. "Maybe. But I'm not used to seeing him worried about that. He usually just tries to make friends."

"How about if you let him off leash?" Mason suggested.

"You don't mind?"

"Does he listen to you when you tell him to stop doing something?"

"85% of the time," Emma admitted.

"Then let him off. Let's see if he calms down a bit."

Somewhat reluctantly, Emma reached down and took the leash off of Chaos' collar. Squatting down to eye level, she scritched his ears and said quietly, "It's OK, sweetheart. Honestly. Are you OK with Mason petting you?"

"Mason may not be OK with this. He won't bite me, will he?"

Emma shook her head. "No. He's gentle. Just reach down and rub his head."

She watched as Mason stretched his hand out slowly, and laid it gently on Chaos' head, gradually reaching out his fingers to scratch the dog's ears.

Chaos looked up at Mason, his tail starting to wag.

"You're doing great," Emma assured him. "Keep going."

She watched as Mason crouched down in front of them and reached out to rub his head with both hands. Chaos closed his eyes, sank to the floor, and promptly went belly up.

"What is he doing?" Mason asked in alarm, half-rising. Emma's hand on his arm stopped him.

"He wants a belly-rub. This is a good thing, Mason," she added. "It means he trusts you."

"Why does he trust me? I'm a stranger."

"Maybe. But he trusts me, and he sees that I trust you. Plus, he has his own instinct. He's fine with you."

"Really?"

"Really."

Emma watched as Mason slowly reached out and started rubbing Chaos on the chest and belly, and the dog just closed his eyes and wiggled closer. When Mason finally stopped, Chaos rolled on his side and looked up at him with love.

"That's it," she said. "You have a friend for life."

"Why was he shaking so badly when he came in?" Mason asked.

Emma shrugged with some concern. "I honestly have no idea. Sometimes dogs react to things in ways we don't understand. And I got him when he was several months old, so there might be something here that caused him to remember some bad experience he had before I adopted him. But it doesn't matter. As long as he knows that he's safe here and that you're a good guy, he'll be fine."

"He seems like a nice dog," Mason said half-skeptically.

And Emma laughed. "Oh, he is. He's a handful sometimes, but he's a sweetheart. You'll see. I have his crate and his things in my car. Can you hold Chaos while I slip out the door and go get them?"

Mason shook his head. "No, you stay here. I'll go get your things. Your bedroom is upstairs - the first door on the right."

Emma took a deep breath. "OK. Thanks, Mason. I have mostly dog things, and one suitcase for me. I'll get the rest in the morning."

"I'll help you," he offered.

"It's not necessary."

"Maybe not. But I'll help you anyway."

Emma nodded. There was no point in fighting over this, especially when he was trying to be nice. "OK. Thanks. I'll take Chaos out back and then we'll go upstairs."

"There's a fenced-in back yard for the dog, and your room has a deck that has stairs down into the yard. So you should be able to let him in and out from there if that's easier."

Emma looked at him with surprise. "Seriously? That's wonderful! Thank you. That will make any late-night bathroom breaks so much easier. Thanks, Mason."

"You're welcome."

As Mason slipped out the front door to go get Emma's things from her car, Emma started up the staircase to the top floor. "You coming, Chaos?" she asked when she was halfway up. But the dog was still sitting in the foyer, waiting for Mason to come back in. When he heard the sound of footsteps on the walk, his tail started wagging, and he was at the door, happily greeting Mason when he walked back into the house.

Emma sat down on the stairs and watched while Mason maneuvered into the house with arms full of Chaos' gear, while still trying to bend down and pat the dog on the head. Chaos stood up and nestled up against Mason, his tail showing his delight in making a new friend. For his part, Mason appeared to be equally interested in the dog. He dropped his load to the floor, bending down to scritch the dog first on the head, and then on the stomach when he rolled over for a belly rub.

Emma just chuckled. "He's got you trained already," she said lightly over her shoulder as she stood up again and started up the stairs.

Mason looked up at her as she retreated, then back down at the dog. This might not be as bad as he'd thought, he realized. Maybe he did like dogs after all.

SIX

As the days went by, Emma found that it was easy enough to talk with Mason and interact if she could pretend that they were not husband and wife. That they were strangers. But now that she had moved her things into his house, that was changing. She was taking on a role that she didn't want, hadn't asked for, and resented. She didn't want to leave her home, her neighborhood, her life. She particularly didn't want to do it because she had been forced into a hole by her sister and this man. This man who seemed like a robot to Emma.

He was being kind enough. He offered her any room in his house for her bedroom if she wasn't pleased with the one he'd initially suggested she use, and any other room for an office. He told her to help herself to anything in his kitchen. To swim in his pool. To use his gym. To raid his wine cellar. But it was so impersonal, and so completely different from anything Emma was used to. She wanted warmth, life, laughter. This home had none of that. Decorated in light wood, stainless steel, and black and white furniture, there was no color.

The kitchen was amazing - full of all the appliances Emma had ever wanted or dreamed of. But the room itself left her cold.

The only place where she felt at home was in the all-season room that was attached to the back of the house. This room was filled with plants and foliage and lawn furniture, and it looked out over an amazing view of the water. It needed a few pillows to make it more livable, but the room itself had a warmth to it that the rest of the house lacked.

Chaos seemed to agree with her. When he wasn't with her, he spent most of his time out in the all-season room, looking out the windows and occasionally barking at nothing.

Mason was never home. It wasn't really a problem for Emma, since she had her own friends and her own job to keep her busy. It was just odd, she thought. It was like being married to a ghost. He came home late, went to his study, then to bed. Seldom stopped by the kitchen, only occasionally checked in with her to see how she was, and he was gone again in the morning before Emma was up. Chaos occasionally barked when he heard Mason moving around downstairs, but that was often the only way that Emma knew that her husband was around.

One Saturday morning, Emma woke up starving. She wanted coffee and breakfast, in that order. Padding down to the kitchen, she looked into the fridge, but saw nothing that resembled breakfast food. Same for the pantry. And the cupboards. Perplexed, she leaned back against the countertop and wondered what in the world Mason ate. She knew that he often ate breakfast on the run, and had business dinners frequently, but this was silly, she thought. And she could not live like this for three years.

After taking Chaos out for a run, Emma showered and changed her clothes, crated her pooped-out pooch, grabbed her purse and headed for her car. After a quick stop for a large cup of steaming hot coffee, she continued up the road to the shopping center. Five hours later, she returned to the house, her trunk filled with groceries, and her back seat laden with purchases from a local home decorating store. She wasn't planning to change all of Mason's house - that seemed extreme. But her living space was going to be transformed, and she was claiming the kitchen. Caterers be damned, she thought.

Letting Chaos out to follow her around and sniff her new things, she looked around in satisfaction. It really didn't take much to make a house feel like a home. A new duvet on the bed, some new sheets, a few throw pillows that had color in them. More pillows for the chair. Some bright towels in the bathroom, and a couple of happy baskets to hold her things. NOW her bedroom felt lived in. Felt like it might be hers. Felt less like a hotel. Felt like a place she could actually enjoy for a while. She'd work on her office next week.

Back in the kitchen, she put away groceries, organized the pantry shelves, and stocked the fridge with fruit, cheese, yogurt, some dips and spreads, and things she would want for baking and cooking - butter, eggs, yeast, milk, cream cheese, and various sauces and condiments. And a bin full of fresh veggies for salads.

Mason wouldn't even notice, she thought with amusement, looking around the room when she was done. Everything was in its place. Besides, the man was never home, and when he was, he was in his office, which was on the other side of the house. Emma wondered if Mason even realized that he had a kitchen some days.

So. It was Saturday. Normally, she went out for drinks or dinner with friends, or met up with a date, or popped in to see her family. But she hadn't planned anything for tonight with her friends, and she was still steering clear of the flammable cargo explosion that was her family's current state. Tonight, she was staying home.

Glancing at her watch, Emma realized that it was close to 4:00. She hadn't seen Mason all day, and since he hadn't made checking in with her a habit, she decided that she was going to do her own thing. And her own thing, at least tonight, involved cooking dinner.

At 6:00, Mason pulled into his driveway. He hadn't meant to spend all day at the office, but things just happened that way. He felt a little badly that he'd abandoned Emma so soon after moving her in, but she was a competent professional woman, and she would figure her own life out. And she was still dealing with her family. Plus, she had just gotten back from a trip, he reasoned. She probably slept in, maybe took a nap later in the day. He'd check in with her tonight before heading into his home office just to be sure that she was comfortable and settled.

The amazing aroma was the first thing that hit him when he walked in the door. It was a combination of tomato, garlic, onion, Italian seasonings, and warm bread, and it hit his senses with the impact of a pile-driver. He stopped for a moment, puzzled. Why would caterers be in his kitchen? They had no event tonight that he remembered. No dinner, no cocktails. Did they get something wrong on the schedule? But then again, he thought, even when the caterers showed up, nothing ever smelled like this.

Dropping his keys and his briefcase in the hallway, Mason pulled off his overcoat and hung it in the closet before making his way to the kitchen. Where his jaw dropped.

Emma's back was to him, but he could see the small beads of sweat that had gathered on the back of her neck. Her hair had been loosely gathered on top of her head, but tendrils of wavy curls escaped, hanging loosely to her shoulders. Her butt was lovingly encased in a pair of worn denim jeans, and they had flour handprints on them where she had wiped her fingers. She had on an old cotton shirt, tied loosely at the waist, and the sleeves were rolled up past her elbows. She was standing over the cooktop, a fry pan in hand, slowly pouring a wet mixture onto the pan and letting it cook dry before removing it to a wire rack and doing it all over again. A big pan of sauce was simmering on the stove, and there were tomato splatters all over the cooktop. Another bowl of cheese and herbs was sitting off to the side, clearly meant to fill something. Chaos was asleep on the floor, apparently resting up for when he'd be called in for clean-up duty, and Emma effortlessly stepped around him.

Mason took all of it in, his emotions churning. The aroma was heaven, and he wanted whatever it was she was making. In her jeans and cotton shirt, with her attention fully on the food she was cooking, she was the sexiest thing he'd seen in a long time. He hadn't realized how curvy she was, and he wondered why he hadn't noticed. But he was noticing now, he thought. And while the mess she had made in his kitchen was positively astounding, he was surprised to find that he wasn't mad. Even when he saw a tomato sauce-filled spoon resting on his granite countertop, his emotions were far from anger. Because the main thing he felt, staring at this woman in his kitchen, was a sense of home.

More than anything, it was that last emotion that caused Mason to retreat. If Emma had looked up while he was standing there, she would have been shocked to see the almost tender look on his face - a look that rendered him human. But by the time he had leaned against the doorway to the kitchen and cleared his throat, his emotions were tucked back in, and all Emma saw when she looked up at him in surprise, was a vague appearance of irritation.

"What, in God's name, have you done to this kitchen?" he asked softly.

She wiped her brow with her shirt sleeve as she deftly moved another manicotti noodle to the drying rack. "I've made kind of a mess," she admitted with a grin as she looked around. "I'll clean it up, though. I always make a mess when I cook. I didn't think you'd mind, since we don't have anything going on tonight. I was in the mood to cook, and when..."

It registered then that he wasn't amused. "You're angry."

"Look at this place."

"Yeah. I know. But I'll clean it up, Mason."

"That's not your job," he growled.

Emma stopped what she was doing then, and looked up at him like he had two heads. "Job?" she asked incredulously. "Do you really think I see this as a job, Mason?" she asked, indicating the mess in the kitchen. "Do you honestly just want me to live here, go to work, come home, stay in my room, and only come out when you want me to go to some function with you? I agreed to be your wife for three years, not to give up my life."

Mason looked puzzled. "This is your life?"

She sighed, willing the anger to seep out of her. "Yeah," she said softly after a few moments. "It is. I love to cook. You'd have known that if you bothered to learn anything about me. I love to cook and entertain and pair amazing wines with amazing food. I love to bake bread, and to experiment with different grains and different oils. Outside of the kitchen, I read. I listen to classical, country and alternative music. I swim. I walk dogs for the SPCA. Oh, and I'm a damn good lawyer, in case you were wondering."

"I wasn't," he said mildly.

"Oh, so that part of my life you checked out."

"Of course."

She sighed. "I guess I'm not surprised."

Leaning against the doorframe and crossing his arms, he asked, "You walk dogs?"

"Uh huh."

"Why?"

"They need exercise. And I like dogs, as you already know."

"Country music?"

"Zac Brown Band."

"I'm more of a Miranda Lambert and Jason Aldean guy."

She just looked at him.

"What?" he asked.

"I would never have pegged you for country music. Classical, yes. Maybe even some classic rock. But not country."

"You don't think I'm a mom and apple pie kind of a guy?"

"Absolutely not."

He grinned then, and Emma felt her legs go weak. This was the first time he'd smiled that kind of smile at her and it was devastating. She had no idea how to respond.

"Seriously, Emma. You've made one hell of a mess. Are those tomato stains going to come off my tile?" But his eyes were still smiling as he asked.

She smiled back. "Yeah, they'll come off."

Pushing himself away from the doorframe, he ventured further into the kitchen. "So what are you making?"

"Manicotti."

"From scratch," he said incredulously.

"Yeah. From scratch. That's why the kitchen is such a mess."

He sniffed at the sauce on the cooktop. "At the risk of sounding desperate, is there enough to share?"

She burst out laughing. "Mason, this makes enough to feed an army. I was going to freeze a bunch for my lunches. So yes, there's more than enough to share."

"Manicotti," he mused, then asked. "May I choose a wine?"

"Absolutely. Dinner won't be ready for another hour at least, though," she warned.

"I'll open the bottle and join you. I assume you drink while you cook?"

"I do."

"Good. I'll be back."

"That might be the most delicious meal I've ever eaten."

Mason had reappeared in the kitchen about twenty minutes after he left. He had changed into a worn pair of blue jeans, and an old grey t-shirt with his alma mater's logo on it. His feet were bare, and he carried a bottle of red wine in his hand. After opening the bottle and pouring them each a glass, he sat down in the kitchen and kept Emma company as she cooked. Occasionally, he would toss Chaos a pretzel or a nut from a container on the counter, and laugh when the dog would skitter over the floor, once nearly taking Emma down with him.

Emma was amazed. This was a side of this very unemotional man that she'd never seen. And she kind of liked, she admitted. Plus, while the man was hot in a suit and tie, he was positively smoking in jeans and a t-shirt. The material was soft and well-worn, and his muscles were clearly defined, even under the loose fabric. She needed to be careful, she suddenly realized. Because what she was seeing here, tonight, could cause all sorts of emotional storms if she let herself think that this man really existed. She needed to remember who he was, and how coldly and ruthlessly he had pressured her into this marriage. She needed to remember that he had no use for her, apart from being able to claim his uncle's voting options on his stock. And she needed to remember that they had no relationship, and never would. The man had the emotional sensitivity of a brick.

Still, watching him tonight as he entertained her dog, she let herself enjoy his company, even while sternly reminding herself that this was a one-time thing. So she continued to work on dinner, instinctively knowing that any commentary from her might end the level of comfort he seemed to be feeling this evening.

In addition to the manicotti dish, Emma had rounded out the meal with a tossed green salad and piping hot garlic bread, fresh from the oven. Now, she was sitting at the table, her face flushed, still sipping from her glass of wine.

"That may be about the most delicious wine I've ever tasted," she rebutted. "Tell me more about it."

Mason smiled. "I'm glad you like it. It's one of my favorites."

The conversation was easier tonight than it had been before. They chatted about wine, about food, and then about how they had each come to love pairings. By the time the bottle of wine was empty and the food was eaten, Chaos was again asleep at their feet. Emma sighed and pushed away from the table.

"OK, I'd better clean up the rest of the mess," she groaned.

"Just leave it for Teresa tomorrow," Mason offered.

But Emma looked around her and shook her head. "Nah, that's not fair. I made the mess, I clean it up. Besides, almost everything just goes into your dishwasher."

"Then I'll help."

They worked companionably for about twenty minutes. Emma rinsed the dishes and loaded the dishwasher while Mason put away leftovers and wiped down the countertops. After adding soap to the machine, Emma started the cycle and bent down to replace the soap under the sink. Standing up, she turned toward the kitchen, only to find that Mason was right behind her.

She stopped abruptly to prevent herself from careening into him, and nearly fell backward into the sink. But he reached out and caught her arms, holding her steady until she found her footing. She thanked him, and then moved to walk around him, but Mason didn't step away. He just stood there, looking down at her with a puzzled look on his face, his fingers still loosely wrapped around her elbows.

"What are you doing?" she asked, silently cursing the breathlessness in her voice.

Reaching up, he lightly caressed her cheek, tucking her hair behind her ears, his expression almost tender.

"That was a delicious meal, Emma. Thank you for letting me join you."

Emma nodded, trying again to move away, but she was cornered between two sides of kitchen cabinetry.

"I'm glad you enjoyed it. Thanks for the use of your amazing kitchen," she added, trying to keep the conversation light, unsure what Mason was doing or why.

When he reached out again to run his thumb over her cheek, Emma pushed away.

"Stop it," she said quietly.

He immediately dropped his hand and moved away, blanking away any expression on his face. "I apologize. I forgot for a moment..."

"That I'm not one of your dates?" Emma smiled to defuse her comment. "Don't worry about it, Mason. I'm sure this is odd for both of us." Turning, she gestured to Chaos and headed for the doorway. "I'll take Chaos out for a walk." Turning in the doorway, she added, "Thanks for the wine, Mason. It was some of the best I've had."

Later that night, Emma looked up from the book she was reading when she heard a tap on the door of her bedroom. She had left the door open to allow Chaos to move around a bit, but she was still surprised to see Mason standing there.

"Your room looks different," he said immediately.

"I made a few changes," Emma admitted, putting the book down and standing up. She needed to be at a more equal height with him while they talked, particularly given what had happened earlier this evening in the kitchen.

He just nodded. If Emma had expected that he'd compliment her on all of her color choices, she was apparently going to be out of luck. The wall was back up, the hardness had returned. She could see it as well as feel it.

"Are you settled in? Is there anything you need?" he asked.

She shook her head. "I'm getting there. I'll unpack my office tomorrow."

"Good." He hesitated, then started to turn away. "I'll be in my office. Just knock if you need anything."

"I'll be fine. Good night."

"Good night, Emma."

Emma sensed that there was more that he wanted to say, so she asked softly, "Mason, do we need to talk about what happened earlier?"

But he shook his head. "There's nothing to talk about, Emma. It was an accident, and I apologize."

"But..."

Mason turned back around, spearing her with a sharp look. "We have an agreement, Emma, and I intend to abide by it. Neither of us wants to change the rules, correct?" He held her gaze, waiting for an answer.

Emma nodded. "No, you're right. I'm fine with things the way they are. Were. Oh, you know what I mean."

His expression didn't change. "I do know what you mean. Good. We're fine then. Good night, Emma."

"Night," she said softly.

SEVEN

Life continued, Emma thought as the days turned into weeks. And hers wasn't much different from what it was before, apart from the fact that she lived in a different neighborhood, and never dated. It wasn't like she was with a different guy every week, but she had a fairly active social life that seemed to have largely ground to a halt, now that she was married to Mason. She missed going to happy hours after work, then out to dinner with a few good friends, but it just wouldn't do for her to never be seen with her husband. She spent a lot of nights alone, or with Chaos. Even her relationship with her family remained strained these days. So she just threw herself into her work during the days, and even found herself bringing work home with her - something she'd been loath to do for the past several years.

One evening, Emma was working in her office when Mason knocked at the door.

"Hi," she said, looking up. Mason was in his work clothes, his dark suit and matching tie making him look especially handsome this evening. "What's up?"

"Can you be free on Saturday night, Emma?" he asked.

"I think so," she said, pulling her calendar toward her and checking to be sure she was free. She was. "What's happening on Saturday?"

"There's a charity benefit at the country club that night. My mother and my sister will be there. We should take advantage of that and introduce you in public."

She hesitated before asking quietly, "You're sure that public is better than inviting them over here?"

"Yes."

Nodding slightly, she sighed, then penciled the information into her calendar. Looking up again, she asked, "Mason, do they know anything about the will or about the circumstances of our marriage?"

"They do not."

"So they think…."

"That we fell in love and I proposed. Or that you managed to entice me into your bed, and trick me into marriage," he said half-seriously.

Emma rolled her eyes. "You have to tell them, Mason."

"No."

"They will wonder what happened to Jen. And they will wonder what the hell kind of a woman I am who would marry you after knowing you for such a short time."

"How good of an actress are you, Emma?"

"Not that good."

"And if I make it worth your while?"

"With what?" she asked incredulously, leaning back in her seat. "Money? Jewelry? I'm not going to be bought, Mason. You've got to know that by now." She closed her eyes and counted to ten. "OK. What do you want me to do?"

"Pretend that you're madly in love with me," he said, only half kidding.

"I barely know you," Emma pointed out. "Even after all this time."

"Then you don't know me enough to hate me," he stated.

"Mason..."

He walked over to the chair in front of her desk and leaned on it, his arms crossed in front of him and his expression once again serious. "Look. I don't think my sister or my mother expect any woman to fall madly in love with me. They both think that the only reason anyone would be with me is for my money. So if you play it up too much, they'll just roll their eyes and assume that you're worse than the rest of the women I normally date."

Some of Emma's surprise must have shown in her eyes. "Good Lord, Mason. No wonder..."

"No wonder what?"

"No wonder you're such a hard man. The two women who are supposed to be 100% squarely in your court, think that no one can love you for you? That any woman who chooses to be with you is only doing so because you're rich?"

"I'm not exactly lovable," he said dryly.

"Well, maybe not at first glance," Emma agreed. "But you have good qualities."

He lifted an eyebrow. "Name one."

"You're smart."

"Is that the first characteristic you look for in a boyfriend?" he asked.

"No. But it's not the last either."

"So what's the first?"

"The first thing I look for? Kindness, I think. Someone who is genuinely nice to others, not because anyone is watching, but because they want to treat others well."

"So that's not me. What's the last?"

"Oh, there are a world of traits that I don't care about at all. Those aren't worth listing."

"So you'd take kind over smart?"

"Probably. I'd rather be with someone dumb and sweet than smart and mean."

"I'm not the nicest man in the world, Emma."

"You may not be the warmest man I know, but you're not mean. Mean is kicking puppies and making people feel small so you can feel bigger. That's not you."

"And you know this how?"

She shrugged. "I'm a lawyer, Mason. I'm a pretty good judge of character. Usually."

He looked at her through narrowed eyes. "Why the qualifier?"

"I've been off once or twice," she admitted. "Look, Mason. I can't pretend to be madly in love with you to your family - it would come off as an act, since I'm not exactly the simpering type. But caring? Yes. Putting myself squarely in your corner? Yes. And I won't say anything that will completely alienate your family or your friends."

Mason was silent for a few minutes before saying, "No, you're not the simpering type, for which I am eternally grateful."

"Trust me, Mason."

"For some reason that I cannot define or name, I actually do."

Emma laughed lightly. "Your mother is going to eat me alive, isn't she?"

"She's going to try to," Mason agreed with a shrug. "But I'll do my best to prevent it."

"The biggest issue, apart from our elopement and hasty marriage, is the money thing, right?"

"That's the only issue."

Emma was startled. "That's pathetic."

"What do you mean?"

Standing up, Emma moved to the front of her desk and leaned against it. "Oh Mason. If my daughter were getting married, I'd be concerned that she marry for the right reasons. I'd want to know that they knew each other well enough to choose each other, and that they knew what they were getting into with a marriage. But most of all, I'd want to know that they loved each other. That's all that matters - everything else falls in line if love is there."

"Well, that's fairly unrealistic in this day and age. But what's your point?"

"If she's only worried about money, she's forgetting the more important piece of marriage - love and respect. She should be concerned that we love each other."

"You have a very romantic view of relationships, don't you?"

"Well of course. Haven't you ever been in love, Mason?"

"You have got to be kidding me."

Emma looked at him somberly. "I'm not kidding. Mason, you worry me."

"I worry YOU? I think it should be the other way around. What the hell have people been feeding you to make you think that romantic love exists? In the end, it's all about what we can do for each other."

"Sex, money, and power? Aw geez. You're serious, aren't you?"

"Very."

She sighed and ran her fingers through her hair in frustration. "Then we're about the most mismatched couple in the galaxy." Taking a deep breath, she continued. "I don't know, Mason. Maybe that's all true in your world, but not in mine. My parents married for love - there was no money or power dynamics at play in their relationship. And no, I'm NOT speaking of my parents and sex in the same sentence. My grandparents - same thing. And same for most of my friends. I'm sorry you don't see that in your circle of friends, Mason, I really am. And I'm mostly sorry that your parents didn't model that kind of a relationship for you. But I believe in love, and that's what I'm going to hold out for."

Mason pushed himself up to a standing position, looking down at Emma with disbelief. "I hate to point this out, but you married for something quite different from love."

"Yeah. I did. But that wouldn't have been my first choice," she answered quietly.

"I think you'll find that our relationship is every bit as successful as these others, where couples married for 'love'."

"We're done in three years," Emma pointed out. "Nobody else I know has a time limit on their marriage."

Mason shrugged. "Maybe they should. Maybe serial monogamy is a better deal than people think."

Emma knew that it was a losing battle to fight this with Mason. She would never convince him that love existed, or that it formed a strong basis for marriage. Unless he ever felt it himself, he'd never believe in it. How sad, she thought. But it was an important truth for her to remember - he wasn't interested in a real relationship. And since she didn't have power or money to rival his, the only thing that he would see her providing in any relationship they formed was sex. So she needed to be very careful that they steered clear of each other. Physically, yes, but on her part, emotionally as well.

Mason was just looking at her, watching the emotions crossing her face and wondering how she could possibly be as good of a lawyer as she was when she was so easy to read. He saw the frustration, the sadness, the resignation that their relationship would never be more than it was. And for just a moment, he felt a twinge of sadness too. But just a twinge, and just for a moment. While the thought of a short-term relationship with her had crossed his mind, even from when he had first laid eyes on her, he realized that he might need to back way off. He had no interest at all in emotional involvement, and this woman had 'emotional involvement' written all over her.

"I'd better get back to work," she said at last. "What time should I be ready on Saturday?"

"7:00 will be fine. It's not far."

Pushing herself away from the desk, she walked around to her chair. "Anything else, Mason?" she asked.

"No."

"Don't worry about Saturday night. We'll pull it off," she said quietly.

"I'm not worried, Emma. If anyone can disarm my mother, it's you."

Emma watched him go, her eyes wary. She knew that she had thrown him with her talk of love. But there was no way that she could or would let him think that she would ever get involved with anyone if she didn't love them. And that included her hot, sexy, and oh-so emotionless husband.

Emma dressed carefully for the occasion, slipping into a sleeveless, long sage green dress that fit her figure beautifully. It was conservative in the front, cut just under her neckline, but it dipped lower in the back and draped softly to her feet. She had added a pair of taupe-colored sandals with heels, and was carrying a matching evening bag. Her jewelry was simple – a thin gold chain with a single pearl hanging from a pendant, and matching earrings. She was just slipping her earrings in when there was a knock on her door. She opened it and glanced up at Mason, who looked stunningly handsome in his tuxedo. His frame filled out the jacket in a way that made her catch her breath.

"Wow. You look wonderful," she said softly. "There's just something about a man in a black tux..."

He smiled politely. "Thank you. And you look beautiful."

"Thanks. I think that might be more of a compliment if you didn't sound so surprised," she grinned.

"You're a lovely woman, Emma."

The serious tone of his voice surprised her, but when Emma looked up at Mason, his expression was neutral.

"Thank you, Mason. That's nice of you to say."

"I've had the car sent around. We're using a driver this evening since the parking situation around the venue is less than ideal. Do you need more time?"

"No. Chaos is crated, and I'm ready whenever you are."

Mason looked over at the crate where Chaos was looking balefully up at him. "He's rather manipulative, isn't he?"

Emma laughed. "OH yeah. He's fine. He got treats and a walk and he just got in from a romp in the yard. As soon as we leave, he'll settle right in for a nap."

"I'll meet you downstairs, then," he said, with one last glance at the dog.

Emma blew Chaos a kiss, then checked her reflection in the mirror. This was as good as it got, she thought. Her makeup looked natural, her hair was tamed, and she had run the lint roller over her dress. The only thing that she needed to deal with before she headed downstairs was the overwhelming attraction she was feeling for Mason. Because, God help her, the sight of that man in a tux was breathtaking.

She knew that she hid her emotions fairly well – not as well as Mason, but that might be because he had no emotions, she thought. So she was pretty sure that he didn't know that he was affecting her this way, and she needed to be sure that her attraction stayed hidden. Because the one thing she'd learned in the past six weeks was that the man was ruthless. If he thought that he could have a sexual relationship with her, and still maintain the agreement they had, he would jump at the chance. Not because she was anything special, she reasoned, but because she had demanded his celibacy. A bone-headed move on her part in some ways, since she was quite sure that the man had a very active sex drive. Which meant that she'd have to be doubly careful, since he may want to sleep with her just to have a warm body next to him. Emma was under no illusions that Mason could be interested in her. She was, quite simply, not his type.

So. Tonight. She would go to the charity event. She would do her best to separate herself from his side after 30 minutes or so, and she would not look over at him. At all. Ever. Even if he was absolutely the hottest man in the room. She would talk to the society matrons and charm the older gentlemen as best she could. And she would refuse to be intimidated by his family. That was her plan.

Chaos looked up at her skeptically. "I know," she said firmly. "But if I have a plan, it makes it easier for me to revert to that when the evening goes to hell. And we'll be walking tonight when I get home, so be prepared," she warned.

Mason was waiting for her in the foyer. To the man's credit, he did not check his watch as Emma descended the stairs, but instead just watched her as she walked down, concentrating carefully on putting one foot in front of the other so she didn't trip.

"You'll be the loveliest woman there tonight, Emma," Mason said as he offered her his arm.

She smiled up at him. "If you're trying to brace me for meeting your mother, a glass of wine would probably be better preparation. Or a few shots of tequila."

"You will want a clear mind when you spar with my mother," Mason warned.

Emma sighed loudly. "Maybe. Though sparring with her drunk might be more fun."

Mason laughed. "You'll be fine."

"Said the spider to the fly.... No, I know I will be. I don't really have anything to lose with her, and I'm not going to pretend to be anything I'm not."

"Including madly in love with me."

"Including that."

The initial buzz around their entry died fairly quickly as Mason's friends and acquaintances came up to greet them and to be introduced to Emma. She was growing used to the surprised looks on their faces when they met her, and just smiled politely as many of them pointed out how different she was from Mason's usual women. She couldn't figure out if it was a compliment or not.

After some time, Emma decided that her plan needed action. She had been hanging beside Mason for too long, and she needed some breathing room. He was a lot to take in – an amazing combination of gorgeous male, entertaining conversation, and good manners. If she wasn't careful, she'd be thinking that she was head-over-heels in love with the guy by the end of the evening. And given his lack of a heart, predatory crocodilian nature, and overall businesslike attitude toward their marriage, that would be a complete and total disaster.

So she excused herself from Mason's side, and headed directly to the ladies' room to buy herself her freedom. When she emerged, she plucked a glass of champagne from a passing waiter's tray, and sauntered over to one of the open windows that looked out on the skyline of the city. It was a beautiful view, she thought, just as she felt someone come up to stand beside her.

Emma knew immediately who the tall, elegant woman next to her was. So this is where Mason had gotten his noble features from, as well as his regal bearing. The woman positively radiated aristocracy. But her expression was rigid, and Emma could sense the displeasure emanating from her like heat from a brush fire. Reminding herself that she didn't really need the woman to approve of her, and that her loyalty in this situation was first to herself and then to Mason, she turned to face the paragon of discontent that was Mrs. Parker.

'So you're Mason's latest." The woman fired off her initial parry, managing to both look down her nose at Emma and to give the appearance that she was ignoring her completely.

"I'm Emma Jameson, Mrs. Parker. It's nice to meet you." She would probably lose at trading insults, she knew, but she could hold her own at well-mannered and gracious. At the end of the day, she needed to be able to live with herself.

"Mason tells me that he was fool enough to marry you," the woman sniffed.

Emma laughed to herself. Mason had warned her that his mother would be difficult, but he may have understated the situation. Still, Emma felt like she'd been thrust into a period movie - and that she was cast as the servant girl in the presence of royalty. Ah well. She really wasn't intimidated, and laughing seemed preferable to crying or getting angry.

"Well, if *he* put it that way, we're already in trouble," Emma smiled. "But yes, we married about six weeks ago. I've been urging him to have you and your daughter over one evening for dinner. I think I've almost worn him down."

If the woman lifted her nose any further, she would drown in a rainstorm, Emma thought. "I do not need my son's gold-digging wife to invite me to his home," the woman said with a loud harrumph.

"Of course not," Emma responded evenly. "Though having the invitation of your son might come in handy," she added.

"That will come."

"I'm sure it will." Emma took a sip of her champagne, and looked around the room, hoping for some escape hatch to open up in front of her. Nothing seemed to be forthcoming, so she sighed and prepared herself for another incoming volley. She didn't need to wait long.

"I hope my son had you sign a pre-nuptial agreement."

"Of course."

"Then you know that you'll not get a penny from him when he divorces you."

And that did it. Emma burst out laughing, to the immense surprise of her new mother-in-law. Looking the dour woman straight in the eyes, Emma simply stated, "Mrs. Parker, you are a piece of work. Look, your son and I are married. I'm not planning to divorce him yet. And I don't think he's planning to divorce me yet either, though you can certainly feel free to ask him."

The woman sniffed again, clearly not done torturing her, but a bit surprised by her new daughter-in-law's responses to her questions. Emma realized that any woman who had dated Mason before had probably gotten this same third degree. The question was, how many of them deserved it, and how many had been nice women, but frightened away by it.

The woman's attention focused on her ring.

"Let me see your ring," she ordered, taking Emma's hand in hers and squinting at it in the dim light. "It's very plain," she at last decreed, dropping Emma's hand.

Emma smiled then, stretching out her fingers to look again at the tasteful band. "Yes. Simple and elegant. Works beautifully for me."

"I assume Mason has ordered you a diamond?"

"Good Lord, I hope not," Emma asserted. "He knows that I don't want one, so I'd hope that he would abide by my wishes."

"You don't like diamonds?" The scornful tone was clear.

"I love them. On other women. I'm not much of a diamond person, though."

Emma waited for it. Three... two... one... The sniff. It was so predictable. This was getting fun.

"What kind of person are you?" the woman asked.

So Emma shrugged. "That, Mrs. Parker, is exactly why you should get to know me. Because I could tell you the truth, and you'd still have to judge it if were true or a lie. Better that you figure out on your own whether I'm the person you think I am, or someone completely different."

"Women are always after Mason's money."

"That may be the case. But why do you immediately assume that any woman who is with Mason is interested in his wealth? I actually find it rather insulting for Mason's sake that you just assume that his financial status is the only appealing thing about him. I've dated rich men before, Mrs. Parker. None of them hold a candle to your son." Emma said this mildly, but from the look in her mother-in-law's eyes, she knew that she had taken it as a rebuke. Ah well. In for a penny, in for a pound, she thought. Time to take off the gloves.

"Do you date wealthy men exclusively?" the woman asked disdainfully.

"My last serious boyfriend was a high school teacher," Emma smiled. "What about you? Did you marry your husband for his money?"

It may have taken a lot to shock the woman, but Emma figured that she'd done it. It was a good 25 seconds before the woman managed to close her mouth to the frown it had been in before, and say, "My dear, you have no idea who you are dealing with."

"Oh, but I do," Emma said quietly. "You came from humble beginnings, and married a very wealthy man. And maybe that's why you assume that everyone who dates your son is in it for that very thing – money. But here's the thing,

Mrs. Parker – your opinion of Mason is wrong. He's far more than a bank account and far more than a titanium card with American Express. He's a good man with a good heart. So despite your own baggage, you've raised him well."

"Do you love him?" the woman challenged her.

"That, Mrs. Parker, is between me and your son. He knows exactly how I feel about him, and I know exactly how he feels about me. And truthfully, it doesn't really matter if I love him. I like him. And that's….."

"…More than a lot of people can say," Mason said, coming up behind them and slipping his arm around her waist. "I keep waiting for the mushroom cloud over here. How are you two getting along?"

Emma looked at the woman across from her, and realized that many of her questions could be construed as protective of her son. She may be a cold and hard woman, and she may have transferred those traits to her son, but Emma realized that the woman loved Mason. In her own way. And that made some of her interrogation OK. Looking up at Mason, she admitted, "I kind of like your mom. She says what she thinks. I might not like it, but at least she's not two-faced."

Mason's eyebrows went up when his mother nodded, her mouth still grim. "I'd say that I'm inclined to give her the benefit of the doubt. So far."

With a slight smile at Emma and a nod at her son, the woman spun around and stalked off, leaving a stunned silence in her wake.

"Did you just do what I think you did?"

"I don't know. What do you think I did?"

"Impressed my mother."

Emma looked at the retreating figure dubiously. "Oh, I seriously doubt that I did *that*. I think she's either running off to clean her shotgun, or to hire a hit man. She's very protective of you. Just in a scary Lady Macbeth kind of a way."

"Protective?"

"Yeah. I'm not impressed with her warm motherly tendencies, but she's like a pit bull in terms of making sure that no woman is taking advantage of you. Go talk to her," Emma encouraged. "That particular encounter made me hungry enough to eat half the buffet table, so I'm going to go dive into the hors d'oeuvres."

Mason just shook his head.

"Hey, do I need to worry about the same kind of thing from your sister?"

At that, Mason chuckled. "Not really. She hasn't liked most of the women I've dated before, but she's more polite than my mother. If you want to take the bull by the horns, Amanda is over by the bar, trying to blend into the woodwork. She hates these things."

"In the black dress?" Emma asked.

"Yes."

"OK. See you later," she smiled as she set her empty glass down on a collection tray and headed in Amanda's direction. On her way over, she discreetly studied her new sister-in-law. While she was well-dressed and her make-up and hair were flawless, there was a discomfort about her that Emma sensed. Mason was right. The woman didn't want to be here. The question was whether she was always uncomfortable at these kinds of events, or whether she was particularly uncomfortable with the thought of meeting Emma.

Making her way to the buffet table, Emma loaded up on appetizers, then headed over to the bar near where Amanda was standing. Plucking a glass of wine from one of the passing waiters, she walked over to stand next to Amanda, looking out at the room in the same direction.

"Do you know everybody here?" she asked, taking a sip of her wine and balancing her plate in her other hand.

Amanda turned to see who was standing next to her, and started in surprise. She recovered well, though. Emma was impressed.

"Not even half," Amanda responded. "But that's still probably a lot more than you know. Are you recovering from your talk with Mother?"

Emma laughed. "That's what the wine is for. She may be moving on to the hard stuff too - I think I may have annoyed her a little bit."

"From the look on her face once or twice during your conversation, I think you may be right."

"Has she ever made anyone cry?" Emma asked lightly.

Amanda grinned. "Yeah. Her rate is at about 65%."

"Holy cow! And what happens to the other 35%? Fleeing the scene? Anger? Laughter?"

"You're the first person I've seen laugh," Amanda admitted. "So welcome to the family. I understand that Mason has kept you hidden for a while."

"A bit too long, probably," Emma replied. "So it's nice to finally meet you."

"How long have you known my brother?"

"Not very long, so I understand a lot of the puzzled looks I'm getting."

Amanda shook her head. "Don't take this wrong, but I think the puzzled part is because you're not the type of woman Mason normally dates."

"Oh, believe me, I know that," Emma laughed. "For one thing, I have a dog."

"You do not."

"I do."

"And he still married you?"

"I can't quite believe it myself."

"Do they get along?"

"Oh, Chaos is beside himself with happiness. He's been following Mason around the house for the past few weeks. I think Mason secretly likes it, even if he complains about the furballs around on the hardwood."

Amanda laughed. "And Mason tells us that you're a lawyer?"

"I am. I practice family law now. I did criminal for a while, but it rules your life. I needed to be able to set my hours a bit more and to have room in my world for more than work. And you? Mason said that you're in a medical field, but didn't really give me any more than that."

"He probably doesn't know any more than that," Amanda said wryly. "If you're not in business, he's not that interested in what you do. I'm a genetic counselor."

"Seriously? Wow. That's got to be an incredible mixture of rewarding and heart-breaking. What got you interested in that?"

"Genetics? Trying to figure out the odds of turning out like my mother and father, probably," Amanda chuckled. "But you're right. It's turned out to be a good choice for me."

Emma set her plate down on a table nearby and commenced munching after offering to share with the woman. "I grabbed too much. Feel free. So Mason seems to think that both you and your mother suspect that everyone he's with is after his dollars. I can kind of see that with your mother, but..."

Amanda nearly choked on the mushroom she'd just placed in her mouth. Emma handed her her glass and patted her lightly on the back. "You OK?" she asked.

"Fine. I'm just surprised. And kind of amused, to be honest. Because Mason thinks that anyone *I* date is after our family's money."

"You're all a suspicious lot, aren't you?" Emma asked with a grin. "I just ask because I think I like you, and I'd like to be friends. But I just want to assure you that while there are many odd reasons for me to be with your brother, his money isn't one of them."

Amanda started laughing. "Yeah. I think I got that from the start. The man must absolutely adore you in order to put up with a dog. And you're too comfortable in your own skin to be looking for your identity through a rich man. So welcome to the family. Again. And this time I mean it."

Emma clinked her glass to Amanda's. "Adore may be too strong of a word," she confided. "But at least Chaos is growing on him."

The ride home that night was quiet. Emma was tired, and her conversations with her new mother-in-law and sister-in-law had worn her out. When they got back to Mason's home, Emma went upstairs to let Chaos out, while Mason locked up downstairs. Emma was in her bedroom, waiting for Chaos to reappear on her balcony, when Mason knocked lightly on her door. Emma turned around to see him leaning in the frame.

"Did you really ask my mother if she'd married my father for money?" he asked softly.

Emma nodded, unable to tell if he was angry or just curious. "I did," she responded.

"Whatever possessed you to do that?"

She shrugged. "She insulted you."

"Me?"

"Yes. As you'd warned me, she insinuated that women are only interested in you for money. I made sure that she understood that you had other charms in addition to a checkbook. She didn't necessarily buy that. So I wondered out loud if she had that kind of thing in her own past. She's just so sure that it's always the case with you, and while that may sometimes be true, she doesn't seem to judge people based on their own merits. So I asked her."

"She was rather offended, but I think she got over it when she realized that you were actually defending me."

"Did your parents have a good marriage?" Emma asked.

The walls went up immediately. Emma could see them fall into place. "Why?" he asked shortly.

"Why what?"

"Why do you want to know?"

Emma rolled her eyes. "I'm making small talk, Mason. I'm not taking notes to write an unauthorized biography. I'm interested in your mother, and in your relationship with her. That's all."

Mason looked at her for several beats before responding, "No. They had an awful marriage. They lived in the same house, but on separate wings, since I was two."

"Were they cordial at least?"

"I don't remember them interacting much, apart from an occasional social event that they hosted. And they played perfect hosts then, but there was no bond between them."

"So is that what you think of when you think of marriage?"

Walls not only up, but defenses in place and offense fully engaged. "Again, why?"

"Because I'm married to you. And yes, it may be a business deal, and it may be for show, but it's still a marriage. And it sounds an awful lot like your parents' marriage," she added, crossing her arms in front of her defensively.

"Are you looking for more, Emma?" he asked mockingly, crossing his arms as he continued to lean against the door frame. "Is this your way of asking for a different kind of relationship? Because I'd be happy to join you in your bed this evening. While it's not part of the contract, I would be willing to work around that."

She blushed, but didn't turn away. He was deliberately trying to provoke her, and she wasn't having any of it. She stated firmly, "No thank you."

Mason watched her closely. She was flustered, and flustered made her absolutely beautiful. Just like the other night, the physical pull he felt toward her was strong. And her quiet refusal irritated him. Women wanted him. This woman wanted him, he was sure of it. But she wasn't doing anything about it, and that bothered him.

Chaos appeared at the door and barked once, shortly, looking for entry. Emma turned away and opened the door for him, and he came bounding in, his tongue hanging out and his tail wagging furiously. His two favorite people in the whole world were in one room. That was nirvana for any dog. Trying to decide who to slobber on first, he paced between them, wagging with joy.

"I'd better let you get some sleep," Mason said finally, after giving the dog an affectionate scritch on the head. "Amanda liked you, by the way."

"I liked her. And your Mom. Good night, Mason."

Mason was in his room pacing. The past few weeks had been different from what he'd expected, but this evening had, without a doubt, been the most trying. Emma was starting to get to him. And for someone who was damn good at keeping his emotions contained, this was more than disconcerting, it was troubling.

It wasn't just the way she looked in her dress tonight, though Lord knew he'd had heart palpitations when she'd opened her door and he'd caught a glimpse of her. And it wasn't just the way that she'd moved, or the way that her hair waved, or the glow on her face as she laughed at a joke. It was the way she had stood up for him. Defended him. To his own mother, for heaven's sake. Emma was right – Mason had never had anyone in his corner before, and this was new to him. New in a way that had him wondering if he might want to think about a relationship with this woman. But also new in a way that made him question whether he needed to cut his losses, divorce Emma, and just take the stock hit.

He found himself testing the waters with Emma – pushing her to define their relationship, and always hoping that she would respond in a way that let him make a move of some sort. He knew that he could push her – that he could probably even get her into bed with him before the weekend was over. But he also knew that if he did that, she'd declare the contract void, and she'd run. So that was a lose-lose situation for him. But damn, he wanted her. Sexually, yes. But it was starting to be more than that.

She honestly didn't see her attraction. Growing up in the shadow of Jen must have made her think that her own natural beauty was somehow less than the beauty of her sister. And while Jen was, indeed, gorgeous, Emma had a glow about her that was more intriguing to him than her sister. He knew, without a doubt, that marriage to Jen would have led to sex. But he also know, without a doubt, that he'd be moving on after three years without a backward glance, and neither of them would expect otherwise. Emma was different, though. If he got involved with her, he'd hurt her. She would fall in love. She would want forever. And she would expect that Mason would want that too.

So he needed to keep his distance. She already thought him cold. He needed to reinforce that, but it was getting harder to keep his own needs and wants in check. She had already won over his sister, and probably his mother. And Chaos had wrapped his paws around Mason's heart. In six weeks, they had each managed to form bonds that he thought were impossible. He never wanted an animal in his house – he avoided the emotional attachment. He never expected a woman to please his mother. And he never had wanted to come home to a mess in his kitchen, a dog on his floor, and dinner on his table. Emma was proving to be far more trouble than she had any right to be. .

EIGHT

Two weeks later, while doing his best to keep distance between himself and Emma, Mason realized that he'd forgotten to inform his wife about a dinner party that he was planning for the weekend. Heading home from work in the early evening on Tuesday night, he found Emma in her office, Chaos gnawing on a chew toy at her feet.

"Cocktail party? This Saturday?"

Mason's feeling of guilt was unusual for him, and he overcompensated. "Is something wrong with your hearing, Emma? That's what I just said."

She looked up at him incredulously. "But I have plans for Saturday."

"Cancel them."

Emma tossed down her pen, leaned back in her chair, and crossed her arms in front of her. "That's not fair. You didn't tell me until just now. I can't sit around and wait for you in case you might have some event. I made plans with friends. I don't want to break them."

"Our agreement…"

"I know all about what's in the damn agreement, Mason. The agreement you forged with my sister, I might add."

"But which you signed…"

She sighed, leaning forward to place her arms on her desk. She looked tired, Mason realized. "Under duress," she said softly. "But yes. Look. I will cancel this weekend. This time. But I will not do it again. In the future, unless there is some huge public relations nightmare that requires an emergency cocktail party, I am going to keep the plans I make, and you'll be on your own."

"You're my wife. If I need you…"

"Then you had better make sure that you remember to *tell* me that you need me. And for the record, stop reminding me that I'm your damn wife." Her steely gaze met his.

That took him aback. "Why?"

"Because this is some crazy business deal. Wife makes it sound much more personal. And this relationship is anything but that."

Mason's eyes narrowed. "Oh it's very personal, Emma. And whether or not you like to be reminded of it, you *are* my wife."

"In name only. It's business, Mason. So make sure that any function that you want me to be at goes into an appointment book. Send me an Outlook meeting request. Anything. Just don't expect me to sit home, twiddling my thumbs, waiting for you to ask me to get dressed up and play wife. We agreed that I'd keep my life and my job. So that means that I get a say in social arrangements."

Mason waited a beat, and then continued. "The caterers are coming at 3:00 to start setting up. You don't need to be here for that if you have things to do. Guests will start arriving at 6:00, and dinner will be served at 7:00."

"Did you hear a word I said?" Emma asked, irritated.

"Every word, Emma. But since you already agreed to make yourself available on Saturday, it seems that the argument is moot."

"For this weekend, perhaps. But not for the future. I mean it, Mason."

He sighed. "This would be so much easier if you'd just accepted the money I offered to you. An employer/employee relationship is less complicated."

"Than a wife? No kidding. And this is exactly why it was so important to me that there would be no funds changing hands. I never wanted anyone to be able to say that I accepted money for this. Or that you needed to buy a wife."

"I didn't need..."

"I know that, Mason. Probably half the female population of the city knows that. But if it got out, it would hurt you."

"It won't get out."

Emma was clearly exasperated. "Look. You and I will never tell. But you never know whether someone in your lawyer's office will see the paperwork, or my sister will decide to come back to town and stir things up, or your mother will put two and two together and figure it out."

"So how did you go from being infuriated with me two minutes ago to being so protective now?"

Emma groaned in frustration. "It's called a relationship, Mason. I can get mad as hell at you, but I can still look out for you. Haven't you ever had a real partnership with someone before?"

Mason paused. "Apparently not," he said slowly, looking down at Emma. "Try to get over being mad by Saturday night. And dress is formal, but not black-tie."

Emma sighed. "So cocktail dress but not long gown, right?"

"Right."

Groaning, Emma pulled her calendar toward her. "I'll need to shop, damnit. And I hate shopping. You'd better be ordering good food," she grumbled.

Mason couldn't help the grin that came to his face. "I always serve the best, Emma. And I'll order extra for you."

She narrowed her eyes at him. "Olives and nuts. You put those on the menu, and I'll stop grousing."

"Done. Have you eaten?"

"Ages ago. There are leftovers in the fridge if you want them," she offered.

"Did you cook?"

"Of course."

Against his better judgment, Mason said, "Come talk to me while I heat up dinner. I'll open a good bottle of wine," he offered as a bribe.

Emma sighed and looked up at him. "Red?" she asked hopefully.

"Of course," he grinned.

"Then I'm in. Give me ten minutes and I'll meet you in the kitchen. Do you remember where it is?" she smiled innocently.

"Ha. See you in ten."

Emma's spirits lifted slightly as Mason left the room. She knew he'd been avoiding her lately, but she wasn't entirely sure why. Part of her wondered if he was sick of having her around, or if Chaos had worn out his welcome. But another part of her was grateful. She needed distance from this man.

Ten minutes later, she hit send on the e-mail she was composing, and turned off her computer. When she'd gotten home, she'd changed into a worn pair of jeans and a cotton t-shirt, and she had a pair of old scruffy shoes on her feet. But she was comfortable, and she didn't feel like changing. So whistling to Chaos, she left the room and headed downstairs.

Chaos, unwilling to abandon his chew toy, picked it up and carried it down behind her.

Mason was nowhere to be seen when she got to the kitchen, but she noted that he'd pulled out two wine glasses and set them on the counter, so she assumed he was down in the wine cellar. Chaos plopped himself strategically next to the counter, looking hopefully up at the sky and waiting for food to fall at his feet. After washing her hands, Emma pulled out the vegetable strudel she'd made earlier that evening. She turned on the oven, cut off a healthy portion, and placed it on a baking tray to warm it up, and to re-crisp the shell. There was leftover salad too, so Emma placed that on a plate and pulled out the salad dressing she'd mixed together and put it on the table as well.

When Mason emerged from the basement, he was again struck by the warmth he felt when Emma was busy in the kitchen. Not only did she cook amazing food, but she enjoyed it, and it showed in the way that she fussed with the dishes. And the extra touches were phenomenal – Mason had never known anyone who made their own salad dressing, for heaven's sake.

"Dinner in about twenty minutes," Emma informed him. "I could microwave it if you're starving, but if you can wait, it will be a lot better if I heat it up in the oven."

"I can wait. Pull out some of those nuts and olives I know you have hidden, and I'll munch until dinner is ready," he said with crooked grin. "I found a nice Pinot Noir that I think you'll like. And it will go very well with chocolate, if you want dessert while I eat."

"Oh! Yes! I think I have some dark chocolate hidden away in the back of the pantry. I'll dig it out."

Mason opened the wine, pouring it carefully into their glasses. "Let it breathe for a few minutes, Emma," he instructed, pushing one glass toward her. "It's good now, but it will be better if you give it a moment."

Emma reached into the pantry and pulled out a container of mixed nuts, then dove into the fridge for the olives. Placing each in front of Mason on the kitchen island, she took her glass of wine, then pulled up a stool at the other end and watched him as he took a handful of nuts and poured them into his mouth.

They sat in companionable silence for a few minutes as the smell of the vegetable strudel began to permeate the kitchen. "That smells incredible," Mason said, nodding his head at the oven.

"It came out nicely," Emma agreed. "I haven't made this before, but I think I'll keep the recipe. I liked it."

"You experiment a lot?"

"I do. Makes cooking more fun. I have my tried and true recipes, like manicotti, but they're more my comfort food recipes – the things I make when I want consistency, or when I just feel blue."

"Is that a good mood barometer for you? If you make something new, you're feeling fine?" he asked, motioning that the wine should be ready to taste.

"Pretty much. Or I might feel fine, but just be thinking of my mom or my Gran. Though these days, if I think of Gran, I'll be heating up a frozen dinner," she said wryly, taking a sip of the wine. "Oh my goodness! That's amazing wine! Can I see the label?" she asked.

He pushed the bottle toward her.

"If nothing else, I'm going to leave here in three years with a solid education in wine," Emma said absently as she read the label, missing the look of consternation that appeared on Mason's face and then was quickly stifled.

Getting up, she pulled the piece of strudel from the oven and placed it on a dinner plate in front of Mason. Adding the bowl of salad and the dressing, she dug in a drawer and found silverware to hand him as well.

"Thanks. This looks amazing, Emma," he said as he took in the feast in front of him.

"I hope you like it." Sitting back down, she pulled her wine glass toward her again, then stood up quickly. "Forgot the chocolate!" Reaching back into the pantry, she emerged with a bar of dark chocolate, and sat back down at the counter. Mason watched surreptitiously as she broke off a piece, placed it in her mouth, and closed her eyes, enjoying the flavor. When she took a sip of wine, she broke into a smile. "Oh wow. This is so good. I'll save you some, Mason - you have to try this combination."

For his part, Mason had already forgotten to eat, but when she opened her eyes and looked over at him, he quickly looked down at his plate. Ah yes. Salad. And dinner. Yes. And wine. Forcing himself to concentrate, he cut off a piece of strudel and bit into it.

He was silent as he chewed, looking up at Emma thoughtfully. "You made this?" he asked.

"Of course."

"From scratch."

"Well, yes. But I bought the phyllo dough. I don't think I could make that without uttering a lot of curse words, and Chaos is a sensitive dog."

Mason looked down at the 'sensitive dog,' who had moved strategically over to be directly under him, ready to catch crumbs.

"Don't you ever feed your dog?" he asked with a grin.

"Seldom. Poor dog. Nothing but skin and bones."

"Seriously, Em. This is delicious. I had no idea that you could make something like this in a home kitchen."

"Well, your kitchen doesn't quite fit the definition of 'home kitchen,' but yes. It's actually pretty easy."

Mason was shoveling food into his mouth at an astounding speed. Emma just watched in awe.

"Do you want me to heat up another piece?" she asked.

He shook his head. "This is plenty. I'm just hungry. But I'll finish this up and I'll be fine. Thanks Emma, this is really good. I appreciate it."

"You're always welcome to whatever I leave in the fridge, Mason," she said quietly.

"Thanks," he responded. "I may start to take you up on that. I don't usually get food this good when I order take-out. But only if you let me buy the groceries."

"Nah. You keep contributing wine, and we're even, I think. Probably more than even – I think I'll get the better end of the deal."

"We're not roommates, Emma," Mason said quietly. "This doesn't have to be an even split. And I think I can put food on the table in my house."

Emma looked up at him in surprise. "Of course you can," she said gently. "But…"

"But what?"

"But you don't need to buy my food or support my cooking habit. And you may decide that you want to go back to take-out, and…"

"Go on."

"And I can buy my own food, Mason. Look," she said, deciding to lay her cards on the table. "I know you've been avoiding me. I'm not entirely sure why, but I know it makes you more comfortable in many ways, so that's OK. But you might feel the need to continue doing that. And I don't want you paying for my groceries if you're not sharing them."

"You're my wife, Emma. I hardly think that my paying for groceries compromises our relationship."

She smiled sadly. "We have an arrangement, Mason, not a relationship. And no, we're not roommates, not exactly. But we're probably closer to that than we are to husband and wife."

Mason drained his wine glass. "Are you asking to revisit the terms of our agreement, Emma?"

She drained her glass as well. "Nope. Good night, Mason. Thanks for the wine. Bring Chaos up with you when you come?"

Standing, she placed her glass in the sink and headed for the stairs. Because if she stayed, she might be tempted to open negotiations.

On Saturday night, Emma dressed carefully in a short black classic sheath dress with high black and red shoes. A simple silver band encircled her neck, simple silver hoop earrings hung from her lobes, and her brown wavy hair was pulled back in a red metal clasp. It was the perfect combination of dressy and chic, and Mason nodded his approval as she came down the steps to join him in the foyer.

"The caterers are nearly set up," he informed her. "Is there anything you'd like to change?"

Her eyes widened. "Oh heavens no. I don't know anything about throwing a dinner party of this caliber! I'm sure it will all be fine."

He took in her jittery hands and her quick breathing, and his eyes narrowed. "You're not nervous, are you?"

Sighing, she admitted, "A bit. These are all your friends this evening, and all of them will be looking at us, wondering why they've never met me before, and why the rush."

"Maybe, but I think they'll be pleasantly surprised. And Amanda will be here, so you'll have a familiar face in the crowd."

She looked relieved. "Oh good. I really do like your sister."

"I think the feeling is mutual."

"Is your Mom coming?" Emma asked with some trepidation.

"I doubt it."

"Did you invite her?"

"Yes."

"And she didn't RSVP?" Emma feigned dramatic concern by moving the back of her hand to her forehead. "Oh my goodness, the rules of society have been broken, the world must be ending. I'd better run back upstairs and say farewell to Chaos."

Mason rolled his eyes. "Speaking of the dog…"

"He's in his crate. I gave him a frozen Kong of peanut butter. If you turn the music up when he starts to whine, you won't even notice he's there."

"And if he barks?"

"I'll go up and comfort him."

Mason looked at his watch. "Does he need to be let out before everyone arrives?"

Emma shook her head. "I let him out about 20 minutes ago. He should be ok, unless guests really linger. In which case, I'll get him leashed and take him out the side door."

Mason seemed to really look at Emma then. "You look nice," he said softly.

"Thanks. I'm recycling. I didn't have time to shop. I hope no one notices, but I don't think people pay as much attention to black, so I think I'm safe."

Mason laughed. "I think you're fine. Lovely, in fact. Would you like a glass of wine?"

"Before guests arrive?" Emma laughed. "Talk about living dangerously. Anything I need to know about the group you've invited?"

"Some are friends, some are colleagues, many are employees."

"Ah, so the obligatory go-to-the-boss's-house evening."

"I'm sure people want to come," Mason said with a straight face.

Emma burst out laughing. "I'm sure you're right," she giggled. "We'll see how late people stay."

Mason grinned. "Go make sure they have your olives and nuts. I want to be sure that we're set at the bar."

Emma wandered out onto the patio and was happy to see that Mason had taken her request to heart. There were bowls of mixed nuts and olives spread around on various tables, and the caterers were moving around, ensuring that everything was set up correctly. When Emma heard the doorbell ring, she reluctantly took one last look around and headed back inside.

"You did well tonight." It was the end of the evening, and the last guests had headed out a short while ago. The caterers were moving around, picking up the remnants of the party, and packing up leftovers to leave in the fridge. Emma had gone upstairs to let Chaos out, and was now back downstairs helping to get things in order. She looked up when Mason appeared next to her.

"Thank you. You sound surprised."

"I was concerned that you might not enjoy yourself, or that you might not feel comfortable with the people I work with."

"Why would you think that?" Emma asked.

"You don't know any of them."

"I'm a lawyer. I schmooze."

He smiled then. A warm, happy smile. It took Emma's breath away.

"You should smile more often," she said softly.

Mason looked at her as if he hadn't heard her. "What?" he asked.

"It makes you more approachable," she explained.

"I'm not approachable?"

"Aw geez, Mason. Not normally, no."

"According to who?" he asked.

"Well, me. And probably a good portion of your staff. I think half of them are afraid of you, and the other half was too scared to tell me that they are afraid of you."

"They told you this?"

"Well, not right off. Some were sure that I was some kind of nasty spy who was going to rat them out to the boss. Others, like your mom, think that I'm a gold-digging vapid idiot who only married you for your money because, seriously, why else would I be with you? And the rest thought I was some poor stupid girl who got sucked in by your sexiness, and that I'm going to find out very soon what a mistake I've made."

"Sexiness?" he asked, his eyebrows raised.

She shrugged. "Well, yeah."

He rolled his eyes. "Did anyone in the room have anything nice to say about our marriage?"

"It will come, Mason," she answered quietly. "People just didn't expect this, that's all. You date supermodels. You don't marry the girl next door."

"I *like* the girl next door," he said in his own defense.

"That's just because I feed you."

He leaned back against the wall and crossed his arms in front of him, looking down at her with a crooked grin on his face. "So you didn't come out looking so good in all of this, did you?"

"What do you mean?" she asked suspiciously.

"Well, you were either a spy, a gold-digger, or a girl with a low IQ who makes decisions based on looks alone."

"Oh. I didn't think of it that way, but you're kind of right. OK, I'm insulted. Except that I can kind of see the sexiness thing."

Mason's eyes narrowed. "How much did you have to drink tonight?"

"Probably a couple of glasses of wine too much," she admitted. "Your friends intimidated me a little. Plus, I was scared your mother would show up."

"So you think I'm sexy?"

"Of course. Anyone with two X chromosomes thinks you're sexy. And some of the people with Y chromosomes. If they're gay. You're kind of appealing across all crowds, I think."

Mason looked at her closely. "Only *two* glasses of wine too much?" he asked.

"Yeah. Only two glasses. It's like truth serum to me. Give me wine, and ask me anything."

"Anything?"

"Sure."

"Why didn't you want money to do this?"

She looked puzzled. "To do what?"

"To marry me."

"I don't marry for money."

He chuckled. "I'm sure you don't make a habit of it. But it would have made your life easier to take the funds. So…"

But Emma shook her head. "I make decent money on my own. I'm living in your house for a while, so I can rent my place out if I choose. And I live the way I want to. So I don't need the money, and it would just cause problems. I don't want to be beholden to you financially."

"Why are you so different from your sister?"

"More truth serum questions? Don't know. She's always been the beautiful and kind of wild one. I guess I needed to make up for her by being calm and responsible. My parents could only cope with one of her."

"Why did you decide to become a lawyer?"

"I like rules." At the look of incredulity on Mason's face, Emma laughed. "No, seriously. I think we have rules for a reason, and people should follow them, and if they don't there should be consequences."

"Do you like to make the rules?"

"Not particularly. I'm more of an enforcer, I think. Especially when it comes to kids. When people break rules and kids get hurt...."

"I can see that." Picking up a half-empty bottle from the table near them, Mason asked, "More wine?"

"Why? What other questions are you planning to ask me?"

"I haven't decided."

"Then no more," Emma stated firmly. "I've had enough, really. But thanks. This was a fun evening, Mason. And I liked spending more time with Amanda. Are you sorry your mom didn't come?"

"She'll show up eventually," Mason said with certainty. "She might be waiting to see what others think of you before making up her own mind."

"Well." Emma wasn't sure how to take that. So she just thought about it for a moment, and then decided that she really should head up to her room. Being a little tipsy in the presence of a man that she was incredibly attracted to might not be the best strategy for her future, she thought. Particularly since said attractive man didn't seem averse to following up on said attraction.

"Good night, Mason," she said as she turned toward the stairs. "See you in the morning."

"Good night, Emma. Sweet dreams."

NINE

Despite her best efforts, Emma's visits to her parents' house were still strained. They were still hurt at how quickly and privately Emma had married a man they had never met, and she couldn't really explain it to them without implicating her sister for a really stupid move. And possibly a criminal one, given that she had signed a contract, taken money, and then reneged on the deal. It wasn't that Emma felt the need to protect Jen from her parents, but more that when her parents found out, and all hell broke loose, Jen should be there to explain herself.

Occasionally, Emma would take Chaos and go for a walk with her father, but their conversations now focused on work, not on anything personal. Her talks with her mother were loaded with unspoken meaning. And her grandmother just looked at her, shook her head in disgust, and poured another martini. So it was with a heavy heart one night that Emma sat in the sunroom of Mason's home, looking out at the beautiful view, and wondering if she'd ever be able to fit in to her old life again. Chaos was resting his head on the seat next to her, and Emma was gently scratching his head and rubbing his ears. He seemed to sense her melancholy mood, and just sat quietly, looking worriedly up at her.

Her day had not been improved by work today. One of the foster children that Emma represented had run away from home, and Emma was trying to work with social workers to determine if it was because of issues the child had, or issues that existed in the foster home. Sometimes it was hard to separate them out.

"Emma?"

"Mason. Hi. I didn't expect you home tonight," she said, sitting up and passing her hands briefly over her eyes to make sure that he didn't see any remnants of tears.

"Are you all right?" he asked gently.

"Yeah. Just a hard day," she admitted. "How was yours?"

"It was fine." He took a hard look at her, but didn't pry. "I'm headed out of town next week for a few days. I leave Monday, but I'll be back by the weekend."

Emma nodded. "Anything you need me to do while you're gone?"

He shook his head. "No."

"OK. Thanks for letting me know."

"Do you want a glass of wine?" he offered.

"Thanks, but I don't think so. Not tonight. But there are leftovers in the fridge for you – and they're fine to be microwaved," she added.

Watching him leave, Emma looked back out the window into the night. Sitting here wasn't helping her frame of mind, she thought. Maybe she'd go down to the kitchen after all. She still didn't really want to drink, since wine would probably just make her sleepy on top of being sad, but she could keep him company while he ate.

When she walked into the kitchen, Mason was standing in front of the fridge with a confused look on his face. She laughed. "It tastes a lot better than it looks," she assured him, as he gazed skeptically at the dish in his hand.

He looked up at her with surprise. "What is it?" he asked.

"A black bean sweet potato chili. It's really yummy. There's salad and cornbread too," she informed him, moving over to take a seat at the counter.

"OK. I'll try it. You haven't made anything that I don't like yet," he added.

She watched as he heated up a plate for dinner, then walked over to join her at the island. His first bite of her food was always fun to watch, since he was always doubtful about her dishes until he tried them. Tonight was no different. After his first bite, he tore into the meal like a starving man.

"So what made your day so trying?" he asked as he ate.

Emma sighed. "I had a bad case at work. And then I went to go see my parents. They still haven't forgiven me for this," she said, waving her hand back and forth between them.

Mason shrugged. "It'll work out."

But Emma wasn't so sanguine. "It might. It might not. Even when Jen comes home, things might not ever get back to how they were."

"Is that a bad thing? If they don't see you for who you are, as an adult able to make your own decisions, why would you want to go back to that kind of a relationship?"

"Because they're my family. And I love them. And I know that I hurt them."

"Maybe, but they hurt you too, by not giving you the benefit of the doubt. You don't need to run everything you do by a steering committee, Emma."

"No, but this was marriage. I think a family can have a reasonable expectation of being informed before their daughter goes off and marries someone."

"Jen appears to have gone off with some guy. They're not worried about that?"

"Of course they are. But that's normal behavior for Jen."

"Then I don't understand the problem here. I see a double standard – what's good for Jen is not acceptable for Emma."

She sighed. "You're right, of course. But just because they aren't applying the same standards to me and my sister doesn't mean that I didn't hurt them, or that they don't have the right to feel left out of my life. We have always had an open and fairly loving relationship, apart from a few months in high school when I was running around with the local bad boy, but that's another story."

He finished his dinner and pushed the plate away. "Is their love for you conditional, then? You do what is expected and all is well, but you do something contrary to that and they withdraw?"

"No. I don't think so. I think I always know that they love me. But they're not always happy with me. Just like you're not always happy with me."

"But I'm not family."

"Of course you are. You're my husband. You're as close to family as you can get."

"Not exactly," he said dryly. "Our relationship is based on a business arrangement, not on anything else."

"I'm aware of that," Emma returned. "But over the past few months, it seems that we've at least approached the boundaries of a friendship."

Mason shrugged. "We're not friends, Emma. We get along well, we're compatible, and we each play our roles well, but we've never strayed from the initial agreement in our contract."

Her eyes narrowed. "Do you even know what a friend is?"

"I have friends."

"Yeah? How do you know?"

"What do you mean?"

"Do you have the same definition for a friendship that you have for a relationship? A mutual acknowledgment of what you can get from each other?"

"Emma..."

"Oh never mind." She stood up and grabbed Mason's plate, putting it into the sink and running water over it. "I've got a few more things to do before I go to bed."

He stood as well. "Emma, you're overreacting again."

For some reason, Mason's words hit Emma hard. After a bad day and a difficult visit with her family, this criticism of her own feelings was like throwing gasoline on a fire. Her words exploded out of her in frustration.

"Overreacting? Because we have different opinions on relationships, you assume that I'm the one who is wrong?"

"Calm down, Emma. This isn't worth getting emotional about."

"No? Then what is, Mason? Are you ever emotional? Other than occasionally showing some slight amount of anger or annoyance or frustration at me? Tell me something, Mason. Do you feel *anything? Ever?*"

And something in Mason seemed to snap in response. He moved faster than Emma had ever seen. In seconds, he was next to her, his hands gripping her arms, his entire body pushing her back until she was up against the kitchen wall. He moved forward, slid his hands down her arms until they reached her wrists, then deliberately raised them up above her head, moving still closer. His face was inches from hers, his eyes burning down at her as he responded roughly, "Feel? Do I *feel* anything? What do you think, Emma?"

She gasped, her eyes flying up to meet his. "Mason, what...?"

But he continued as if he hadn't heard her. "For months, I've watched you in my house. Out with my friends. Talking with my sister, and even my mother. For months, I've seen you in shorts, in dresses designed specifically to increase my blood pressure to boiling point, even in your bathrobe. And you ask me if I *feel* anything?"

Still holding her hands above her head with one hand, he moved the other down the side of her face, to the side of her neck, causing waves of sensation to radiate out from her core. She closed her eyes, moaning softly.

"What about you, little Emma? What do you feel?" he asked softly, his voice husky with need. He gently kissed the side of her neck, behind her ear, moving softly around to her chin. She writhed against him. This man, this hard-hearted man, was making her feel things she'd never felt before. He was expertly making her want him. And that was the problem. He was completely in control. She was completely at his mercy.

Turning her head, she began to struggle against him. Without a word, he let her go, stepping back. She fought for breath, cowered against the wall. He simply straightened his tie.

"Don't do that again," she said quietly, once she'd caught her breath.

"You asked, little Emma. I was just responding," he replied evenly.

"No. You were making a different point entirely. And I get it," she said with a sigh.

But Mason just pinned her with his gaze. The same predatory gaze that had caused chills to run up Emma's spine when she first met this man.

"I'm not sure you do. I want you, Emma. True, that wasn't part of the original deal, and I'm not the kind of man who forces himself on others."

"No. I know that," she acquiesced.

He nodded, moving away from her toward the door. "Good night, then."

Emma couldn't sleep. She was sitting in the comfortable chair in her room, legs curled under her, staring out the patio doors into the night. Despite the cool air, she had the doors open, so a breeze blew in through the screen. But every time she thought about what had happened downstairs, in the kitchen, a wave of heat rushed over her – the cool air helped to beat that back down.

She knew that Mason was delivering a message – that any closeness she felt from him was sexual. That he would be happy to have her join him in his bed, but that was the extent of his emotional engagement. They weren't friends. They weren't anything more than friends. They were two people who were shackled together via a business arrangement. And if they got additional 'benefits' out of that, it would be fine with him. But if she was looking for white picket fences, children, a playmate for Chaos… she was barking up the wrong tree.

And intellectually, Emma understood. She had known from the start that Mason was unreachable. That he tucked his emotions in so deeply that it would take a warehouse of dynamite to break through the walls he'd built. She had accepted that, even welcomed it, since it meant that there would be no real strings between them. After three years, she would be done.

But his touch had nearly undone her. Even knowing that it was expertly and coldly applied, he had still known just what buttons she had, and how to push them. In the space of about fifteen seconds, he had her twisting in his arms, nearly begging him to take her on the countertop. It was shameless, she thought. But she knew and understood that she could go no further than that. If she did, if she allowed their arrangement to progress to a sexual relationship, he would destroy her. He wouldn't mean to, but he would. After three years, he would quietly divorce her, and show her the door.

A door that she was looking to with longing now. Not even a year was up. Oh hell, not even half a year was up. She would need to survive this for a lot longer than she'd survived it so far. Could she do it without destroying her heart? Emma wasn't sure. Because, as hard as Mason was, as emotionally distant as he made himself out to be, there was something inside him that pulled at her. She saw pieces of this occasionally – with Chaos, with his sister, even with her. But only pieces, and they were quickly tucked back into place.

Looking out into the night, Emma replayed his touch. Replayed his words to her. Wondered what would have happened if she'd let things go on. But she didn't wonder for long. She knew. She would become his sexual release, and he would become her world. She needed to stop it when she did, and she needed to make sure this didn't happen again.

Mason was leaving on Monday. Today was Thursday. As far as she knew, they had no plans this weekend. Time to make herself scarce, she thought. By the time they saw each other again, this day would be truly behind her, and her emotions would be back in check.

The next day, after a quiet morning doing laundry and relaxing in her room, Emma decided to take the bull by the horns and deal with her family. Throwing on an old pair of sweats, a t-shirt, and some tennis shoes, she loaded Chaos into her car and headed for the dog park. After throwing the ball so many times that Chaos began to look the other way when she threw it in hopes of getting some rest, Emma gave him some fresh water and a handful of treats. After stopping at the local coffee shop for a drink and a snack, she headed over to her grandmother's house.

Knocking lightly on the front door, she pushed it open and stepped in, calling out as she entered. "Gran?"

Her grandmother appeared in the doorway, her feet encased in a pair of old tennis shoes, and her hair tied back in some crazy fashion to keep it out of her eyes. "Emma, what on earth are you doing here?" she asked.

"Came to talk," Emma responded, kissing her on the cheek. "Is it a bad time?"

Gran shook her head vehemently, nearly dislodging one of the pins that was holding her hair in place. "Oh Lord no. I was just settling in for some stupid afternoon TV that always makes me infuriated at the low depths to which our society has shrunk. And then I realize that I'm watching it and that just makes me madder. Come on in. Where's Chaos?"

"He's in the car, napping. I'm parked in the shade, so he's fine for a bit."

"You can bring him in, you know," her grandmother offered.

"I know. But then he'll wake up and just start getting into everything. I just took him to the dog park, and he ran about a million miles there, so he's worn out. He's happy."

"But you're not," her grandmother said, looking closely at her.

"Not what?" Emma asked.

"Happy."

She sighed. "Not particularly, no."

"Well come on in and sit down, and tell me what's going on. Is it that man?" she asked with a frown.

Emma shook her head. "Mason? Not really. That's pretty much going exactly as I expected it would. No, I'm more unhappy with how things are with us," she explained as she plopped down on the couch next to her grandmother. "I miss my family."

"You should have thought of that before you ran away and married a man behind our backs," her grandmother sniffed.

Emma looked over at her grandmother. "Oh just stop," she said firmly. "If Jen had done this, you'd all have thrown a party. I had my reasons, which none of you ever considered, or even asked about. It was just all about you. So enough of this crap. You either love me and trust me enough to know that I did what I did for a very good reason, or you boot me out on my butt. What's it gonna be, Granny?" she challenged with a grin.

"Do not call me Granny," her grandmother groused. But then she sighed. "You're probably right. We'd celebrate until the cows came home if Jen came home married to a man like Mason."

"So what's the issue with me?"

Her grandmother looked thoughtful. "You've always been the responsible one, Emma. We all somehow expect that Jen will come home one day with a shaved head, a tattoo on her back, and some motorcycle-man in tow, and announce that they eloped. You, we expected the white dress and the party and the bouquet tossing. It's just something we need to work through, I guess. Plus the fact that you didn't include us in any of this. I guess we felt left out. We never even knew you were dating, for God's sake."

Emma leaned back in her chair. Of all the members of her family, she was closest to her grandmother. Boxed stuffing, frozen pie, and all. She had gotten her love for cooking from this woman. She had spent hours at her house when she was little, curled up next to her, watching episodes of Seinfeld. Maybe it was time to confide in her.

"Well, I wasn't," she said at last.

"Wasn't what?"

"Dating. I just met him two days before I married him."

Her grandmother looked over at her, then over at her well-stocked bar. "Do I need a martini for this conversation?"

Emma gave a half laugh, and said, "Maybe."

But Emma's grandmother shook her head. "No. I'll wait. Go ahead. Explain."

So Emma told her the story. Told her about Jen, about the contract, about Mason's threats. Told her about the quick marriage, the social events, meeting his mother. Told her about the slow building up of a friendship. Even told her about what had happened last night. And through it all, her grandmother just held her hand and listened.

"Well," she said when Emma finished. "We've certainly been giving you hell when you didn't deserve it. Sounds like you've been living through a hell of your own."

And for the first time since this whole fiasco began, Emma broke down in tears. Her grandmother just held her and let her sob her heart out.

"So let's figure this out, you and me," she said at last, when Emma was at last reduced to a hiccupping mess.

"First, you have your family support system back. I won't say a word to your parents about all of this, since I know you're trying to keep Jen's ridiculous behavior quiet, but I'll do what I can to make sure that things go back to normal. And you should bring Mason over with you from time to time. We need to meet the young man. That will help. But it seems to me that you have a few things to deal with, the first being your own feelings for your husband."

"My feelings for him are ambivalent at best, Gran," Emma admitted. "I'm attracted to him, but I don't really know if it does, or if it could, go any further than that."

"You could sleep with him," her grandmother suggested.

"Gran!"

"Oh come on. I watch nighttime television. I know what happens between kids these days. But if you sleep with him, you'll probably fall in love with him. It's the way you're built, Emma."

"OK," Emma responded somewhat moodily. "So no sleeping with the husband. Check."

"No need to be grumpy, young lady," her grandmother said sternly.

"Sorry Gran," Emma said with the beginnings of a grin. It was the first time she'd felt like smiling in days.

"So no sex," Gran continued. "But that means you need an outlet for all of that temptation. And having seen your husband's photo in the paper, I can see how that temptation might be rather.... strong. How about an affair on the side?" she suggested.

Emma crossed her arms and looked sternly at her grandmother. "Gran! Nighttime television plots are not a good tool to use to plan my life!"

"No prospects?" Gran asked sympathetically.

Emma shook her head. "I'm *not* sleeping around just because my husband makes me... well..."

"Why not?"

"Because when I sleep with a guy, it means something. And how the heck am I going to build a relationship with one man when I'm married to someone else? That even sounds awful, just saying it!"

"How about building a relationship with your husband?"

Emma stopped and sighed. "I don't think he has the capacity for that."

But Gran looked at her thoughtfully. "Maybe he does. Maybe you just need to pull it out of him."

"I can't do that, Gran," Emma responded softly. "I can't invest in someone to that extent, just to fail. It will kill me."

"And if you don't try? Will you regret it?"

She shrugged. "Maybe. I don't know."

Her grandmother patted her knee. "Well that's one thing to think about. Now back to your outlet... do you have toys?"

Emma nearly flew off the couch. "Gran! I am not discussing this with you!"

"Well then go to the gym," Gran said in disgust. "Work off your frustration. But you'd better seriously tire yourself out, because if he pushes you up against a wall again, you're not going to be able to walk away that easily."

Emma sighed, leaning back into the couch again. "No kidding," she said softly.

"You're always welcome over here, Emma. If you need a break. For as long as you want to stay."

"Thanks, Gran." Emma smiled mischievously. "Will you bake me cookies? From scratch?"

Her grandmother shrugged. "Maybe. Or maybe from a mix."

Emma laughed. "Thanks, Gran. For listening and understanding."

"Watch out for yourself, Emma. Listen to your heart. And bring that man by. Not only do I want to be able to admire him, but I'd kind of like to get to know him for myself. Because now, after what you've told me, I'm a little worried about you."

"He's safe, Gran. Honestly. He won't hurt me."

"Not physically, Emma. But I'm worried about your heart. So bring him by, ok?"

Nodding, Emma agreed. "OK. But not yet. I'm avoiding him this weekend, and he's gone all next week. So after that?"

"After that. And if you're avoiding him this weekend, how about taking me to my beauty parlor appointment tomorrow?"

"On a Sunday?"

"Sally opens in the afternoon for me. That way, nobody else comes in, and we enjoy a good gossip. You can come along. It might get your mind off of things, and also give you some ammunition for when you're dealing with some of those society people."

Emma grinned. "OK, Gran. What time?"

"Pick me up at 12:30. We can grab a quick lunch at the diner before we go over to Sally's."

"Deal." Emma stood up, then leaned over to kiss her grandmother on the cheek. "Thanks again, Gran. I love you, you know."

"And I love you too. I'm sorry that I didn't just trust you on this, dear. It won't happen again."

"It's OK," Emma answered truthfully. "This one was a lot to take in. See you tomorrow."

Heading back to her car, feeling better than she had in weeks, Emma woke up an exhausted Chaos and took him to the local pet store, where he roamed the aisles with glee, vacuuming up any and all pieces of food that had fallen to the floor. After loading her cart with his dog food, dog treats, chew toys, and a new dog bed, she headed for the checkout, dog in tow. Chaos looked up at her approvingly as she loaded his new items into the trunk, and then handed him a dog biscuit.

The next stop was the grocery store. Since Chaos was separated from the dog food by a metal dog gate, Emma felt OK about leaving him in the car with the food. Parking in the shade again, she did a quick run through the store, picking up food for the week, remembering that she was cooking for one again.

Then the dry cleaners. Suits dropped off, suits picked up.

Then the drugstore for a few items.

Then the gas station.

By the time Emma looked at her watch again, it was close to 6:00. Time to go home, drop everything off, feed Chaos, crate him, and then head out again. She had plans for the night with some old friends from college who lived about an hour away from her. She was grateful - staying home tonight was not an option, and she was looking forward to just relaxing with some people she knew really well, without having to answer questions or be defensive. Margaritas were definitely on the agenda.

Emma got home late. She was amazed when she'd looked at her watch in the restaurant and realized that it was nearly midnight. It had been a fun night, she thought. Old friends were the best - they caught up on each other's lives, laughed about old times, and just comfortably bantered over a couple of pitchers of margaritas. They switched to coffee or diet coke by 10:00, since all of them needed to drive, and enjoyed sharing a few decadent desserts. Emma nearly told them about Mason, but couldn't bring herself to do so. After spilling everything to her grandmother earlier that day, she found that she was surprisingly at peace with where she was, and where she was was in a business arrangement.

After waving goodbye and promising to get together again soon, Emma settled into her car and headed home. The drive was a pleasant one, and Emma just listened to music and let her mind drift around. To work, to her family, to Mason. She sighed. She'd figure it out, she thought. And for now, she was one day closer to his business trip, so she may not even need to see him again before he left.

Pulling into the garage, Emma collected her purse from the passenger seat and lowered the garage door before getting out of the car. Quietly opening the door to the kitchen, she let herself in. She grabbed a bottle of water from the fridge, and was just starting to head for the stairs when she realized that a light was on in the living room. Mason was sitting there, nursing a scotch, and from the looks of it, he'd been there a while.

"Where have you been?" he asked quietly, almost menacingly. It rubbed Emma the wrong way.

"Out," she responded simply. "Why do you ask?"

"Out where?"

But Emma shook her head. "Mason, I've never had to account for my whereabouts to you before. Has something changed?"

He looked pointedly at his watch. "You've never been this late before."

"Good point. I need to go let Chaos out. Excuse me."

"I let him out about an hour ago. He's fine. He's back in his crate, asleep." Mason stood up then, approaching where Emma was standing. "Where were you, Emma?" he asked again.

"What's the issue, Mason?" she persisted.

"Were you with someone?"

She rolled her eyes. "Of course I was. Do you honestly think I'd stay out until 1:00 in the morning alone?"

But Mason wasn't letting up. "Who were you with?" he asked.

Emma sighed. "Mason, it's late. I'm tired. I'm home safely, and I didn't do anything to embarrass you tonight. Good night," she added softly as she turned toward the stairs.

His hand on her arm stopped her. When she turned to look down at his grip, and then up into his eyes, she was shocked at the raw anger she saw there. It froze her in place, and sent a quick frisson of trepidation down her spine.

"You're my wife," he said evenly. "Were you with a man tonight, Emma?"

"Of course not," she responded softly, instinctively speaking quietly in an attempt to calm his anger.

He ran his eyes over her slim form. "That's not a coffee and movies outfit," he pointed out, his eyes roaming over the lower-cut-than-usual black shirt she was wearing over a red camisole, down to the short black plaid skirt with a touch of red, and on past her black hose to her two-inch heels. Emma looked down at her outfit again, as if reminding herself what she had on. When she looked back up, she met his eyes. The anger was still there, but it was joined by solid need.

Shaking slightly, Emma quietly responded. "No. It's a girls'-night-out outfit. We went to a restaurant. We had a few drinks. We had a few appetizers. We drank coffee and ate chocolate desserts. We talked and we laughed."

"Where's your wedding ring?" he asked, his eye zoning in on her bare finger.

Emma's eyes flew up to his. "Upstairs on my dresser," she admitted.

There was silence for a moment. Emma was fascinated by the tick that appeared on his jaw line.

"So let me get this straight. You went out to a bar with a bunch of women, drank, and passed yourself off as a single woman. Did you pick anyone up while you were at it?"

Emma would have laughed if she weren't so aware of his fury. "Oh for heaven's sake, Mason. I'm not exactly the kind of woman who picks men up in bars. I'm kind of a straight arrow, in case you hadn't noticed. And I don't cheat. Even on my in-name-only husband. Now can I please go to sleep? It's late."

But Mason had latched on to her straight arrow allegory, looking her in the eye with an intensity that stirred her. "Are you a virgin, little Emma?" he asked softly, his hand slowly reaching up to caress her cheek with his knuckles.

She flushed bright red and pulled back from his touch. "That's a rather personal question."

"Are you?" he persisted, stepping closer to her as he asked the question.

"No," Emma said, taking a step back.

"So you know about sexual need. And pleasure," he stated, his eyes dropping to her mouth.

"Where are you going with this, Mason?" Emma asked, trying to speak firmly.

His look was intense, and it was doing all sorts of things to Emma's composure. Slowly reaching out his hand, he gripped the back of her neck with his fingers, reminding Emma of his strength and his authority. As he pulled her toward him, she thought of all the reasons this was a bad idea. She remembered what her grandmother had said about the next time he had her in his arms, and she remembered her own assessment of their relationship. None of it was enough. She let herself be pulled slowly into his embrace.

The hand at her neck slowly tipped her face until she was looking directly at him. His eyes stayed locked on hers, the heat from his body reached out and encircled her, causing any thoughts of pushing back to melt away.

As he lowered his mouth to hers, he whispered quietly, "If you want a man, you come to me, Emma. Is that understood?"

She tried one last time to employ reason. "Mason..."

And then he kissed her. And her entire world exploded. Because Mason Parker, cold and stoic man that he was, had a passion burning inside of him that reached into her soul, and send flames of desire burning through her veins.

Where Emma had thought there would be control, there was a decided lack of restraint. Where she had expected cold expertise, there was hot abandon. And she was lost. She opened her mouth to him, pulling him closer.

But as suddenly as Mason had pulled her to him, he just as quickly thrust her away. Holding her arms to keep her steady while she caught her breath, he watched her as she slowly came back to reality, looking up at him with a combination of wonder and unease.

"Are you OK?" he asked gently when her breathing had returned to some semblance of normal.

"I'm fine," she responded, pulling carefully away.

"I apologize. That was..."

"It's OK, Mason. It's late." She averted her eyes. "Good night."

She was moving away when she felt his hand reach out and capture her left hand. He fingered her ring finger.

"Why did you leave your ring here?" he asked quietly.

She answered him honestly. "Because I met some old friends who live a few towns over. And I wanted a night where I didn't need to explain for the hundred and fifth time why I married a man I just met."

The anger had left his eyes, but the tick was still present in his jaw.

"I was worried about you, Emma."

"There's no need," she assured him quietly. "I've taken care of myself for years."

He ignored her response. "Next time you're out so late, let me know where you'll be. I didn't know whether to call your office, the police, the hospitals, your parents..."

"My cell phone?" she suggested.

"You didn't answer."

"Oh. I'm sorry, Mason. It was loud there."

"Good night, Emma," he said, releasing her hand.

She nodded, then headed for the stairs. For the second night in a row, she needed her own space. And she probably wouldn't be getting a lot of sleep tonight, either.

TEN

The next morning, Emma was out in the yard, tossing a ball for Chaos, when she caught a glimpse of movement through one of the slats in the fence. Looking over, she thought she saw a pair of eyes peering through at them. She tossed the ball, and moved closer to the fence as Chaos brought it back. Yup. Definitely eyes. And from their height, they probably belonged to a little kid.

She slowly worked her way over to the fence, until she was a few feet away. Throwing the ball again, she glanced over to see if the eyes were still there. They were.

"What's your name?" she asked casually, throwing the ball again.

At first, she didn't think the kid would answer. But then she heard a response. "Malcolm."

She tossed the ball again. "That's a lot of name for a kid. What do your friends call you?"

Again a pause, then, "Malcolm."

At that, she turned to look at the fence, her hands on her hips. "Seriously?" she asked.

"Yeah. It's a hard name to shorten."

Emma stifled a laugh, still watching the fence. "OK. Can I call you Mal?" she asked.

"Doesn't that mean 'bad' in Spanish?"

"Yeah. If you pronounce it 'mahl'. I'll pronounce it like Mel. Besides, don't you sort of want to be a badass kid?"

She heard a hoot of laughter from over the fence. "Yeah. I guess. OK. You can call me Mal. But no one else."

"Can Chaos call you Mal?"

"Chaos?"

"Chaos is my dog."

"Dogs can't talk."

"Mine sort of can. I channel him."

"You what?"

"Talk for him. You know, translate dog to English."

"You can do that?"

"I can."

"How come you can have a dog in this neighborhood and I can't?" the child asked suspiciously.

Emma rolled her eyes. The boy's parents probably told him that the neighborhood didn't allow dogs. Oh well. It wasn't her job to perpetuate a lie, she thought. "Because I don't have to live with parents who tell me not to," Emma admitted. "But you can share Chaos with me if you'd like."

"OK. I'd like that. I like dogs."

"Me too."

"I didn't think that Mr. Parker liked dogs," the boy said.

Emma grinned at him. "He doesn't. But Chaos is growing on him."

"Oh."

"So do you want to come over and toss the ball for him sometime?" Emma asked.

"Can I really?"

"Sure. You'll need to ask your mom and dad if it's OK, but anytime you see me out in the yard with him, you're welcome to come over."

"They're in Europe. But I'll ask Michelle if I can come over."

"Who is Michelle?"

"My nanny."

"Well OK. You ask Michelle, and I'll see you over here sometime."

"OK. What's your name?" the boy thought to ask before he headed back inside.

"Emma."

"Can I call you Em?" Malcolm asked mischievously.

"Oh sure," she agreed. "But only you. No one else."

The boy laughed, then waved at her. Chaos poked his nose into her hand, wondering why the ball-throwing had stopped. But Emma was watching Malcolm as he headed back inside the huge house next door. It seemed miles away to Emma, since each house had a huge amount of property associated with it, but she just felt sad watching Mal run. He seemed like a poor little rich boy, she thought. She hoped there were other kids in the neighborhood for him to play with, but she realized that she never heard kids' voices. Ever. Never saw kids. And never saw any other animals. What a place, she thought.

From that day on, Mal came over frequently when Emma was out in the yard with Chaos. Some evenings, he even joined Emma on her walk with the dog, after Emma made sure to introduce herself to his nanny. Michelle seemed fine with having Emma take over some of the child-care responsibilities for Malcolm, which just made Emma even sadder for the boy. But Mal seemed happy enough, and happier still when he was walking Chaos with Emma. A few times, Emma even took him to the dog park with her, and the boy was absolutely in his element. He loved animals. He even talked to Emma about becoming a veterinarian some day.

"I don't think my father would be too happy though. He keeps talking about me taking over his business."

"What does your father do?" Emma asked curiously.

"He owns a meat distribution company," the boy said. When Emma burst into laughter, Mal rolled his eyes. "Yeah. Even I get the irony, and I'm just a kid."

"Malcolm, listen to me. I'm going to tell you something that your parents would kill me for if they heard me. You spend a huge chunk of your life working. You need to love what you do. OK? If that means that you're disinherited, you live with it. Don't ever make your decisions based on money - yours or someone else's. You'll be disappointed."

"Vet school is expensive," Mal said thoughtfully.

"So you take out loans and live in a group house. Or sleep on my couch, that's fine too. But don't compromise on your career. You'll regret it."

"What about you?" Malcolm asked. "Do you like what you do?"

"Every second of it," she replied. "There are some days that are crummy, like when a kid gets sent into a situation that I'm sure is not best for him or her. But I feel like I'm making a difference. And that's important."

"Did your parents support you?"

"Yeah, at least in terms of emotional support. I still needed to pay for law school - we didn't have that kind of money."

Malcolm thought for a few minutes. "I think I'd rather have the emotional support than the money."

Emma grinned, then reached out with her arms and crooked his head into her, rubbing the top of his hair with her other fist. "You're a smart kid. And you've always got my support, if that means anything." Letting him go, she pointed to the other end of the park. "Race you!" And she was off.

"Cheater!" Malcolm cried from behind her. She turned and grinned, running backward until the kid sped by her. She caught up with him at the other end of the park and they both fell to the grass, laughing. Chaos ran around them, sniffing and chasing leaves.

"Thanks, Emma," Malcolm said.

She smiled at him. "Anytime. Hey, Mason is out of town tonight. I'm going to see if I can light myself on fire by cooking burgers on his incredibly complicated grill. Want to come over and bring Michelle? I'll let you man the fire extinguisher."

Mal laughed. "I'll ask her."

Malcolm became a regular fixture at Mason's house. Mason was traveling a lot for work, and Emma was glad for the company. Michelle would come with him a lot, but some nights she liked the break from her childcare duties, and Mal would just come over and play with Chaos. As the nights got a little cooler, they'd sit in front of the fire, play cards or scrabble, and eat. There was always food involved in an evening with Emma.

One Saturday, Emma and Mal were out in the yard playing Frisbee when an errant throw landed the disk on the roof of the garage.

"It's your fault," Emma said to Malcolm as they stared balefully at the Frisbee.

"Mine? You're the one who tossed it."

"Yeah, but if you ate your Wheaties, you could have leapt the eight feet into the air and caught it," she contended.

"You're kind of a crazy lady. You know that, right?"

Emma sighed. "Yeah. I'm aware. OK. Let me see what's in the garage. Maybe I can still get it down."

When Mason arrived home ten minutes later, it was to Emma on his garage roof, and a little kid in the yard, staring up at her. He parked his car, and got out, just staring up at the woman standing ten feet above him. Oh dear Lord, what was that woman doing now? he thought. If she fell... his heart leaped into his throat.

Emma rolled her eyes when she saw Mason pull up. Five minutes later and she would have been down. Instead, she saw the thunderous look on his face and tried to head his lecture off at the pass. Looking down at Malcolm, she made the introductions from the roof.

"Mal, this is Mr. Parker. Mason, this is Malcolm from next door."

"Hi Mr. Parker," the boy said dutifully, as he inched his way toward the gate in the fence.

"Hello Malcolm. Emma, what in the name of all that's holy are you doing up there?"

"We were playing Frisbee and I tossed it onto the roof of the garage. I'm fetching it."

"Get your pretty little butt down here before you break something. For God's sake, Emma. You could hurt yourself."

"That's why Malcolm is here. He's ready to dial 911. Right Mal?"

But Malcolm had skedaddled when Mason showed up. He waved from the other side of the fence, almost apologetically, then disappeared.

"Traitor!" Emma yelled, laughing.

"Can you please get down?" Mason asked, with what he felt was a world of patience.

"Sure." She tossed down the Frisbee. Chaos expertly caught it, then realized that it wasn't food. He dropped it. She swung onto the ladder and was down on the ground in seconds.

"Where did you find the ladder?" Mason asked evenly.

"The garage."

"What were you doing in the garage?"

"Looking for a ladder."

Mason counted to ten. Slowly.

"Emma, you could have fallen. Broken something."

"Unlikely. I do ladders well," she said. "It's throwing Frisbees that I'm not so good at."

"But suppose you did fall?"

"Then Malcolm would have called 911, the ambulance guys would have come and yelled at me for being on the roof, and they'd have taken me to the hospital. And my health insurance would cover my mishap, though my rates might go up."

"Are you done?" Mason asked with a sigh.

She grinned. "Mostly. And I'm hungry. Mal and I worked up an appetite. I was going to ask him to stay for dinner, but you scared him away."

"What's he doing over here, anyway?"

"Hanging out with me. His parents are away, and Michelle is watching TV, so he came out to play in the yard."

"Michelle?"

"His nanny."

"I'm not sure that his parents will want him over here," Mason pointed out.

She shook her head in exasperation. "Oh for heaven's sake. His parents wouldn't notice if he boarded a barge for Argentina and didn't return until he was 25. He's fine. And I like him. Do you want dinner, or not?"

He sighed. Heavily. "Yes. I want dinner. I especially want dinner if you've cooked. Have you?"

"Yes."

"Good. And I need wine. So I'm going to go pick out a bottle. Red or white?"

"White tonight," she said with a smile. "As much as I love red, white will go better with dinner."

"White it is. Dry, I assume?"

"Yes. Please."

With a wave at Mal, who was still hovering near his back door, Emma headed inside.

On Thursday night, Emma got home late after a discouraging day at the office. She was tired, she was hungry, and she was in no mood for anything but dinner and a run with Chaos. On her way to the kitchen, she poked her head into Mason's office to ask if he'd fed the dog. Because really, there was no other way to tell. Chaos would eat supper over and over and over again with the same amount of gusto.

"I did. About an hour ago. That dog is a vacuum," Mason grumbled.

"No kidding," Emma said as she rolled her eyes. "Thanks for feeding him. I'll take him out for some exercise in a bit," she added. "You've eaten?"

"I have, yes. There's leftover Thai food in the fridge if you want it."

"Thanks. I'll take you up on that. I still have some work to do tonight, so that will save me time. Thanks, Mason."

He nodded. Leaning back in his chair, he crossed his arms over his chest and informed her, "You had a phone call tonight."

Emma was surprised. Nobody ever called her here. That's what her cell was for. "Really?" she asked. "Who called? Gran?"

Mason's gaze pinned hers. "Some guy. Some guy named Will."

Confused, Emma responded, "Will? Will called here?"

"Who is he, Emma?" Mason asked conversationally.

"He's a lawyer," she responded, absently, wondering what Will could have wanted. "He worked one of my recent cases with me. Did he say what he wanted?" she asked.

"He left a message, yes."

"Is it still on the phone? Should I listen to it?"

"Sure. Feel free."

Mason's response had her looking at him more closely. He seemed annoyed. No, more than annoyed. He seemed irritated. No. Not that either. Angry? Why would he be angry that a colleague had called her at home?

"For heaven's sake, Mason. Just tell me. I have a million things to do before tomorrow. If Will has information that I can use on one of my cases, I need to know."

But Mason shook his head slowly. "It wasn't a work-related message, Emma. Did you forget to tell him that you're married?" he asked casually.

She looked over at him, puzzled. "It never came up. We're colleagues. Strictly business."

"Not according to the message he left."

"What? What did he say?"

"That he enjoyed dinner the other night, and was hoping to do it again. Soon. Perhaps on Friday night."

Emma was flabbergasted. "What?" she said again, with a touch of annoyance.

"Did you go on a date with the man, Emma?" Mason was asking.

"Of course not!" she said incredulously.

"So what dinner is he referring to?"

"A dinner that about ten of us went to after we closed a case. He seriously called here?" she asked again.

"Yes, Emma. He did."

She shook her head. She really didn't need this tonight, she thought. "And because of that, you went straight to the conclusion that I'm dating him?"

"Are you?"

Emma sighed heavily. "Mason."

"Because he also happened to mention that he found the restaurant that the two of you were looking for in San Diego."

"Well, that's awesome, since I'll be going back there in a few weeks. But if you're thinking that I was there for any kind of romantic rendezvous, or that I'm headed back there for some kind of secret liaison, you're wrong."

Mason just looked at her, before asking evenly, "Are you seeing him, Emma?"

She responded through clenched teeth. "Again. No."

"Does he think so?" he persisted.

Emma threw up her hands. "If he does, he's way dumber than even you are. For heaven's sake, Mason..."

He ignored the insult, standing up and moving to the front of his desk. He leaned back against it, looking over at her intently. "Why were you having dinner with him in San Diego, Emma?"

"Because we were both there, and we were both hungry. We're colleagues, Mason. That's all. We occasionally work on the same cases together."

"You'll tell him that you're married."

"Well apparently I'll need to!" she said in exasperation. "I had no idea he was thinking of me in any way but as a lawyer. Good Lord."

Mason continued. "Because if you don't, I will. Right after I call my lawyer, Emma, and invoke the additional two-year clause."

That got her attention. She turned and faced him, the expression on her face one of disbelief and fury. "You *can't* do that. I did *not* cheat," Emma said vehemently.

But Mason did not back down. If anything, his response was more intense. "I can, Emma, and I will. I do not expect to be listening to messages on my phone asking my wife out on a date. *My* wife."

But the possessive tone in his voice just got her mad. She was still tired, she still hadn't eaten, a colleague had made a phenomenally ridiculous move (in her eyes), and she did not want to be blamed for it. But more than that, she did not want Mason to be calling her his anything. And she told him so.

"I'm not your wife, Mason. Except in name only," she added scornfully. "We might be married, we might share a house, but that's all just semantics and paperwork."

"Semantics."

She crossed her arms stubbornly. "Yes."

Mason pushed himself off from the back of his desk, straightening up to his full height. Too late, Emma realized that he was furious, and that she had just stirred up a whole nestful of hornets.

"Mason..."

He strolled over to where she was standing, then reached out and took her chin in his hand and lifting her face to his. She stared at him, defiant, willing herself to stay still, not to run, not to struggle. He took a step forward. When she held her ground, his body moved up against hers. She couldn't help herself - she stepped back. He followed. In two more steps, her back was against the wall of his study, his hips firmly holding hers in place as his hand gently moved down her face and over her cheek, his thumb stroking roughly over her lips.

Emma kept silent, her hands gripping the wall behind her, certain that anything she could say would only exacerbate Mason's fierce anger. With sure intent, Mason pushed back the hair from her face, then gripped the back of her head firmly as he growled, "You're my wife, Emma. For three years. During that time, you belong to me."

Emma could no longer keep quiet. "Why?" she asked fiercely, glaring at him, even as he held her firmly in his grip.

"Why what?"

"You don't want this, Mason. You don't want me, or a relationship, or anything that looks like a relationship. You want a wife, long enough to get your voting stocks. That's it. So you don't need me to belong to you - you just need it to look like I do. So fine," she said softly. "You've won on all those counts. Now let me go."

But Mason just looked down at her with a thoughtful expression, before his gaze settled on her mouth. Heat flared in his eyes as he lifted them to hers. "No, I don't think I'm going to do that, Emma. Because you need to remember something about me."

"What?"

"I don't share." Mason moved his other hand up to grip the other side of Emma's head, her body held in place against the wall by his. Firmly, he lifted her face to his, and leaned down to cover her mouth with his own.

His kiss was hard, and he forced her own softer lips open for him. When his tongue penetrated her mouth, she gasped with surprise. And found herself kissing him back. She didn't want to. She didn't want to be attracted to him, or to let herself show him that she wanted him, but she seemed to have no choice. She couldn't feel anything but him. Couldn't think of anything but him. And when he lifted his head from hers, she simply leaned forward, her forehead resting lightly on his chest.

"Here's the bottom line, Emma," he said quietly. "I want you, badly. So if sex is what you want, you can have it. But you can't have it with anyone other than me. Not while we're married. You belong to me, just as I belong to you. For three years. Nobody else, Emma. Just me. Is that clear?"

"But..."

"Here's the *semantics* of it," he continued without pausing. "You are my wife. And as un-romantic as it may seem to you, we have a contract." He gripped her shoulders, bending down until he was sure that she was looking at him. "There will be no Will. There will be no other men."

She pushed away from him, and he let her go. She leaned against the arm of one of Mason's chairs as she looked over at Mason.

"You're right," she said at last, the fight having gone out of her when he kissed her. "There is no Will - there never has been. There is no other man. You need to have *some* trust in me, or this is going to be a miserable existence for three years. And later, when we're feeling a little less frustrated than we are right now, we might want to revisit this celibacy clause. Because here's the thing - you can't keep kissing me. You make me crazy when you do. You show emotion, you show a part of yourself. But when you stop, your defenses go back up again. I can't see-saw, Mason. It's not who I am."

Standing up, she moved carefully around him and toward the door. "Will is a colleague. I did not cheat. I do not cheat. I did not break your damn contract," she added furiously. "I will fight you on this one."

Mason just stood against the wall, his arms crossed, looking down at her. Finally, he nodded. "I believe you. Just tell the guy that you're married before he calls here again."

She sighed. "I will." And she quietly left.

Things had changed subtly between them since that night. Emma was more guarded when she talked to Mason, and he had gone back to the quiet hard man she'd first married. He didn't come home much. She spent more time at the office, often coming home at dinner time to change and run, then going back to the office with Chaos.

The attraction between them was out in the open, but neither would act on it. Emma wasn't willing to put her emotions on the line for a man who seemed to have none, and

Mason did not want to push himself on a woman who obviously wanted more than sex. Sex was all he was willing to give.

When Emma knew that Mason would be out of town, she spent more time at the house, frequently inviting Malcolm and Michelle over for dinner or a movie. When Mason knew that Emma would be out of town, he poured himself a scotch and settled into his den, doing nothing but staring at the TV. They avoided each other, unless there was a social event that they needed to be at. And those evenings were incredibly hard for both of them. Mason, because all he wanted to do was peel Emma out of whatever dress she appeared in, and Emma, because she felt like the world's biggest fraud. She hated pretending to be happily married to a man she barely knew, and she was sure that the entire room could sense the tension between them. She only hoped that they attributed it to sexual tension of newlyweds, and not to anything more.

One evening, after a long and fairly boring dinner, complete with speeches and presentations, Emma leaned back in her chair, and felt Mason's arm encircle her shoulders. She had worn a slate blue evening gown this evening, which left her back and shoulders bare, with thin straps holding up the bodice and criss-crossing her back to fasten at the waist. Mason's warm arm felt good in the chill of the room, and she leaned back against him, settling into his shoulder. His fingers lightly clasped her upper arm, and he gently stroked her skin as they watched the final speaker close up the evening.

"You feel good," Mason breathed into her ear quietly.

She shivered at both his words and the feel of his breath on her skin. "You're keeping me warm," she said in return, attempting to keep things light.

"I'm glad," he said simply.

She pulled forward and away from him then. "Mason..."

"Shhh. People are watching." He continued to stroke her shoulder, his movements sure as he pulled her back against him.

And indeed they were. Speculation about Mason and his wife had only grown as time went on. Emma was not who any of them had expected, and she was sure that people watched them with skepticism. So she forced herself to lean back naturally, and to look up at him with an adoring smile. He answered with a smile of his own - one that would look natural and loving from anywhere but where she was. She alone saw the chill in his eyes.

At the coat check, Mason kept her tucked close. As they waited for their car to be brought around by the valet, he kissed her lightly on the temple, and kept her encircled in his arms. But once they were in the car, the silence returned. Mason drove, Emma stayed tucked in on the passenger side, and they had little interaction on the way home. When they got home, Emma let Chaos out while Mason checked his e-mail and then closed and locked the house. Emma called a polite goodnight to him as she shut her door. He grunted a response.

Back in his room, Mason paced. Emma had raised the clause about seeing other people a few weeks ago, and they'd never revisited it. Mason knew that she was right about one thing - remaining celibate for three years would be damn near impossible. But the thought of her with someone else, anyone else, was unacceptable. If anyone saw her in public, his own reputation would be at risk, as well as hers. And as discreet as she could be, he couldn't imagine any man dating Emma and not wanting to show her off. And the same held true for him. Unless he was willing to either tell a woman the truth about his relationship with Emma, he'd have to resort to running around like a cheating husband, and that just was not in his blood. The only alternative was to seduce Emma. As much as he wanted that, wanted *her*, he just didn't know if that was wise. She would get attached. Want to talk and share feelings. Want to plan for a family.

For just a moment, he was distracted by the thought of her pregnant with his child. Of a little Emma running around the house. Of a miniature Mason, throwing a football. For just a brief period of time, he wondered if he was pushing away the best thing that had happened to him. But then he remembered his own childhood, and his own father, and realized how like his father he'd become. So no, he wasn't capable of being a normal guy with a normal life. Three years with Emma, stock options intact, and then back to the life he was leading before. Back to seeing different women, sleeping with them as he wished. The thought left him cold, but he saw no other option. He needed to resist his attraction for his own wife.

As Mason paced and pondered, Emma was sitting in her own bedroom, her thoughts scattered. All it took was a seductive word from him, a slight act of tenderness, and she was drawn to him again. Until she saw his eyes, and realized what an amazing actor he was. He felt nothing for her, she was sure of it, but he was able to convince the entire world that he did. It was exhausting, she thought. And she was very sure that she wouldn't be able to do two more years of this. Something would have to give. Two weeks later, it gave. Jen returned to town.

ELEVEN

Emma was at work on a Friday afternoon when she got a call from her grandmother. Gran never called her during the day, preferring to wait until the evening so she could watch her daytime shows and have plenty of time to regale her granddaughter with what she'd learned in the infomercials.

"Gran? Everything OK?" Emma asked when she picked up the receiver.

"Jen's coming home."

Emma was silent.

"Emma? You there?"

"I'm here, Gran. Nice lead-in there, by the way. So now I'm just debating about whether I should stop and pick up a boxing glove or a gallon of red wine on my way home from work tonight."

"Definitely the wine," her grandmother advised. "She sounded nervous on the phone, so I think she's expecting the hit. And you've never been able to take her without the element of surprise on your side, so I think you should let that thought go."

Emma sighed. "OK. So she's going to Mom and Dad's?"

"Evidently she's going to your house first. She called me to make sure that you're still at work - she intends to surprise you at home, only you're not living there anymore, so she'd be waiting there a long time."

"She doesn't know I married Mason?" Emma asked.

"Apparently not. I sure didn't tell her."

Emma put her head in her hands and rubbed her temples between her thumb and middle fingers. "Thanks for the heads-up Gran," she said quietly. "I appreciate it."

"Call me later. I don't have enough money to bail you out of jail if you do something stupid, though, so try not to kill her."

Emma laughed then. "I'll behave. You playing bingo tonight?"

"Not a chance. I'm sitting by the phone waiting for my granddaughter to call."

"Got canceled, huh?"

"Yeah. Some other event at the Moose Lodge tonight. Come by if you need me."

"Love you Gran."

"Love you too, baby. Good luck."

Hanging up the phone, Emma swiveled in her desk chair to look out her office window. This was going to be an interesting evening, she thought. Jen had stayed away a long time. Had she done it because she was having such a good time, wherever she went, that she just didn't want to return home? Or had she done it to be sure that Emma had gotten over her initial fury at being left in this situation?

She wanted to see her sister. She loved her sister. She had missed her sister. But they needed to hash out this whole Mason Parker thing first. Emma had no illusions that Jen felt any guilt about walking out on her deal with Mason, but her act had consequences, and it was Emma who was paying them. This wasn't just another 'Emma will fix it' situation - and Jen needed to realize that her actions had indeed impacted someone.

Things with her husband hadn't gotten any easier lately. If anything, she and Mason were even more cautious around each other. Chaos helped, since he loved them both, but it was still awkward. Mason went out of his way to avoid her, never returning to their conversation a month ago about revisiting their contract to allow some sort of sexual release. For him. Emma wasn't really interested in getting involved with anyone - she had way too much on her plate as it was, and she sensed that Mason would make that impossible anyway. If he had exploded over the thought of a phone call, he was going to have apoplexy at the thought of her going on a date.

But that was for another time, another discussion, another argument. For now, she needed to go meet Jen.

As soon as Emma walked in the door of her home, she knew that Jen hadn't been there yet. It still had the feel of a house not lived-in. She moved around, opening windows to let in some air, and generally dusting things off a bit. She missed it here, though not as much as she did at first. She was just opening up the curtains in the kitchen when she heard a quick knock on the front door, followed by the sound of the door opening. She turned to see her sister, framed in the doorway, her long hair flowing over her shoulders, a gauzy shirt covering a camisole and tight leggings, and three-inch heels. And a huge smile on her face.

Emma couldn't help it. She smiled.

"Jen," she said in relief, glad to see her sister in one piece.

"Emma," her sister grinned back at her.

Hands on her hips, Emma shook her head. "I don't know whether to hug you or strangle you."

"I'd probably prefer the hug, but would understand strangulation," Jen admitted.

Emma reached out and pulled her sister into a bear hug. God, she'd missed her. Even as she had wanted to kill her.

"Do you have any idea what you did to me, Jen?" she asked, releasing her sister and putting it all right on the table, needing everything out in the open from the start.

"I do, Em. And I want to explain. I mean, I knew he'd be mad and all. I hope he wasn't too mean to you. But I figured you'd be able to calm him down if anyone could."

Emma collapsed down onto the couch, tucking her foot up under her. "Why did you send me over there, Jen? There were no things to pick up. Did you want me to be your replacement?"

Jen dropped her purse on a table and sank down next to her sister. She reached out and squeezed Emma's hand. "No. No, Emma, no. Of course not. I just know that you're a calm and sweet person, and a lawyer. I figured that if anyone could tell him nicely, it would be you. And since I took $300k of his money, I wanted you to maybe buy me some time."

"Why did you need that money, Jen?"

She looked embarrassed. "Leo and I were going to open a motorcycle repair shop in California. I figured that would get us started, and I didn't think he'd miss it."

Emma shook her head. "Jen, you didn't need to know Mason well to know that he wasn't going to just let $300,000 go."

"I kind of figured that he wouldn't pursue it. That maybe he'd be too embarrassed. You know, for having to buy a wife and all."

"You've met the man."

"Sure."

"And you still think he would need to buy a wife."

"Yeah, I kind of wondered about that. Thought maybe he had issues."

"He probably does," Emma admitted. "But nothing that would prevent half the single women in this town from marrying him on the spot."

"So he must have found someone else," Jen said immediately. "Good. I figured he would. I mean, with all that money and all."

"Um, Jen...?" Emma said, holding up her left hand and pointing to the ring on her finger.

Jen turned white. "*You* married him?"

"I didn't really have a choice, Jen. Remember that pesky little contract you signed?"

"That thing? But that didn't mean anything, Emma! It was just a paper that said that I wouldn't financially gain from the marriage. Well, beyond what we'd agreed to, anyway."

Emma looked at her incredulously. "Did you even read it?"

"I glanced at it," Jen said defensively, her eyes focusing on the straps of her purse.

Emma leaned back against the back of the couch and closed her eyes. Without opening them, she asked her sister, "Do you remember me telling you once that you should never sign anything without letting me read it?"

"Yeah, but this..."

"This was a legally binding contract, Jen. It stated that you would go through with the marriage. If you didn't, you needed to find him a replacement 'wife'. If you didn't, he could sue for breach of contract."

"Oh Lord. Emma, you should have let him sue," Jen said seriously, reaching out again to grasp Emma's hand. "Why did you marry him?"

"It was sort of a forced issue, Jen. Given that you had $300,000 of his money, and he had a contract that you'd signed and reneged on. Jen, this is serious. He could have done more than sue you. He could have had you arrested."

"But he didn't, Emma. I still can't believe you married him. This wasn't your problem - you should have just let him deal with me directly. I could have talked my way out of it."

Emma shook her head. "Jen, he was not so much in a talking mood. He was definitely in a suing mood. And he would have taken all your assets."

Jen shrugged. "I don't have that much."

"Including the house."

If Jen could go any whiter, she did. "Oh no. Emma."

"Yeah."

"Emma, I'm sorry. I'm so so sorry. I had no idea. Look. I'll pay him back. Or you. Since you now deserve all of the money for actually marrying the guy."

"I'm not making any money for marrying him, Jen. He already paid you, and there was no way I was taking money for this. It was bad enough that my sister stiffed him."

"You're giving up $750,000?" Jen asked incredulously.

Emma turned her head and looked her sister in the eye. Softly, she said, "Jen..."

She had the grace to look sheepish. "OK. You're right. I'm sorry."

The two sisters sat quietly on the couch for a moment, before Emma asked quietly, "What happened to the shop?"

Jen looked down at her lap. "Leo and I split up," she admitted.

She looked so morose that Emma's heart melted a bit. Just a bit. "I'm sorry, Jen," she said quietly.

Jen nodded. "Me too." After a few more moments, she asked, "Did you tell Mom and Dad about all of this?"

"No. Not their business. Gran knows, though. She was giving me the cold shoulder for way too long and I caved."

Jen looked chagrined. "Does she hate me?"

"Of course not. Nobody hates you. Not Gran, not me."

"And Mason?"

"Nah. Some days he probably wishes he'd married you and not me, but we're coexisting."

Jen took a deep breath, and then offered, "Em, if you want me to, I'll step in."

"I don't think it works that way. I think he needs to be married to the same woman for three years. So while I appreciate the pinch hitting offer, there's no need."

Jen's eyes filled as she looked at her sister, and realized the mess she'd put her in. "Emma, don't be mad at me. I love you. You're my sister."

Emma gave her sister a small smile in return. "I love you too, you moron. But I think I might stay mad for a while."

Her sister looked over at her with a calculating expression on her face. "You're good for him, I think. This might work out in ways that you don't even realize yet."

"What?"

"He's cold. You're warm. Some of that warm needs to rub off on him."

"Maybe the cold is rubbing off on me. He's a reptile, Jen. He has cold blood in his veins. The only thing that warms him up is the damn sunshine."

But Jen just snorted. "He's a hard man, that's true. You can see that by just looking at him. But I think there's more there, Emma."

"Now why would you say that?"

"He asked me to step in to marry him to seal a business deal, Em. We met at a party, and we got along pretty well. We hung out a bit - nothing romantic at all. And then one day, he asked me if I wanted to make some money, and I said yes. So that's what started all of it. If I'd said no, he would have found another solution. That's just the way Mason is."

Emma just looked puzzled. "But that makes no sense. If that were the case, he would have just gone after the money you took from him, and let the contracted agreement disappear."

"That's what I'm saying, Emma. And that's why I was so surprised not only that you married him, but that he pushed it so hard."

"You must have misread him, Jen. A man does not draw up a contract like you signed if he's not completely serious about his intentions."

Jen shrugged. "Maybe. But here's the thing, Emma. Mason and I got along fine, but we both knew that we were too much alike for there to be anything between us. Ever. I like the guy, don't get me wrong, and I think he's sexy as hell, but we'd never survive a real relationship. But you, on the other hand..."

"What about me?"

"He didn't need to marry you, Em. He could have yelled at you, told you to get back the money I took, and run you off his property. But instead, he pushed you into taking my place. It may have made things easier for him, but I'm not convinced that it was the only way for him to get that stock."

"What's your point?"

"You and I are different, Emma. A blind man could see that after spending ten minutes with each of us. I'm completely wrong for him. But I think you may be completely right for him."

Emma just looked at her in disbelief. "What are you saying? That he took one look at me and thought, hey, I'd like to marry that woman and give it a three-year test run?"

Jen shrugged. "Maybe," she said softly. "It's possible."

Emma snorted. "No way. Not in a million years. I do not inspire that kind of behavior. I inspire exasperation. I inspire frustration. I do not inspire that kind of impetuous act, and certainly not from a man like Mason Parker. Who, I might add, is still as cold as the day I married him."

But Jen shook her head. "I kind of doubt that. But we'll see. Can I come over sometime?" she asked with a sly grin.

Emma picked up a pillow from the chair and threw it at her sister. "You're a crazy, terrible, horrible, rotten person. I love you anyway, you fruitcake."

Jen caught the pillow easily and tucked it under her leg. "I know you do. Listen, Emma, I really am sorry that you got stuck with this. It was never my intention..."

"I know, Jen. But next time you have a contract in your hand that you're thinking of signing, even if it's just an agreement box for downloading software on your computer, *call me*."

"I will. I promise." She crossed her heart with her index finger.

"So are you around for a while?"

"Yeah, a few weeks anyway. I might stick around for longer if I can find a job."

"I'll let you know if I hear of anything. It'd be nice to have you here for a while."

Jen sighed. "I should go over to Mom and Dad's. You coming over this weekend?"

"Not sure yet. They're still a little mad at me for marrying Mason without any warning. And I haven't actually introduced him to them yet."

"Emma, why didn't you just tell them the truth?"

Emma shrugged. "Why should they be mad at both of us? And at this point, they'd be doubly mad at me for not telling them sooner. They'll get over it eventually. But don't be surprised if they tell you how disappointed in me they are."

"I'll tell them, Emma."

"Nah. Honestly, at this point it's a moot point. Let it go and bask in being the prodigal daughter," she said with a grin.

After Jen left with a big hug and a promise to see her soon, Emma moved around the house, reclosing and locking the windows and drawing curtains on the lower floor. When she was done, she sat back down on the couch and thought about what Jen had said. She knew that maintaining his uncle's voting rights was critically important for his business. And the absolute airtight contract that Jen had signed made it clear that he took the marriage a lot more seriously than she had. No wonder she'd backed out, Emma thought. Jen had assumed that Mason could weather the hit that her disappearance would cause, or that he'd find another way to deal with the requirements of his uncle's will. But Emma wasn't sure there was another way.

Or was there? Did he have a backup plan, in case Jen didn't show up? Or was he just so annoyed and angry at being walked out on that he took it out on Emma? There was way more going on here than she had initially thought. The problem was, Mason was not exactly the kind of guy she could just ask. He'd shut down. He'd freeze her out. Because as much as Jen assumed that he'd warmed up a bit, Emma knew he hadn't. The only time she saw him show any emotion was when he was kissing her, and that was raw physical attraction. There was no soul connection between them. Made clearer, Emma thought, by his reaction every time - he retreated.

Well. This was a fine mess. She'd have to unravel it all eventually. And it would take a talk with Mason to figure it out. So unraveling it any time soon was unlikely. Oh hell, she thought to herself. A serious mess. Standing up, she grabbed her keys and headed for the door.

When she got back home that night, she let Chaos out into the back yard to scout the perimeter and look for any morsels of food that might have been tossed over the fence by some benevolent stranger that day. Grabbing a bottle of water from the fridge, she went in search of Mason, finding him working in his office. She knocked lightly on the door, then walked in when he looked up to see her in the doorway.

"Emma. This is a surprise."

"Jen's back in town," she said without any preamble.

Mason dropped his pen onto the papers he was reading and gave her his attention. "Oh? Did you kill her and weight the body down in the lake?"

"Nah," Emma responded, collapsing into one of Mason's comfy office chairs and tossing her legs over one arm. "I threw her body in the cement at that new construction site downtown."

"Oh, good thinking. Water is unpredictable - cement is forever. You ok?" he asked.

She shrugged. "Yeah."

"Did you lay into her?"

"A bit. Not completely."

"Why not?"

"Felt disloyal, believe it or not. If I'm too mad at her, it means that I'm hating life with you. And that's not exactly true. And even if it were, that's between you and me."

Mason nodded. "So what happened with her and this guy?"

"They split up."

"Oh."

"Does that bother you?" Emma asked, swinging her legs around and straightening up to look at him.

"Should it?"

"You were going to marry her. This other guy came between you."

Mason leaned back in his chair and pinned her with his gaze. "Emma, if it hadn't been that guy, it would have been something else. Jen got cold feet. And not cold 'I don't love him enough to marry him' feet. Cold 'I don't want to tie myself down for three years' feet."

"She's back though," Emma reminded him. "Do you want..." she stopped, unable to really articulate what she was asking him.

"Are you asking me if I prefer Jen to you, Emma?"

"Not exactly," she said seriously, refusing to be embarrassed. "Look, she's my sister. She's gorgeous. She's a little commitment-phobic, but she's sweet."

Mason stood up then and moved around to the front of his desk, leaning back on it with his hands in his pants pockets.

"And?" he asked.

"I'm serious, Mason. If you want to get back together with her, I'm sure that we can figure out a way to quietly make that happen."

"Why would I want that, Emma?" he asked, seeming to be genuinely puzzled.

"Were you not listening to me? Gorgeous? Sweet?"

"I like you," he said, a slight smile playing on his lips. It threw her for a moment before she gathered her thoughts enough to respond.

"Well, that's nice. But I'm not exactly in Jen's league, and we both know it. But you and I could still be friends, Mason."

"Friends?" Mason's hands came out of his pockets, and he pushed himself away from the desk, striding over to where Emma sat, perched stiffly on his chair. Standing over her, he looked down at her as she looked back up at him cautiously.

"Friends?" he asked again, incredulously.

"Yeah, friends. What?" she asked, almost belligerently.

But he was shaking his head in disbelief. "For such a smart woman, you really don't get it, do you?"

"Get what?"

"Jen is not sweet. She's cold and cynical, like me."

Emma was appalled. "No, she's not!"

"She is. And that's why she and I *can* be friends. But you and I? We're not friend material."

Emma felt stricken, and tried to hide her reaction, but Mason was nothing if not perceptive. Reaching down, he grasped her by the arms and pulled her up beside him. Holding herself stiff, she tried valiantly for nonchalant, but couldn't quite pull it off.

"Damnit, Mason, what are you doing?" she said at last, her arms sandwiched between them as he pulled her still closer to his long form.

"Showing you why you and I *can't* be friends."

And with that, he lowered his mouth to hers, one hand splayed across her back, holding her tightly to him, while the other moved up to hold her head as he simply took. His lips slanted across hers, moving fiercely, possessively, while his tongue invaded her mouth. His kiss was one of passion, one of need, but certainly not one of friendship. The hand around her back was equally possessive, moving up under her shirt to find bare skin, and caressing it with a sense of ownership.

Emma realized that her own hands were clutching the front of his shirt, using it to pull him closer, into the kiss that he was pressing on her. Their breathing was audible, their movements more frenzied than sure.

It was only when Mason's hands started to move around under her shirt that Emma realized that she needed to put a stop to this. But God, it was hard. He was making her feel things that she badly wanted to feel - just not with this man. Not with a man who had ice in his veins. Only now, she had to admit, it felt like fire.

"Mason, wait," she managed to breathe out as she pushed away from him at the same time. He released her immediately, but didn't move away. Instead, he leaned down and asked softly, "Do you still think I should try to make a move on Jen?"

"Um." Emma couldn't think straight, especially since Mason was not giving her any space. He inched forward, until he was nearly touching her again.

"Or that you and I can just be friends?" he added. "Because it won't work, Emma. It never would have been like that between us, but especially not now."

Emma backed up a step. "It would have been, Mason. There was nothing between us when we met, and we should have kept it that way. Because this won't work either. We're like two fighters circling each other in a ring. We go at it for a while, then retreat and circle again."

Mason moved forward. Again. "Maybe we shouldn't retreat."

Emma sighed, looking up at him resignedly. "Then we'd probably kill each other."

"You're already killing me, sweetheart," he said quietly.

"That seems mutual, Mason," she said, looking up at him seriously.

He nodded, reaching out a hand to run his knuckles over her cheek. "We're going to need to deal with this at some point, Emma."

But Emma turned, moving away so that he was no longer touching her. She couldn't think straight when he was so gentle – it churned her up inside, and made her want things she shouldn't and couldn't want. "I can't, Mason. This is has to be business, and nothing more. If we can't have a friendship, then we need to keep this professional. Because, honest to God, I can't be your wife for three years and then quit when the contract is up. I can't. Don't ask me to."

"Then what *are* you asking for, Emma?" he asked, turning to face her with his hands back in his pockets.

She looked at him closely, sure she'd see some sense of panic in his eyes at the thought of anything resembling a relationship. But she saw nothing – just the same thoughtful expression he'd worn for most of the evening. She sighed then, and answered, "Nothing. Really, Mason, I'm not asking for a thing. I'm just trying to put down a boundary or two." She paused, then pulled her sweater tighter around her middle. Smiling slightly, she added, "And I'm staying out of your way for a while - I'm going to go get Chaos and go for a run. Good night, Mason." Backing out of his office, she headed for her room to change.

Mason watched her go. Breathing deeply, he settled back down into the chair behind his desk, and leaned forward resting his weight on his forearms. God he wanted that woman. But he wanted her with no strings attached and with Emma, there would be strings. With Jen, there would have been nothing – maybe not even sex, he admitted, because despite her beauty, there was no attraction between them. They would have signed a contract that enabled both of them to meet their needs on the side, not one that forbade either of them to cheat. Whatever had possessed him to agree to that? he wondered. Not that he wanted to go out and bed the first woman that walked across his path, but to not have that option for three years? No wonder he was cornering Emma every chance he got. Maybe he needed to revisit the idea of changing their contract.

But as soon as he thought that, his visceral reaction was one of absolute denial. No, he couldn't do that. He wanted Emma. And it was *Emma* he wanted, not just any woman. It was Emma he had wanted since the day he'd opened his door to find her on his stoop. It was Emma he'd wanted from the second he'd heard her explanation as to why Jen wasn't coming. He could have just let Jen go, sent her a message through his lawyer that he expected repayment of the money he'd given her up front, and decided that his uncle's voting stock wasn't worth the hassle. To be honest, it may not have affected his business as much as he'd been concerned about.

Thus far, he'd had more than enough support from his stockholders to have majority votes any time he wanted it. Sure, it was nice to have the additional votes in his back pocket, but unless things changed drastically in the future, it may not have hurt him to lose them.

But when Emma had shown up, all sympathetic and feisty, he knew he had to have her. And rather than ripping up the contract, he'd used it to rope her in. And he hadn't regretted it, not even when they were at each other's throats. She made him feel alive. Truth was, if Jen hadn't left when she did, Mason would have been thinking up ways to ditch her and grab Emma anyway, if his initial reaction to her was any indication.

And she wanted him. Physically, anyway, but it was a start. And he had three years. Three years to break down her defenses. The question was, what would he do once he broke them down? He knew what Emma would want - marriage, children, a home. Could he give her that? Or would he just want her for a period of time, then grow weary of her? He doubted it, though. Because she was still the same feisty woman he'd met, and she challenged him. She wasn't impressed by his wealth, she wasn't intimidated by his personality, and she wasn't frightened of his mother, by God. That took a special kind of woman. He'd never ever considered a long-term relationship before. Could he consider it now? With Emma? She appealed to him more than any woman ever had, but was that enough?

Recalling his parents' marriage, Mason grimaced. There weren't many happy days in that household when he and Amanda were growing up, but Amanda had somehow come out of their childhood with more optimism and more... normality than he had. In all of his relationships, he looked for what the women wanted from him - money, power, sex. His mother had taught him that, perhaps without even meaning to, because that's how his father had acted. But Amanda still looked for love. How had she escaped the same household that he grew up in, looking at life so differently? He knew that she had gone her own way after college, refusing to bend to the iron will of their father and join the family business. But business was all Mason had ever wanted to pursue - to show his father that he was just as good at building and managing a company as the older man ever was. But had Mason lost his humanity at the same time?

Shutting down his computer, Mason stood up and looked down at the paperwork on his desk. It would wait, he thought. He needed a break. Moving out to the kitchen, he grabbed a bottle of water from the refrigerator, and then headed into the family room. Football, he thought. That was exactly what he needed to take his mind off Emma. He heard her come in right before halftime, climbing the stairs with Chaos at her heels. In a different world, she'd join him. They'd sit and talk, maybe share a bottle of wine or a few beers while watching the game. But that would be a world that Mason didn't inhabit and didn't know how to get to. Turning his attention back to the game, he sighed. Maybe he needed to spend some time figuring that out.

TWELVE

A few weeks later, on a Saturday afternoon, Emma was in the kitchen making bread when she heard a knock on the back door. She opened it to find Malcolm standing there, holding something in his jacket. After Emma let him in, he opened up the front of his coat, and Emma saw a little black and white furball looking up at her with huge eyes.

"A kitten! Oh, he's so cute! Where did you get him, Mal?" Emma asked, hoping against hope that his parents gave in and let him get an animal.

But Malcolm's answer made her heart sink. "I found him. He was hiding under a bush in the front yard. Do you think he's OK? He's awfully little."

"He is. But I think he looks fine. Let's take a look. Come on inside," she invited, motioning toward the kitchen.

Following her in, but still clutching the kitten, Mal walked back to the kitchen with Emma, looking down at the little bundle of fur in his arms adoringly.

"Do you think we can keep him?" he asked.

"Let's look first to see if he has a tag," Emma said, but she realized quickly that the animal had no collar. She sat down on one of the stools and looked seriously at the boy.

"Mal, you know I love you, and you know I want you to have a pet almost as much as you want one. But do you think your parents will let you have a cat?"

Malcolm shook his head. "I don't know," he said softly, already knowing in his heart that the answer would be no.

"You can ask," Emma suggested gently. "In the meantime, he can stay here. You and I can take him to the vet this week to be sure that everything is OK, and we can make sure we don't see any fliers for a missing kitten. OK?"

The look on the boy's face nearly broke Emma's heart. She knew that he badly wanted this animal as his own, but she also knew his parents. There was no way they were letting this little furball of destruction into their showcase of a house. Even if it was something their son badly wanted. So she could take it in, if she could convince Mason that this was a good idea, and Mal could see it all the time. Whenever he wanted. She sighed. It wasn't ideal, but it was an option.

When Mason got home a few hours later, Emma was waiting. She had put the kitten in her room in case it got destructive, and met him in the living room, before he had a chance to escape to his study.

"You want to what?" he asked, when Emma was done telling the story.

She rolled her eyes. "I want to keep the cat."

"But why?"

"Because it's cute. And little. And alone. And because Malcolm loves it."

"So why doesn't Malcolm keep the cat?"

"You've met his parents. Do you really need to ask?"

Mason crossed his arms and looked sternly down at Emma. "So because his parents are not cat lovers, I have to take in a cat?"

Emma looked up at him suspiciously. "No, you don't have to do anything. But have you seen a kitten lately?"

"No," he admitted cautiously, not sure where this might take him.

"Well, you can't make a decision until you meet him."

He rolled his eyes. "OK. I'll meet him. But then if I say he goes, he goes."

The stubborn look on her face was back. Mason sighed.

"Oh hell. As long as it stays in your room. And as long as Chaos doesn't create havoc by chasing it all over my house."

She grinned. "No promises. But I'll try. Hang on. I'll go get him."

She was back seconds later with the tiny little black and white kitten. It was probably the smallest animal that Mason had ever seen, and it was absolutely the cutest thing he'd ever laid eyes on. When Emma held the kitten out to him, he backed away. He didn't know how to hold a cat!

"Oh for heaven's sake," she said. "Sit down."

He sat. She placed the cat in his lap. "He's a kitten. You really can't hurt him unless you try to. Here. Let him crawl on you."

The cat was all over him. In his lap. Up his chest. On his shoulder. Around his back. On the other shoulder. Back down. And Mason was enchanted. This little creature was adorable.

"What are Chaos' thoughts on this?" he asked dryly.

"Dunno. Haven't introduced them."

"Has he been around cats before?"

"Not much. This will be new."

"In my house?"

"Relax, Mason. We'll take it slow and easy."

He leaned his head back on the couch. "Why do I let you talk me into these things?" he asked through gritted teeth.

"Because your life would be boring otherwise," she grinned. "I've got to go pick up some food and a litter box for him."

He gave in. "Go. Take Chaos. I'll watch the little crazy feline."

"You sure?" Emma asked.

"No."

Emma grinned. "OK, OK. I'm going. I'll be back quickly. If you need something to do while I'm gone, you could come up with a name for him."

"Malcolm should name him," Mason said immediately.

"OK then. His name is Max. I tried to advocate for Havoc, but Mal wasn't amused."

Mason laughed then. "Havoc might be more appropriate, but Max is a good name. Go. But please tell me you have something in the fridge that I could heat up for dinner?"

"I do. It's on the top shelf. I'll be back in half an hour," she assured him, scritching the kitten on the head and briefly squeezing Mason's shoulder. "Try not to step on him," she called as she and Chaos bounded out the door.

Emma couldn't sleep. She kept listening for sounds of the kitten on the stairs. She worried that he had gotten lost, or that he was stuck somewhere. She worried that he was lonely. Finally, at 11:00, she surrendered. Climbing out of bed, she shrugged into her robe and padded down the stairs. She'd start in the kitchen, where they'd set up a little bed for the animal, near the window so he could look out. If he wasn't there, she'd start looking around.

When she looked around the corner of the kitchen, she nearly laughed. Mason was sitting on the floor, cross-legged, letting Max climb all over him. As she watched, he picked the kitten off of him and set him on the floor, but Max immediately climbed back up until it was sitting on his shoulder. She smiled softly at the sight, and started to quietly back away, but as she moved, she must have made a sound. Mason's gaze swung over to where she was standing. The look on his face was one of sincere happiness. And it melted Emma's heart.

She moved over to where he sat and gently plucked the kitten from his shoulder. She cuddled it closely, kissing its tiny belly and rubbing her nose into its fur. He squirmed, but his paws reached out to pull her closer. Giggling, she handed Max back to Mason, who set him back on his shoulder. He shrugged. "It's a losing battle," he said with a grin. "What are you doing up?"

"Apparently the same thing as you. I wanted to make sure Max was OK. I wasn't sure if he'd make it up the stairs if he got lonely."

He chuckled. "The cat's fine. A little energetic, but fine."

"I can hear him purring from here. So you're OK with keeping him?"

Mason turned his head to regard the kitten on his shoulder. "WE are keeping him. This is joint custody."

She smiled and reached down to scratch the little kitty head. As she did so, her robe gaped open, and Mason caught a glimpse of the dark blue silk nightgown she had on underneath. His gaze moved down to her long legs, peeking out from under her robe, and when he raised his eyes to hers, the laughter was gone.

Emma nearly gasped at the intensity of his stare. His eyes locked on hers, he slowly pushed his way to his feet. He gently set the kitten back into his bed, then turned and moved toward Emma. His shirt was unbuttoned at the neck, and his tie was loose, but even in his state of slight disarray, he was the sexiest man Emma had ever seen. And at this moment, he was completely focused on her. She lifted one hand to catch her hair in back of her neck, and watched as he approached her, stopping only inches from her. Reaching out, he wrapped his fingers around her neck, gently using his thumb to lift her face toward his.

Pulling her mouth to his, he kissed her. It was rougher than his kisses had been before, and Emma felt the controlled passion behind it. He explored her mouth with his tongue, his lips moving over hers, fierce and demanding.

"Emma," he said as he lifted his head, his voice low and gravelly. "You have to know that I want you."

She nodded solemnly, her breathing unsteady. She knew. She wanted him with equal passion.

"Tell me," he commanded softly. "Tell me that you want me too."

"I do. I want you too, but..."

"Emma, I don't want this to be one-sided or for you to feel coerced," Mason continued.

She nodded. "Mason, I know that the contract…"

But he interrupted her. "To hell with the contract," he said fiercely. "This is between us. I don't want to do anything you don't want, Emma." He ran his thumb gently over her lip. "If you tell me to stop, I'll step away."

She closed her eyes. She wanted this man. Badly. But there would be consequences.

"Mason, I don't take this lightly," she whispered.

"Nor do I."

But Emma pulled away, and Mason reluctantly let her go.

"What I mean is..." She took a deep breath. "Look. If this is just because you need a woman in your bed, then you need to stop this. I've offered before - we can renegotiate the contract so that you can sleep with other women."

"You're offering me an outlet."

"Yes."

"And if I tell you that I don't want an outlet? That I want you?"

"Do you?"

"Emma…"

"Because I'm not like Jen. Or like the other women you've dated before me. I'm not asking for a ring and a promise of forever, but if you're just in this for the sex, I can't do this."

He looked intently down at her, without touching her. "You have the ring already," he reminded her, reaching out to brush a strand of hair back from her face. "And neither of us knows what tomorrow will bring, or if forever is in the cards for anyone."

Still standing a foot away from her, he held her in place without touching her, just by the strength of his gaze. "Will you let me make love to you, Emma?" he asked gently.

She stared up at him, her need for him consuming her, making it hard for her to think. Would she regret this in the morning? she wondered. But some part of her simply didn't care. She'd deal with the consequences the next day. And there would be consequences, she knew. Still, she didn't have a choice, really. She wanted this man like she wanted air to breathe. "Yes," she whispered.

With a groan of relief, Mason reached out and pulled Emma into his arms. There was no finesse to this, not tonight. Not now. Not when he finally had her in his embrace. His kiss was passionate, bordering on obsessive. There was no expertise to his touch. He simply had to have her. But she was matching him, touch for touch, kiss for kiss. She wanted him too. And while he badly wanted to slow down, to take his time, to show Emma how good it could be between them, the need was too great.

Without lifting his mouth from hers, he swung her up into his arms, and carried her easily up the stairs and into his bedroom. Laying her on the bed, he gently followed her down.

Emma awoke to the feel of little tiny kitten paws walking over her face. Opening one eye, she giggled at the sight of the kitten hopping over her to the space next to her on the bed, and flopping down, raising his paw for a belly rub. She happily obliged. Turning around in the bed, expecting to find Mason there beside her, enjoying the antics of the cat, she found nothing but an empty spot. It was cold – he'd been up for some time.

Fighting the wave of anxiety that hit her, she pulled on the robe that Mason had pulled off of her last night. Picking up Max, she walked down the hallway to her bedroom. Mason had already let Chaos out – his crate was open, and he was nowhere to be seen. So Emma placed the kitten on the floor of her room, and went into the bathroom to take a shower.

It was a bad sign that Mason had gotten up this morning without waking her. Emma knew that. She knew that it was likely that he was regretting last night, or that he was wondering how to tell her that things had gotten out of hand, but that he was very sorry. She also knew that he'd probably be cold this morning. The walls would be back up. She needed to be ready for that. She might have broken through for one night, but she was kidding herself if she thought that once they were down, they'd stay down.

After showering and pulling on a pair of jeans and a t-shirt, she pulled her wet hair back into a ponytail and applied just a dusting of makeup. Looking at her watch, she gave a sigh of relief. It was almost 9:00. She was due at her grandmother's at 11:00 to take her to the grocery store. If she needed to, she'd go over early. Gran would understand, especially once she explained why.

Heading downstairs, Emma found silence. No coffee brewing, no breakfast cooking. Any last hope that she had that Mason was just kindly letting her sleep in disappeared. Moving into the kitchen, she started a pot of coffee, then let Chaos in and fed him. She put down food for the cat. She poured coffee. She drank one cup standing at the counter. She poured herself a bowl of cereal. She ate it. She drank another cup of coffee. She cleaned up after herself.

Going back upstairs, she made the bed in Mason's room, then went into her own room and straightened up. At 10:30, she crated Chaos, shut Max in her room with food, water, and a clean litter box, and headed for Gran's.

Gran took one look at Emma when she opened the door to her granddaughter. "You slept with him."

"I did," Emma admitted as she walked into her grandmother's home and made herself comfortable on the couch.

"Didn't go well?"

"The actual sleeping with him part went very well. It was the morning after that seemed to go downhill."

"What happened?"

"Absolutely nothing. He was gone by the time I got up. Not a note, not a kiss on the forehead, not even a pot of coffee brewing. He was just gone."

"Hmm."

Emma leaned forward, her head in her hands, and looked up at her grandmother with a pained expression. "What have I done, Gran?" she whispered.

"What any sane red-blooded woman in your place would do, Emma. That man is temptation personified. Don't beat yourself up over it."

Emma shook her head ruefully. "I'm an idiot."

"He's the idiot for not appreciating my beautiful granddaughter. Now come on. Let's go get a cup of coffee and put some Bailey's in it. It'll make you feel better."

"You're going to make me an alcoholic yet."

"The day that you say you'll put some coffee in your Baileys' will be the day I worry."

But Emma just sighed and leaned back on the couch. "So what do I do now?" she asked.

"You've got a lot of options, Emma. You can stay here with me, but that's called running away. You can go home this evening and let him have it between the eyes, but that might be overreacting. And I've never been an advocate of the silent treatment. If something bothers you, you deal with it. So I'd suggest either option b or c, which are somewhere in the middle of a, d, and e."

Emma gave a slight smile. "OK. I'll bite. What are options b and c?"

"B is going home later today and pretending that last night never happened. No furtive glances, no silent treatment, just treat him like you treated him last week. It will require every ounce of willpower and sincere acting ability, but it will make him crazy."

"And option c?"

"Talk to him. Not aggressively, not like a scared little girl, but like an adult with an issue to deal with."

Emma thought about it for a moment, then asked, "Can't I just sic Chaos on him?"

"Probably not, since that crazy dog now loves him almost as much as you."

Emma sighed. "I should have known this would happen," she said quietly.

"Emma. Relax. If he acts like a jerk, you learned early on what he's like, and you can deal with the rest of your time with him appropriately. But he might just have needed time to think. So give him that time. See what happens."

"You're right. Of course you're right. OK. Option b it is. Because if I try option c, he'll shut down. We'll talk when he's ready."

"Good choice. OK. Let's go get coffee. And then we'll hit the grocery store. PowerBall is up to $78 million, so I'm playing."

"For a smart woman, you're kinda overly optimistic on your chances with the lottery, Gran."

"Oh shush," the old woman said as she stood up and patted Emma's knee. "A girl can dream."

Pulling into the garage a few hours later, groceries in tow, Emma took a deep breath. This was going to be the hardest thing she'd ever done, she thought. But she would do it. Pulling the tote bag full of produce from her trunk, Emma hefted it over her shoulder and walked into the house.

Mason was home. His car was in the garage, and she heard vague sounds coming from his office. But Emma thought back to what she would have done last week. She headed upstairs to let Chaos out. Opening the door to her room, she giggled. Max had done a number on the room. He'd evidently climbed curtains, knocked things off her dresser, and then fallen fast asleep in the middle of her bed.

"Am I going to need to crate you too, little man?" she asked as she picked up the kitten and then let an exuberant Chaos out of his crate and out the patio door into the back yard. Carrying the little squirmy guy on her shoulder, she picked up the mess he'd made of her things, and then went downstairs to put the groceries away, carrying the cat with her.

In the kitchen, she set Max down on his bed, and moved around the room expertly. She was going over to her parents for dinner that night, so she wasn't cooking. Everything went into its place. When she was done, she looked at her watch. 2:30. She had more than enough time for a run. Changing into her running clothes, she shut Max back into her room, whistled for Chaos, and they set off down the street to the local park.

She loved watching her dog run. Of all the things he loved most in life (food, balls, running, food, her, her family, food, Mason), running seemed to be the one thing that put a huge smile on his face. His gait was goofy, but efficient, and he always seemed to be pulling her along on the leash, no matter how fast she moved. Now, following behind Chaos, she was again struck at how happy he was. No worries, no cares, just a drive to go forward. The possibility of food being in front of him was enough to give him incentive.

She took a longer run than normal. She had time, the day was amazing, and she had a lot of stress to work out. When she finally walked back in the door of Mason's home, it was after 4:30. After letting Chaos out into the backyard to sleep on the deck, she headed to the kitchen to grab a bottle of water. When she walked in, Mason was standing at the sink, looking out the back window. Max was perched on his shoulder.

Here we go, she thought.

"Hey," she said as she strolled over to the fridge. "How much damage did Max cause this time around?"

Mason turned when she walked in, his face tight, obviously expecting her to ask him about last night. But Emma just reached into the fridge, grabbed a bottle of water, and then walked over to reach up and scritch the cat's head.

"When I left him this morning, he managed to pull down one curtain and clean off all the stuff on my dresser. Please tell me that he just slept this afternoon."

Mason handed Max over to her, and she took him gladly, turning away from Mason and rubbing her face in his little kitten fur.

Mason's response sounded cautious, like there might be hidden meaning in her words. "I think he slept. I didn't see any damage, but I just opened the door to let him out. I didn't really look carefully."

Emma sighed. "OK. I'll go assess. Let's go, little man. Hopefully you didn't do any permanent harm." Kitten in one hand and water in the other, Emma headed for the stairs. She felt Mason's eyes on her, but he didn't say a word. Gran was right, Emma thought. This was the way to play it. They'd talk when he was ready.

Opening the door to her room, Emma was pleased to see that Max had indeed slept for a good chunk of the afternoon. The bed had a little kitten-sized indentation on it, and she saw no other signs of mayhem. Placing Max back down on the bed, she grabbed her robe and headed into the shower.

Under the steaming water, Emma replayed her short conversation with Mason. She had guessed right that morning when she woke up - Mason was uncomfortable around her now. He may have wanted her last night, but it was clear that in the light of day there was nothing between them. On his side, anyway. Her reaction to him was as strong as ever, and hiding it was more difficult than she'd thought it would be. But it was important, she knew. If she, in any way, displayed neediness or possessiveness, he'd retreat even further. And two-plus years of cold silence was more than even she could handle. They might not come out of this as lovers, but they needed to come out as friends.

That was the thing, Emma realized. Mason needed her. He didn't know it, but he did. He needed a friend. He needed someone on his side. And even if it hurt, even if he never touched her again like he had last night, she would try like the dickens to support him.

Stepping out of the shower and toweling off, she let Chaos back into her room. He walked over, sniffed Max, then settled down suspiciously on the floor next to his crate. He wasn't sure yet about the cat, but Emma wasn't worried. Chaos would adjust.

She put on a pair of worn blue jeans and pulled an old University of Michigan t-shirt over her head. She quickly blow-dried her hair, then pulled it back into a ponytail. After slipping into an old pair of tennis shoes, she was ready to go. She made sure that Max had plenty of food and fresh water, kissed him on the head, told him to be good and not destroy too much, and whistled for Chaos.

The two of them traipsed down the stairs, Chaos immediately heading for the kitchen in search of food. Emma laughed at the sight of him vacuuming the floor near where Mason had been standing. The dog was convinced that anyone standing in the kitchen was likely to have dropped food, and Emma did not disabuse him of that notion. He was usually right.

As she was picking up her purse and her keys, she looked up to see Mason coming down the stairs, dressed to the nines in a dark suit and tie. Her heart clenched. He looked amazing, and sexy, and... well, kind of angry.

"You're not ready yet?" he asked.

"Ready for what?"

"The cocktail party at the Alvarez's."

Emma thought hard. She was sure she would have remembered if he'd told her about this. She always marked social events on her calendar, and she had checked before agreeing to go over to her parents' home.

"When did you tell me about this?" she asked cautiously.

"Last week. You forgot?"

"Exactly when last week, Mason?"

"I don't know," he said dismissively. "I probably mentioned it over dinner one night."

"You weren't home for dinner last week, Mason. And I would have remembered a cocktail party invitation, because it would have thrown me into the usual state of panic as I tried to figure out what to wear."

"Well, we still have time. Just wear anything. Nobody will notice."

Emma looked up at her husband and blinked. He was an insulting, rude, and incredibly frustrating man. Too bad for her that she still liked the man. But too bad for him - she wasn't changing plans this time. Her relationship with her family was just starting to mend, and she was not going to risk messing it up again.

"No. I'm not going with you. You did not tell me about it. I have plans. You'll have to go without me tonight."

Anger flashed briefly in his eyes. "Our deal..."

"If you can't be bothered to tell me about social events on your calendar that you'd like me to accompany you to, then I can't be bothered to change my plans. I'm not going. Deal with it."

His eyes narrowed. "If this is because..."

Emma interrupted, her own temper flaring. "Do NOT go there, Mason. Do not. Have a nice time tonight," she said, turning around and reaching for Chaos' leash and her purse. She looked over her shoulder at him. He was positioned in the doorway, imperiously. Her heart sank. The cold and emotionless man was back. And he was just standing there, watching her. Gripping her keys, she opened the back door to let Chaos in, then clipped the leash to his collar, holding him tightly so he wouldn't jump up on Mason. Without another look, she headed for her car.

Mason was stunned. He had expected that she'd offer to change her plans for him. After all, what could her plans involve if she was dressed like that, and if she was taking Chaos? Truthfully, he couldn't remember if he'd told her about tonight or not, but she was normally free when he asked her to attend events with him, so he hadn't really thought it would matter.

She'd just taken the dog and walked out.

He was also surprised that she didn't seem to want to talk about last night. Or this morning. She was acting like it had never happened. Any other woman he knew would have wanted to analyze it to death, and would want to know why he'd left her bed this morning and disappeared for the day. And his response would have been coldly sardonic - he had things to do, and didn't plan to just lie around all morning.

The problem was, he had badly wanted to lie around with Emma this morning. She had been amazing last night, and he had gratefully taken what she offered with such humor and kindness. But this morning, feeling the way that he did, he had slipped out of bed and run away. Despite his feelings for Emma, he still didn't know if he wanted a relationship. He had never wanted an emotional connection with anyone, and she would demand that, at the very least, if they continued to have a physical connection.

He rubbed his face. What in the hell had he been thinking last night? Other than that he wanted this woman more than he wanted air to breathe? And still did, if he was honest with himself. But her reaction to him, her complete lack of interest in what had happened last night and this morning, surprised him. She had had a good time last night, he was sure of it. And she had given herself to him freely, willingly, passionately. But maybe that's all she wanted - one night.

So now what?

Well, he was obviously going to the party alone. That was pretty clear. But the more important question was, what in the hell was he going to do about Emma?

Just wear anything. Nobody will notice. The words cut deep, even now, hours later, as she pulled into the driveway of her home. HER home. Not Mason's. She wasn't going back there yet. She would have to, eventually, just to ensure that Max didn't wreak holy havoc in her room. But she needed her time, her space, and her silence for a while.

Her evening with her Mom, Dad, and Gran was nice. They still weren't back to normal completely, but Gran was helping everyone to get there. Still, she would eventually either need to come clean with her parents about why she'd married Mason, or she'd need to show up with him in tow one night.

Nobody will notice. The implication being that nobody really looked at her anyway. Nobody really cared. Nobody saw her as anything but the woman on Mason's arm. She knew it wasn't true, but she understood that people saw her and what she wore *because* she was with Mason, not because she was someone special in her own right.

She didn't feel at all badly that he went off on his own tonight. Maybe now he'd be sure to check with her when he made plans. And if he didn't, she had no problem with telling him no again in the future.

Letting herself in the back door of her house, she stood in the doorway and just breathed. This was still home to her. The smells, the sounds, the feel of it. Even after months of living with Mason, this was still her refuge.

She walked through the darkness to her couch and sank down onto it. Home, she thought.

Home was not with Mason. Home was not in that stark, cold, emotionless house on the other side of town. True, the kitchen was phenomenal, and Max and Chaos helped to make it more comfortable for her. And true, she loved that crazy little boy next door with all her heart. But those were surrounding characters in her life, and those same characters would still be in place if she were living back here. Where she belonged.

Not yet, though. If she tried to broach the subject with Mason now, he would think that she was angry about last night. Or hurt. And while that was kind of true (the hurt part, anyway), she knew that her longing to be home had little to do with one night with Mason. It had more to do with the fact that she saw the writing on the wall. She was not ever going to be the love of his life. She was not going to be the one to break down the barriers around his heart. And she needed to just accept that and figure out a way forward. All of that would be easier to do if she weren't living with the man. If she weren't, herself, falling in love with him.

And that was the problem, really. Despite everything, Emma was finding herself more and more drawn to Mason. Sleeping with him probably hadn't been the best idea she'd ever had, since it just confirmed what she already knew - he could make exquisite love to her body, make her feel things she'd never felt before, ever, but he wouldn't give his heart. Leaving her the next morning had been his way of reminding her of that. And still, when she saw past the ice around his heart, she saw a man who had the capacity to love, but chose not to. And she needed to both know that, know it deep in her heart and in her soul, and to accept it. If she had hope of any kind, her heart would be crushed.

Sighing, she stood up and made her way through the rest of her small house. It was exactly the way she'd left it after talking to Jen earlier that month. And while the economically sound thing to do would be to rent it out while she stayed at Mason's, she couldn't bring herself to do that. She needed to be able to come here occasionally, to reconnect with who she was.

Picking up a photo of her and her sister, smiling at the camera, she felt her eyes well up. Damnit, Jen, she thought. Why did you do this to me? You could have dealt with this man so much better than I can. You would never let yourself get emotionally invested in him. Like I've done. Like I'm doing.

Setting the frame back down onto the table next to the couch, she took another look around. Chaos was waiting in the car. It was time to go.

Letting herself into Mason's home, she opened the back door for Chaos, and then headed upstairs to her bedroom. Max was wide awake, busy doing kittenish things, like climbing the bedspread, scratching at his scratching post, and generally creating havoc. She grinned. There was nothing like a kitten to make you laugh.

She was sound asleep when she was awakened two hours later. She wasn't sure at first what had pulled her from her sleep, but the footsteps in the hallway told her that Mason was home. The soft giggle she heard after that caused her to sit up straight. Silently slipping from her bed, she padded over to the door and leaned her ear against it. The giggle came again, followed by a low chuckle.

So Mason had brought a woman home. That voided the contract. She waited for the sense of relief to come, and was surprised when all she felt was sad. She went back into her room and dressed quietly, then opened the door to her bedroom. The voices she'd heard were now coming from downstairs, so she took a deep sigh and descended the stairs. She had no desire to embarrass Mason or to cause a scene, but she needed to be sure before she called her lawyer in the morning to get her out of this situation.

"Emma?"

"Amanda?" Mason's sister was here?

"I'm sorry, we didn't mean to wake you," Amanda said, giving her a quick hug. "Mason wanted to show me Max, but he forgot that he'd be in with you. Can I see him?"

Emma was still reeling. There was no other woman. Her expression must have concerned Amanda, who just looked at her carefully. "Are you OK?" she asked.

Emma nodded. She'd sort out her feelings later. For now, she needed to step up her game. "I'm fine. Just a little groggy," she smiled. "Come on upstairs. I'll get Max."

Over Amanda's shoulder, she saw Mason smile. It was his predatory smile again, she thought. The damn man had known just what she was thinking, and he was enjoying her discomfort. Carefully steeling her face to hide her feelings, Emma turned away. Oh Lord, she thought. I don't have the emotional resources to deal with this man. He'll win, she thought. Every damn time.

Morning came quickly. Emma took a quick shower, then went downstairs and brewed a pot of coffee. Max and Chaos followed her down, and sat in the sunshine while she waited for the percolator to stop percolating. She felt, rather than heard, Mason come in behind her.

"Morning," she said quietly, looking over her shoulder at him.

"Morning," he replied, reaching into the fridge for an orange. "Come into my study when you have your coffee," he told her. "I'd like to talk to you."

She nodded. "OK," she agreed softly, wondering what this would be about.

A few minutes later, after stirring creamer into her coffee, she took a large comforting sip from her mug, and made her way down the hall to Mason's office.

Leaning in the doorway, she asked, "What's up?"

He motioned her into the room, and then asked, "What are your plans for today, Emma?"

She shrugged as she pushed herself away from the doorframe and sat down on the edge of the couch cushion. "The usual. Church later this morning. Gran. Chaos. Maybe a walk with Malcolm. Why?"

"Can I convince you to spend the day with me?"

She looked at him for a long moment before asking, "Why?"

"We have some tension between us to work out. I want to do that before it gets worse."

"Tension?" she repeated disbelievingly.

He looked at her sharply. "You don't feel it?"

"I just wouldn't characterize it as tension. I'd probably call it pile-driving pressure. But that's me. And no. I'm not abandoning my grandmother for you."

He shrugged, leaning back in his chair. "I could go with you," he suggested. "I haven't met her yet."

Emma shook her head. "You can meet her any time. Except today. I'm not putting her in the middle of whatever the hell it is that's going on between us."

"What is going on between us, Emma?" he asked softly.

Emma bit back a number of unhelpful comments, and just sighed.

"I don't know that anything is really going on, Mason. I think maybe we both got carried away the other night. I think maybe you started worrying that I'd go looking for china patterns and want us to sit on the couch and stare into each other's eyes and talk about our feelings."

His eyes narrowed. "Was I wrong?"

She laughed. "Yeah, you were wrong. Mason, look. What happened the other night was mutual. It happened. It's done. And while it meant something to me, I know that you don't want a relationship. I knew that going in. So my heart is well and truly guarded - I'm not going to fall in love with you and look for more out of this marriage than we've agreed to. OK?"

He looked at her shrewdly, and then slowly nodded. "OK. So what happened last night?"

"Last night? You mean when I let you go to the party alone, or when I woke up to find Amanda looking for a cat and you laughing at me?"

He looked taken aback, but didn't react in any other way. "First, the party."

"You didn't tell me. I made other plans."

"With who?"

"Why is that your business?"

"I guess it's not. I'm just curious what you prioritized above me."

"My family. I'd agreed to go have dinner with them, and then to help my dad move some furniture around."

Mason looked surprised. "Furniture? Emma, I don't want you moving furniture around. You could hurt yourself."

Emma shot him a look of annoyance. "I've been moving furniture around my parents' house since I was twelve. I appreciate the concern, but I'm a little stronger than I look."

"You couldn't have canceled?"

"I could have. I would have if it had been important. But it wasn't important enough for you to have given me warning. So I didn't."

He nodded. "I'll try to get better at remembering to inform you when these things come up," he said, figuratively holding out an olive branch.

"I appreciate it."

He looked at her shrewdly then. "You thought I'd brought another woman home with me last night," he challenged her.

"I sure did."

"And you thought you could get out of our contract."

"I did."

"Sorry to disappoint you," he grinned.

She laughed back. "Me too. But it was good to see Amanda."

Mason hesitated, but then said quietly, "Emma, I'm not a nice man. But even I wouldn't stoop so low as to bring a woman back to the house after the night we shared. And for what it's worth, I'm sorry I didn't stay around the next morning."

Emma nodded her acceptance of his apology. She instinctively knew that even saying that much had been hard for him. "I need to go, Mason. Are we good? For now?"

He eyed her for several seconds. "I'm not entirely sure that we are, Emma. But we can talk more later."

She nodded. "Mason, also for what it's worth, I'm not unhappy here with you. I'm just not completely content. That's not your fault, and I know that. And I'll figure it out. I just have one request."

He raised his eyebrows.

"Don't touch me again."

If Emma hadn't been watching him carefully, she would have missed the flinch. But she *had* seen it. So she explained.

"It's not that I don't like it. I do. But it gets in the way. We need to live together for a long time yet. I can't do that if I'm walking on eggshells around you. So if you touch me again, you need to mean it."

Mason nodded slowly. "Fair enough," he said after a moment.

She got up from the couch. "You're a hard man. We've established that. But I don't have that kind of hard to me. And I need to survive this relationship."

Walking over to the door, she turned and gave him a slight smile. "See you later, Mason. Have a good day."

Don't touch me again. Until she had said that, he wasn't aware of how much he wanted to. He wanted to do more than touch her, he realized. He wanted to kiss her everywhere, to touch her, to lose himself in her. But he saw her vulnerability, and he understood. He had behaved like an ass the other morning, and she was right to protect herself.

He still didn't want a relationship. Or did he? The happiest he'd felt in years was when he was sitting in the kitchen, eating her food, drinking good wine, and having a conversation with Emma. He liked having her by his side at parties, and had genuinely missed her last night. And he'd been surprised that so many people had asked him where she was. She was liked, he realized. People he seldom talked to and barely knew inquired after her. His sister loved her. His mother was warming to her, albeit slowly, and had seemed disappointed when he told her that Emma couldn't make it last night. Her suspicious look made him feel like a kid, particularly when she had said something along the lines of 'She's good for you. Don't let her go', which was completely uncharacteristic of the woman.

What had he said to Emma last night? Something about people not noticing her. He had said it offhand, without thinking, but he now realized that it had been cruel. And wrong. People noticed. He wasn't entirely sure that he would have been so missed if Emma had shown up last night without him.

He couldn't pursue her unless he was sure. Sure that he wanted her in his life, sure that he wouldn't actively kick her out the second she got past his defenses. Until then, he needed to leave her alone. As much as he wanted her, physically, he needed to back away.

.

THIRTEEN

"You sure you're up for this?" Emma asked with some trepidation as they pulled up in front of her parents' house.

Mason turned to look at her, puzzled. "How bad can it be?"

Emma looked worried. "Um. Could be bad. You married their daughter without asking their permission," she pointed out. "Six months ago. This is the first time that you've bothered to meet them. So yeah, expect a few fireworks."

Mason chuckled. "Well, I brought flowers for your mom. And candy for your Gran."

"She will love that. Not as much as a bottle of scotch, but still. And for Dad?" she asked, just to toy with him.

"Emma," he said with a warning tone.

She grinned. "Just kidding. Look. Just weather it. They'll likely get in a dig or two, but you can take it."

"Isn't your Gran on my side?"

"I don't know. She's probably mad at you for holding me to Jen's contract, but she knows that this is an important night. I think she'll be on good behavior."

"We should have brought Chaos."

"Maybe. But this way if we need to run for the hills, we don't need to find the dog first."

"He'd be easy to find. He'd be in the kitchen."

Emma laughed. "You know him well. You ready?"

"Will Jen be here tonight?"

"Nope. She and I talked about it. Decided it was better for her to make other plans. It'll just be you, me, Mom, Dad, and Gran."

"Anything else I should know, other than to expect unconditional animosity?"

The corners of Emma's mouth turned up slightly. "Nope. They're nice people, Mason. They just expected more from me is all," she admitted.

"Do they think we're madly in love?"

"Gran doesn't. She knows the whole story," Emma confessed. "And don't look at me like that. It was the only way to get an ally in the family, and Gran likes knowing stuff nobody else knows. She's an excellent keeper of secrets."

"And your mom and dad?"

"I don't know what they think. But yeah, probably that I fell head over heels and you suckered me into marrying you."

"Suckered...?"

"They don't know anything about you. They may think you're a drug dealer or something."

Mason sighed. "Couldn't you have prepped them just a bit?"

"Nah. More fun this way."

"For who?"

"Me and Gran. OK," she said as she saw the front door open. "Showtime."

Helping Emma from the car, he reached into the back and grabbed the gifts he'd brought for Emma's mother and grandmother, then offered his arm to his wife. His wife, he thought. He didn't often think of Emma that way, but he had to admit that it had a nice ring to it.

She took his arm, smiled up at him, and together they headed up the walk to the front stoop of her parents home. Her father was standing in the doorway, her mother right behind him peeking over his shoulder. When they got to the top of the steps, Emma immediately performed the introductions.

"Mom, Dad, this is Mason," she said.

"So you're the man who swiped my daughter," her father said, eyeing Mason with a mixture of suspicion and distrust.

Mason just nodded. "I did. I'd apologize," he added, "but I'm not really sorry."

Her father seemed initially taken aback by that comment, but then his eyes narrowed as he realized that Mason was complimenting his daughter.

Emma's mother spoke up from around her husband. "Come on in Mason. We're glad to finally meet you."

He smiled then. "And that I do apologize for. I should have been here much sooner than this. But between getting Emma settled in, and work, and figuring out how to dog and cat-proof the house, and..."

Her father spoke up again, sternly. "You should have made the time, son."

Mason agreed. "You're right. But I'm glad to be here now. Mrs. Jameson, these are for you," he added, holding out the flowers he'd purchased earlier.

She reached for them with a smile. "They're lovely, Mason. Come in. Please. Emma, put these in water?"

Emma took them from her mother and moved around her parents, stopping to kiss them each on the cheek. "Sure, Mom." Over her shoulder, she added, "Mason, that's Gran over there, hovering over the martini glass. Gran, this is Mason."

"Well, you're even hunkier in person than in the papers. Come on over here and let me have a look at you," her grandmother commanded, peering at him through her glasses.

Emma rolled her eyes. "Gran, leave him alone. He's already a bit unnerved by all of you."

"Fine," the old woman huffed. "Mason, can I offer you a martini?"

"Take her up on it," Emma called from the kitchen. "You'll need the alcohol in your system. Trust me."

"I'd love one," Mason said to Gran, handing her the box of chocolates. "These are for you. Emma says that you have a sweet tooth. Or two."

She grinned in delight. "Emma is right. And thank you."

"So Mason. Tell us about yourself."

Emma rolled her eyes. The interrogation was beginning. Mason was right, they should have brought Chaos.

By the time dinner was served, Mason had charmed her mother, talked her father down from killing him, and even managed to get in a few spirited jabs at her grandmother, which completely endeared him to her. Emma wasn't sure if the evening was going to be a success or not, but at least nobody was going to end up in the emergency room tonight.

As dinner was winding down, and Emma was just starting to think that they'd made it through the evening unscathed, her mother looked over the table at Mason, and asked, "So, Mason. How did you and Emma meet?"

Mason looked up in startled surprise, his eyes flicking over to Emma. "You never told them?" he asked, hoping she'd pick up on his code for HELP.

She shrugged. "Not really. I just told them that Jen introduced us."

"Well, looks like you have a lot to thank her for," her mother said to Emma, pointedly looking over at Mason. Emma glanced over at her grandmother, who was taking a healthy sip of her martini in an attempt to smother her laughter.

"So Mason," Gran said, leaping in to rescue her granddaughter, who looked ready to spit rocks. "Tell us about adjusting to life with Emma. She can't be easy to get used to, especially with Chaos around all the time."

Emma rolled her eyes. So much for rescuing her granddaughter, she thought. This night was not turning out as she expected.

But Mason, gentleman that he was, was saying incredibly kind things. He was talking about Chaos, about Max, about her obvious love for animals. He was telling them about how lucky he was to come home to her cooking. About how Malcolm adored her.... Listening to him, she felt... cared for. She couldn't go so far as saying loved, but Mason was talking about her as if he admired her. Liked her. Was glad she was in his life. Gazing at him over the rim of her own martini glass, she smiled slightly.

Her parents were flummoxed. She realized that she had never had anyone talk about her this way. Everyone, always, talked about her in conversations punctuated by laughter and eye rolls, saying, 'oh that's just Emma' to any implied criticism, but this man was showing her family how much he valued her. And they had absolutely no idea how to respond.

"Well," Gran said when Mason stopped talking and just smiled lovingly over at Emma. "Who wants dessert?"

An hour later, Emma crawled back into the car next to Mason, and turned to face him. "Holy crap," she said. "That was absolutely amazing."

He just looked over at her, puzzled. "What?"

"What you did in there. I don't think I've ever seen my family speechless."

He shrugged. "They take you for granted, Emma. They love you, but they don't have any idea who you are."

"Except Gran," Emma said quietly.

But Mason shook his head as he turned the key in the ignition. "No, even Gran. She loves you, maybe even with more voracious strength than your parents, but she's also fallen into the habit of laughing at your antics. You're more than that, Emma. You know that, right?"

She just looked at him.

"How often do they ask about your work?" he asked, checking in the mirror and pulling out into the street.

"Um. My Dad does. Sometimes." Emma replied, trying to think of the last time they'd really talked about a case she was working on.

"And how often do they ask your opinion of something serious?"

"Oh, not very often. We usually talk about Chaos, or people we know. But that's just the way my family is."

"What about Jen?"

"What about her?"

"How do they treat her when she's home?"

Emma shrugged. "They usually ask lots of questions. About where she's been, who she's met."

"Exactly. They undervalue you."

"They see me all the time. They don't really need to know where I've been or who I've met - they probably already know."

"Emma."

She sighed. "Yeah, maybe. OK. Probably. But they love me."

"They do, Em. They really do. But they need to see you through a different lens sometimes."

"And that's you?"

He smiled slightly. "For now."

"OK. I can live with that."

"Good." He reached over and squeezed her hand as he drove them home. "Do you think Max has destroyed the house?"

"I locked him in my room."

"I let him out before we left."

Emma shook her head. "Oh, you poor misguided man."

After that night, Emma felt a little more comfortable in Mason's presence again. She still knew when he was home, even if she didn't hear him come in, just because she could sense him. And she still avoided spending a lot of time with him, but the tension between them had dissipated. So when Mason knocked on her bedroom door one evening and told her that he'd like her to accompany him to a charity event that coming weekend, she just nodded.

"OK. Formal?"

"Not black tie. A cocktail dress is fine."

She sighed and leaned against the doorframe. "Can I get away with something I've worn before?" she asked.

He looked down at her, lounging in a pair of yoga pants and a t-shirt, and fought back the sudden want that consumed him. Even in such casual clothes, she drew him in. When he raised his eyes to hers, she was startled at the need she saw reflected in them. She took a step back, drawing in a breath. He closed his eyes, willing himself to stay where he was, even as he wanted to pull her toward him, close his mouth over hers, and drag her to her bed.

"I don't think so, Emma," he said at last, his voice huskier than usual. "Many of the same people will be there from previous events. And it's rather a big deal. I'm sorry, but I think you'll need a new dress."

She forced her eyes away, looking down at her bare feet, poking out from under her pants. "If I wear black, maybe they won't notice."

Mason reached out gently and lifted her face until she was looking him in the eye. "Emma, they'll notice. I was wrong when I said before that nobody would. People watch you closely. They like you. They miss you when you're not there. And I'm willing to bet that many people watch to see what you wear, and then copy your style."

Emma shook her head, even though her chin was still in Mason's grip. "I don't think so, Mason. My style is what you see on me right now. It's not what I wear to events. But I don't want to embarrass you. I'll shop this week."

He let her go with a gentle caress. "Emma, I'll deposit some funds in your checking account this week. You've been spending a lot of money on your clothes, and that's because of me."

But Emma refused. "No."

"Why not?"

She shrugged. "Doesn't feel right. I have the money. If it gets out of control, I'll let you know."

"Emma...."

"I'll be ready on Saturday night, Mason. What time?"

Mason gave her a long look, before replying evenly, "7:00."

"Good night," she said softly, shutting her bedroom door and leaning against it. Damn, he made her want him. Just seeing him standing in her doorway, his long lean body lovingly clothed in a suit that was tailored for him, made her want to rush into his arms and demand that he make love to her. For as long as he was interested, even if it killed her when he eventually left. She had more pride than that, but she stayed for a long time with her back to the door, knowing that if she moved, she might go in the wrong direction.

On Saturday night, Emma was ready at 7:00. She'd fed and crated Chaos, left out kitty food for Max, and dressed in a new bright magenta side-drape sheath dress that she'd found on sale. It fit her curves lovingly, and she paired it with silver sandals and a matching shawl, in case it got chilly. With her brown curls carefully swept up into a loose chignon, she looked, she thought, as good as she was going to.

When she stepped down the stairs at exactly 7:00, Mason was standing in the foyer, checking messages on his smartphone. He looked up when he heard her on the stairway, and did a double take. This was Emma? She looked absolutely beautiful, he thought. She always looked lovely, but this color brought out the rosiness of her cheeks, the soft highlights in her hair, and accented the curves of her body in a way that caused his heart to skip a beat. He nearly dropped his phone as he waited for her to join him at the bottom of the stairs.

"Mason?" She looked uncertain. He was looking at her very strangely, she thought. "What's wrong? Do I have fur somewhere I shouldn't? I thought I'd done a good job with the lint roller," she added, trying to stretch to see her backside, in case she'd missed anything. As she curled around, Mason thought his heart might be going into palpitations.

"No. No fur," he managed to say. "You look amazing, Emma. Beautiful."

She smiled up at him. "Thank you. That's sweet. You look amazing yourself," she added. And he did. There was something about seeing this man in a suit. A black suit. A black suit with a crisp white shirt and a brightly striped tie. He looked... Predatory, she thought. It was a look she hadn't seen for a while, but it was back. He was looking at her with eyes that seemed to see into her soul.

"Mason?" she asked tentatively.

"There will not be a man there tonight who won't be wishing he were me," Mason said, his voice gravelly.

"They always wish that," Emma pointed out lightly. "You're handsome, rich, and incredibly sexy. Who wouldn't want to be you?"

"None of that will matter, Emma. It will be about you tonight." Reaching out, he gently ran a hand over her cheek, then reached down to take her hand. "Ready to go, sweetheart?"

His tenderness was nearly her undoing. She wanted so badly for this to be real. For him to mean it when he called her sweetheart. For him to take her hand because he loved her. Fighting back a sudden wetness that seemed to be gathering in her eyes, she blinked hard and nodded. "I'm ready."

Once they arrived at the country club, Mason disappeared to go in search of drinks and Emma mingled around the room a bit, waiting for his return. She was uncomfortably aware that people were watching her, and she wondered why. She'd been to events with him before, and she'd been dressed to the nines before. She had no idea why she was undergoing such scrutiny tonight.

When Mason appeared back at her side with a glass of red wine for her, she breathed a sigh of relief.

"What's wrong?"

She shook her head. "Nothing. Just feel conspicuously on display tonight. I know my dress is bright, but it's more than that. Any idea what's going on?"

Mason just looked down at her incredulously. The woman really had no idea how gorgeous she was. Many of the women he'd dated in the past had known they were beautiful, and fished for compliments shamelessly. But Emma honestly didn't seem to have an arrogant bone in her body.

"What?" she asked, when he didn't say anything. "Did I split a seam or something?" she asked, trying to cautiously feel along her sides to ensure that her dress was still in place, while balancing her wine glass in the other hand.

Mason just laughed, then reached out and caught her hand in his. "No, no split seam. And nothing is going on. You just look beautiful, and people are noticing. That's all."

Emma's face turned nearly as magenta as her dress. "No, Mason, that's sweet to say, but that can't be."

"Of course it can. Come on. Let's go and find you some olives and nuts, so that wine doesn't go straight to your head."

"You know me well. What kind of wine did you get me?"

"It's a California Pinot Noir. Their selection was limited, especially for such a wine snob as yourself," Mason teased her.

"Ah yes. Once you've tasted from Mason Parker's wine cellar, nothing else seems to do," she laughed.

They were headed toward the small tables of finger food when Mason got waylaid by a business associate. Holding up one finger to Emma to let her know that he'd just be a second, Mason bent his head to listen to the question his colleague was asking. Emma wandered off a ways, wanting to give him privacy to talk. She hadn't gone far when Mason's mother appeared at her side.

"Hi, Mrs. Parker. Nice to see you again," Emma greeted her with a smile.

"Emma," the other woman acknowledged. "We haven't seen you in a while."

Shrugging and taking a sip from her wine glass, Emma responded, "I guess not." Noting that the woman was dressed beautifully tonight in a turquoise dress with a matching jacket, Emma added, "You're looking well."

Mrs. Parker turned and looked over at her shrewdly. "Don't kiss up to me, young lady," was her stern response.

Emma rolled her eyes. "Oh for Pete's sake. I like your dress and I like that color on you. Can't I say that?"

The woman looked at her with a half smile. "Certainly. I like that way of saying it better than the polite 'you're looking well' comment."

"Point taken," Emma grinned back at her.

"Who are you wearing?" Mrs. Parker asked, looking Emma over as she asked.

"Ann Taylor. On sale, even."

The woman out and out laughed. It stunned Emma. "Emma, I think I like you. No. I do like you. Amanda keeps telling me that I've misjudged you, and I think perhaps I have."

Emma just stared at her. And blinked. "Because I shop at Ann Taylor?"

"Because you're not afraid to say so. Here. To me. You didn't marry my son for his money, did you?"

"Hell no," Emma said with assurance.

"Emma," the older woman admonished her quietly.

"Sorry. *Heck* no. No. I didn't."

"So why did you marry him? And don't tell me true love. I know my son. Nobody falls in love with him that fast."

"It was more of a gradual thing?"

"Truth time, Emma."

Emma sighed. "He's a good man, Mrs. Parker."

"Dorothy. You can call me Dorothy. As long as you tell me the truth."

But Emma shook her head. "I can't quite do that. You need to ask your son that question. But the most important thing to know is that we both went into it with good reasons."

The older woman looked piercingly at Emma, then shook her own head. "I don't believe I'll ask him," she said at last. "I want to see how this plays out. You're good for him. I'm staying out of it."

Emma shrugged and took a sip of wine. "Suit yourself. But come over for dinner sometime. Seriously. You and Amanda. I've wanted it for months, and since he's not going to ever ask, I'm going to. I'll even cook."

"Doesn't Mason have caterers?"

"For parties, yes. But not for everyday dinners. I love to cook. Will you come?"

Again, the woman looked her up and down. "I do believe I will," she said decisively.

"Good. I'll find Amanda and ask her too. Next weekend?"

"I'm out of town, unfortunately. Perhaps the following weekend?"

"Perfect. I'll let Mason know."

"You asked my mother for dinner?" Mason looked at her incredulously.

"Yeah."

"And you told her you'd cook?"

"Yes again."

"You realize that she's used to haute cuisine," Mason pointed out.

Emma looked up at him with a perturbed expression. "What, my cuisine isn't haute enough for you?"

Mason just smiled. "I love your cuisine. My mother may be critical."

But Emma shook her head. "Nah. It'll be fine."

"I can get the caterers," Mason offered.

"Nope."

"You're stubborn."

Emma grinned at last. "Yeah. So are you."

"So when is this major event?"

"Not next weekend, but the following."

"Amanda is coming too?"

"Yes. And I told her to feel free to bring the man she's been dating."

"You what?"

Emma just shrugged. "Mason, they've been dating for longer than you and I have known each other. It's about time you and your mother met him, and this way, Amanda gets a buffer. Besides, why should all the attention be on us?" she laughed.

As Emma prepared for entertaining her mother-in-law, she realized that she hadn't yet invited her family over to Mason's home - not for dinner, not for drinks, not even for a game of Yahtzee. It was an oversight that she badly needed to address, particularly if she wanted to keep the hard-earned peace that seemed to have settled over them since they met Mason earlier that month. Plus, Gran was angling for an invite - she wanted to meet Max, see where her granddaughter was living, and assess the overall possibilities for lawn bocce later in the year. Her own yard wasn't big enough for a good game.

So Emma made a mental note to call her parents later that weekend and ask them about their schedule. And in the meantime, she carefully scoured her recipe collection for food she felt sure that Dorothy would like. And she then whittled those down to those that required most preparation in advance so that she could spend time with her guests, and not in the kitchen. By the time Saturday night rolled around, Emma only had a few things left to do, so was looking forward to a glass of wine, and some good conversation with Mason's family.

Mason had spent most of the day in his office, working on a legal issue that had kept him tied up for most of the week. Emma let him be, taking Chaos for a long run in the afternoon to wear him out a bit, and then tending to things in the kitchen. She pondered the table for some time, finally deciding on a dark brown tablecloth, ivory dishes, and a centerpiece of sage green candles in a glass bowl. It was simple, but lovely, and she felt sure that it would please Dorothy.

At around 6:00, Emma heard Mason leave his office and head to his room to get ready for the evening. She realized that she needed to do the same, and climbed the stairs to her own room, taking Chaos with her. After a quick shower, she dressed carefully in a pair of black trousers, a red embroidered tank top, and a matching red flowing sweater. She was looking for casual but elegant, and felt like she'd chosen the right mix of color and texture, particularly when she added black pearl earrings and a pair of soft black leather flats.

Heading back down the stairs, she checked on dinner and began assembling the appetizers she would put out for her guests. Olives and nuts, she grinned to herself, but also a delicious eggplant appetizer, served warm with crusty bread that she'd made earlier that day. All she needed was a decent wine to go with everything, but she would leave that up to Mason.

As if on cue, the man appeared in the kitchen doorway, and Emma nearly dropped the knife she was using to cut the bread. He was dressed in a pair of dark trousers that fitted him perfectly, and had a black turtleneck sweater under a dark grey jacket. He was dressed far more casually than Emma was used to seeing him, but he looked gorgeous. Sexy. Amazing. Emma forgot to close her mouth as she stared at her husband.

But he was staring too. Emma was normally a very pretty woman, and when she was dressed in her cocktail finery, she was gorgeous. But she too was dressed in much more casual clothes than usual, and the red suited her. Oh hell, it didn't just suit her, it was like the color was made for her. With her dark hair and her creamy complexion, the red brought out the color in her cheeks in a flattering way. She was beautiful, he thought. Absolutely beautiful. And if his mother wasn't due to arrive any second, he had no doubt that he would be hard-pressed to keep his hands off her.

"Wow," Emma breathed at last. "You look fantastic."

"I was about to say the same to you," Mason said quietly. "You should wear red more often."

She smiled then, moving her eyes away and breaking the spell that he seemed to have momentarily cast on her. "Thank you. I didn't want to wear a dress tonight. I hope your mother won't mind."

"I doubt she'll mind in the least," Mason shrugged, just as the doorbell chimed.

"I'll get the door," Emma offered, wiping her hands on the kitchen towel and heading for the foyer, Chaos at her heels.

Dorothy was well-dressed as usual, and she accepted Emma's compliments on her color choices graciously.

"I like red on you. Is that Vera Wang?"

"Close. J.Jill."

Dorothy rolled her eyes. "Well, I'd rather have a daughter-in-law who makes off-the-rack clothes look designer, than one who makes designer clothes look off-the-rack."

Emma laughed and leaned forward to kiss the older woman on the cheek. "I'll take that as a compliment. Come on in, Dorothy. Can I take your coat?"

"Where is Mason's maid?"

"She doesn't work nights," Emma replied, taking the coat from her mother-in-law and hanging it carefully in the closet. As she turned, she saw Dorothy eyeing Chaos, who was sticking close to Emma's side.

"What is that?" she asked imperiously.

"It's a dog," Emma responded cautiously.

"Well, I can see that. What is it doing in the house?"

Not sure how to answer, Emma responded, "Keeping the cat company?"

The look on Dorothy's face was priceless. "Cat?" she asked.

Grinning, Emma took Dorothy's arm to lead her into the living room. "Max. He's around here somewhere. Just look before you sit down."

As they moved from the foyer to the living room, Dorothy commented, "The house looks different."

"Really? I've just added some color here and there," Emma said. "Mason didn't even notice."

"I noticed," came a deep voice behind her. "But I liked it, so I didn't complain. If you'd loaded up my house with crocheted doilies, I might have had something to say about it."

Emma grinned. "Well, I'm glad you like it."

"Mother, can I offer you some wine?"

"Sounds delightful," Dorothy said, still looking around her with pleasure.

Mason turned to Emma. "I'll go down to the cellar and choose a bottle. What are we having for dinner?"

Emma shrugged. "I haven't decided yet," she said airily.

It was fun watching Mason go from zero to sixty in seconds. "What?" he said, gritting his teeth to prevent himself from saying something he shouldn't.

She laughed and patted him on the arm. "Oh relax. I'm kidding. We're having roast pork, and it's in the oven. So we have plenty of time to chat. Come on out to the sunroom, Dorothy. It's lovely out there right now, and Mason started a fire in the chimnea."

"Chimnea?"

"It's like a little fireplace for the outdoors. I've got some appetizers out there."

The doorbell rang again, just as Emma had gotten Dorothy seated in a comfortable chair next to the fire.

"That must be Amanda," Emma said, heading for the door. Sure enough, Amanda was standing on the stoop, looking hesitant. Standing beside her, one hand in his pocket and the other arm around Amanda's waist, was a nice looking young man.

Amanda took care of the introductions right off the bat. "Emma, I'd like you to meet Greg. Greg, this is Emma, my sister-in-law."

"It's really nice to meet you Greg," Emma said, smiling her welcome. "Come on in you two. Your mom is here, Amanda. I just sent her out back. Mason is in the basement, rustling up a bottle of fine wine. Can I take your coats?"

Greg helped Amanda out of her coat, and shrugged out of his own, handing both to Emma. She hung them in the closet, then turned back around. Greg was holding Max.

"Nice looking little fellow," he said, holding him up and looking at him closely. "Just a few months old?"

"We think maybe about four?" Emma responded.

"SPCA adoption?"

"Neighbor-found-him-under-a-bush adoption. One look in those eyes and we were both lost. You like animals?"

"Greg is a vet," Amanda said quietly.

Emma burst out laughing.

"What's so funny?" Amanda asked, not sure whether to be amused or hurt.

"The way your mom turned up her nose when she found out about Max and Chaos. This is going to be entertaining. Don't worry, Greg," she turned to hastily reassure her guest. "I am 100% on your side. Any lover of animals is a friend of mine."

"Chaos?" he asked, eyebrows raised questioningly.

"Our dog. He's probably out on the patio, watching hopefully for Amanda's mother to drop crumbs. But seriously, I'm so pleased that you're a vet. The boy next door desperately wants to be a vet. Can I have you both over again sometime and ask Malcolm to join us? I think he'd probably spend the entire evening interrogating you..."

"Oh, so no different from tonight," Greg said dryly, setting the kitten down on the floor.

Emma grinned. "Well, maybe a little different. But I'm really glad you both came."

Turning to Amanda, Emma asked, "Do you want to go face your mom, or do you want to hide out in here with me for a bit?"

"Can Greg hide for five minutes while I go out and break the news to mother that I brought a date?"

"Oh, I already told her you were bringing someone!" Emma said with chagrin, clasping her hand to her mouth. "I'm so sorry, should I not have said anything?"

But Amanda looked relieved. "No. That's perfect. Thanks, Emma. Was she appalled?"

"No, I don't think so. Curious, maybe."

"Uh oh."

"Amanda," Emma said seriously, grabbing one of her hands in hers. "Mason and I have got your back. And I'm sure that Greg does too."

She smiled then. A real smile. "Thanks. Really. Thanks."

Two hours later, Dorothy was leaning back in her chair, daintily wiping her lips with a napkin and sighing with delight.

"Dinner was delicious, Emma. Can I ask you to give that recipe to my caterers?"

"Sure. I'd be happy to. I'm really glad you enjoyed it, Dorothy. I hope you saved room for dessert?"

"Oh my."

"Blueberry pie," Mason said from across the table. "Her specialty, and my favorite."

"How are you not gaining hundreds of pounds?" Amanda asked her brother.

"I've doubled my workout," he said, laughing.

Emma was watching as her mother in law slipped Chaos a morsel of food that was left on her plate. When Dorothy looked up to find Emma watching, she looked guilty, but Emma just smiled and winked.

Straightening up, Dorothy cast a mischievous look at Emma and said, "I swear. I don't know what the world is coming to. All these animals in the house."

"Yeah," Mason drawled. "So much for keeping Chaos crated."

"He's behaving himself," Emma defended him.

"He's one of the best-behaved dogs I've seen in a while," Greg stated firmly. "Especially for being so food-driven."

Emma laughed.

"Where's the cat?" Amanda asked.

"Ask Emma," Mason rolled his eyes. Emma guiltily picked the kitten up from her lap, where it had been sitting since dinner began.

"How did you know he was there?" she asked with a grin.

"Because you kept your left hand below the table the entire night. I assumed it was because the cat was in your lap."

"Guilty," she murmured, setting Max on the floor and standing up to clear the plates. Amanda got up to help her, and they made quick work of loading the dishwasher.

"Is your mother appalled that we don't have help to do this?" Emma whispered to Amanda.

"No. I think she's comfortable at a dinner party for the first time in a long time."

Several glasses of cognac later, Dorothy announced that she was calling her driver and heading home. She was half-snockered, she stated primly, and wished to go before she got fully snockered and made a fool of herself in front of her children. When Greg asked if he and Amanda could see her home, she looked up at him with approval and stated, "That would be delightful."

Amanda rolled her eyes, but good-naturedly helped her mother into her coat, and they all headed out the door, leaving Emma behind holding the cat, and Mason gripping Chaos' collar so he didn't follow Greg out into the night. Greg was apparently Chaos' new best friend.

"I'd say that was a successful evening," Mason drawled. He let Chaos out into the back yard and turned to face Emma, who was cleaning up their dessert plates. "I'm not sure I've ever seen my mother have seconds."

"Really? Wow. She ate almost as much as I did."

"It was delicious, Em. You outdid yourself tonight. If you ever want to have caterers for something like this, all you need to do is ask, but I'd be happy eating nothing but your cooking from here on out."

Emma beamed. She loved it when people ate her food, and ate it with gusto. When she spent hours in the kitchen, she wanted people to enjoy what she produced.

"Yay. Lots of leftovers too, which is wonderful. So what did you think of Greg?" she asked, changing the subject as she loaded the dishwasher with the last of their plates.

"I liked him. You?"

"Very much. He seems really protective of your sister too, and they seem happy together."

"They do. But so do we."

Emma almost asked what he meant by that, but really, she knew. They did seem happy together, from the outside. It was only once they were here, alone together, that the tension resurfaced.

She sighed. "Yeah, you're right. We do. Even your mom is starting to think that we might have married for a reason other than money." She stood, looking straight at him. "If nothing else, that's something good that came out of all of this. Your mom sees you for who you are, and likes you."

"More than that, Emma. Your parents see you for who you are too. And Malcolm has a champion."

"Two. You're on his side too. I can tell."

"Max has a home. Chaos has more people to feed him."

Emma smiled.

"I have a more diversified diet than take-out."

She laughed. "And I'm learning more about wine every day. I'm going to have one hell of a wine cellar one day."

"It's all to the good, then."

"Yes," Emma responded. "All to the good."

She closed the door to the dishwasher and pushed the button to start it, then turned, running straight into Mason who had moved to stand behind her.

"Oooph," she grunted as she ran into him. Instead of moving back, he reached out a hand to steady her.

"Thanks for tonight, Emma," he said softly, reaching up to gently touch her cheek, pushing a strand of hair back behind her ear.

Flustered, Emma stammered, "Oh. Well. I..."

Lowering his lips until they were a hair's breadth away from Emma's, he whispered softly, "Don't worry, Em. I remember my promise. I'll keep it."

She closed her eyes and breathed, wanting so badly to move that short distance and kiss him. For real. But she knew what that could lead to. "Thank you, Mason," she said softly.

He pulled away slightly, looking down into her eyes with tenderness. "But Emma..."

"Yes?"

"The promise was conditional."

Her heart skipped a beat. "I know."
He bent down and kissed her cheek. "See you tomorrow."

FOURTEEN

"**Your** uncle left a codicil to his will."

Three months later, Mason was sitting in the office of his deceased uncle's lawyer, having been summoned there earlier that day. He was leaving later that week for another business trip, so decided that there was no time like the present. He had his secretary cancel his late-afternoon appointments, and he headed to the other side of town to find out what the older gentleman wanted. Now, with this news, Mason said nothing, waiting for the lawyer to continue.

"He instructed me to wait until just before your 41st birthday before revealing the addendum to you," the lawyer said, clearly uncomfortable with what his client had asked of him.

"Go on."

The lawyer leaned back in his chair, crossing one leg over the other and grasping his ankle with one hand. "Your uncle was concerned that you may marry in haste in order to get his voting shares. As, indeed, you did," he added. "But he did not wish you to be bound to a woman for three years if you were unhappy."

Mason shook his head. "I don't understand," he stated firmly. "He is the one who put the three year time commitment on this to begin with."

"Yes. He did that so that you *would* commit. And hopefully choose a woman that you could see spending time with. If he'd said one year initially, he was afraid that you wouldn't put any time into the decision. Any woman would have done."

Mason was silent for a moment before asking, "So what is in the codicil?"

"If you choose to end your marriage after one year, there will be no penalty."

Mason leaned forward, spearing the other man with a sharp look, "Say that again."

"You can divorce Emma at the end of this year, when you turn 41. You will keep the voting shares. Is that what you wish to do?"

Mason leaned back in his chair, his eyes still on the lawyer. Slowly, he asked, "Is there a time limit on this decision?"

The older man shook his head. "Not at all. Your uncle wanted you to be free to make plans if things were not working out."

"I see. And I do not need to marry another woman and do this whole thing again?" he asked sarcastically. The lawyer took him seriously.

"You do not. Your uncle just wanted to push you in what he called the right direction."

Mason laughed without humor. "The right direction, huh. What a stand-up guy my uncle was. So I can terminate this marriage."

"Yes."

"And nothing will change."

"Apart from you being a divorced man, nothing. However…"

Mason grimaced. "However what, Howard?"

The lawyer hesitated. He knew that his client, from the grave, was controlling the lives of two people, one of whom remained completely in the dark, and he was uncomfortable with it. Still, it was his job to continue, and continue he did.

"The codicil to your uncle's will also stipulates that if you and Emma stay together, if you have a family, you will inherit the remainder of his estate."

"If we have a family," Mason repeated.

"Yes."

"I see." He was silent for a good long while before saying slowly, "It was my understanding, Howard, that the remainder of his estate was being held in trust for unnamed charities of his choice."

The lawyer cleared his throat. "Yes. Well."

"Howard." Mason's voice was even and low, and the lawyer felt his anger from across the room. "What other tricks does my uncle have up his six-feet-under sleeve?"

Shaking his head quickly, he responded, "That's all that I know of, Mason. And I'm aware that this is unconventional…."

But Mason had already made up his mind. "I don't want the money, Howard. I don't want his estate. Whether Emma and I stay together or split up, whether we have children or not – none of that can be dictated by a dead man. Not even my uncle. What happens to the estate if there is no family?"

"It goes into the trust described in his original will."

"It should do that, then. Now. Or as soon as legally possible. Can you draw up papers in that regard?"

"I can, Mason. Are you sure that's what you want?"

"Quite sure. While I wished to retain his voting rights for my own company's sake, I have no wish to inherit his estate."

"Very well. About the other matter…"

Mason shook his head slowly. "Let's keep it between us for now. I'm not yet sure how this will all play out. And I need time to think about it, and probably time to talk to Emma."

The lawyer looked surprised. "Talk to Emma? But…"

"She's my wife, Howard. This affects her."

The older man nodded, unable to completely hide his shock at Mason's statement. He knew this man well, and was accustomed to him taking charge in all situations. Talking to his wife? A wife he'd met and married in a matter of days as a business decision? This was unheard of. Looking more closely at Mason, he sighed. "Take all the time you need, Mason. And just let me know what you decide. I'll start drawing up the papers for the rest of the estate."

Standing, Mason reached out his hand to shake Howard's hand. "Thanks for taking the time, Howard. Give my best to your wife."

Howard watched him go. It was the first time Mason had ever mentioned or sent greetings to the lawyer's wife. Maybe this marriage had really changed him.

Two weeks later, Mason was back from his business trip, and ready to talk to Emma. He had had a lot of time to think about his meeting with his uncle's lawyer, and decided to fill Emma in on the details. One thing was certain in his own mind - divorce was not an option. He told himself that it was for social reasons - it would reflect badly on both of them if they were to split only one year after a hasty marriage - it would call to question his ability to make decisions, and make them well. But deep down, he knew it was more than that. He needed more time with her. The thought of his house without Chaos, without Max, without Malcolm and Michelle, but most of all, without Emma, made his heart hurt. No, he wasn't ready to call this marriage over yet.

Back in his home, after letting Chaos out to scour the yard for anything edible that he hadn't managed to find on his previous 600 trips out there, he picked up Max and scritched him before calling his wife at work. Emma's secretary put him right through.

"Mason, you're home! How was your trip?"

"It was fine, but I'm glad to be back. Listen, are you free for dinner tonight? I have a few things I'd like to discuss with you."

Emma paused, hearing something new and slightly strained in his voice. "Sure. I'll be home by 6:00. Do you want me to cook?"

"No. I've made a reservation for 7:00 at The Attic. Will that suit you?"

"Of course." She hesitated before asking, "Mason, is there anything I need to be worried about?"

"No," he said shortly. "I'll meet you at the restaurant." And he was gone.

Emma worried a bit about his call, but had a full afternoon of work to take her mind off him. By the time 6:30 rolled around, she was rushing to finish up some last minute details and to make it to the restaurant on time to meet him. She was a few minutes late when she walked in the front door, where Mason was waiting patiently for her.

"I'm so sorry I'm late," she said as she walked up to him.

He leaned down and kissed her on the cheek. *OK, that was new*, she thought. *But nice.*

"Are you OK, Mason?" she asked right away. "You sounded rushed on the phone. Or stressed. Or something."

"I'm fine." His hand was on the small of her back as the hostess led them to their reserved table. "It's just been a busy day. You look nice," he added as he pulled out her chair for her.

"Thanks."

As Emma settled herself at the table and took a sip from her water glass, Mason glanced at the menus in front of them. "Wine?" he asked.

She looked over at him. "I'm not sure. Do I need a clear head?"

He signaled the waiter. "I'll order a bottle. You can have as much or as little as you choose."

After ordering a bottle of Shiraz, Mason turned to Emma and said, "I want to talk to you about my uncle's will."

NOT what Emma had expected, though she really had no idea what she *had* expected. "His will."

"Yes."

"OK. This is the same uncle that insisted on your marriage, just to be clear."

"Yes."

Emma nodded. "OK. Go on."

"His lawyer called me before I left on this business trip, so I went to see him about two weeks ago, right before I left. Apparently my uncle left a codicil to the will, to be read before my 41st birthday."

Emma leaned back in her seat, eyeing Mason carefully. "Good heavens. Please don't tell me that you now need to have a passel of kids in order to inherit."

"Not exactly," Mason stated evasively.

Her eyes narrowed. "What does 'not exactly' mean?"

They were interrupted by the waiter, arriving with the bottle that Mason had ordered, and Emma had to wait through the ceremonial uncorking, tasting, and pouring of the wine before Mason could answer.

"It means that he essentially gave me choices," Mason stated as the waiter left the table.

"Well isn't that nice of him, given that he's, um, how do I say this nicely...? dead."

Mason laughed. "He's more involved in my life now than he was when he was alive," he admitted.

Emma took a sip of her wine and asked quietly, bracing herself for more craziness, "OK, what are the choices?"

"We can stay married, as originally dictated by the will. Nothing changes."

"OK."

"We can divorce, go our separate ways, and I retain the voting stock."

She raised her eyebrows.

"Or we can stay married, have a family, and I inherit, fully, my uncle's estate. Worth several million dollars. Or more."

Emma blinked.

Mason looked over at her intently. "Emma, I told my uncle's lawyer that I did not wish to inherit the estate. His original will had it going into a charitable trust, which would be managed by a board. I stated that I wished for that to occur as had been originally planned."

Emma set her glass down and looked across the table at Mason. She wasn't sure how to take this statement. On the one hand, she was relieved that he wasn't trying to romance her into something that would provide him with financial gain. But on the other... was he essentially saying that he saw no future with her? Despite the fact that she frequently counted down the days till the end of their contract, she knew that a part of her hoped that there might be some spark of... something... between them.

Mason was looking back at her with a serious expression on his face - one that she hadn't seen before. Oh, she'd seen him serious to be sure, but this was different. There was an intensity here that was unusual.

She leaned forward on the table, studying Mason carefully. Something was happening here that made no sense, and she wasn't even sure what questions to ask. She started carefully.

Quietly, she asked, "Is there more?"

"I need to decide between my first two choices," he stated, taking a sip of wine and watching her as he did so.

"Stay married or divorce me."

"Yes."

"And I have no say?"

Mason shrugged, his eyes shuttered. "Not really, no. The contract stands, unless I choose to void it."

She shook her head, trying to figure out what all of this meant. "I know what the contract stipulates, Mason. Believe me, I practically memorized that thing. But that's not really what I meant. What I meant was, this involves me. It involves my life. Why are you choosing not to discuss it with me?"

"I chose to tell you about this, Emma. I could have kept you completely in the dark. I may have even been able to talk you into staying married to me, having children with me," he added, his eyes boring into hers, acknowledging their mutual attraction.

Emma flushed and reached for her water glass.

"I removed that piece of the equation completely by instructing my uncle's lawyer to revert to the original will. My uncle removed the other financial piece from the equation - the voting rights are mine, regardless."

"So you have no financial incentive to stay married to me," Emma said quietly, her eyes searching his for whatever he was trying to tell her.

He seemed to hesitate for just a moment before leaning forward over the table. Keeping his voice low, he firmly stated, "I may not have a financial incentive, but I do have a social incentive. It will not reflect well on either of us for us to marry and then divorce a year later. And for me, it will be particularly difficult since you seem to have charmed every one of my business acquaintances, my sister, and my mother. So while the reasons for the initial marriage have been voided, I see no reason to, at this time, void the marriage itself."

Emma was trying hard to control her temper, but it was getting harder. Nowhere in this equation was there talk of feelings, or contentment, or even physical attraction. It was all about his business, his social world, his reputation. Nothing about her, her family, her needs, her future. Damn him, she thought. She took a long drink of water, then leaned back in her chair, looking around the room. He had brought her here tonight so that she wouldn't yell, wouldn't make a scene. He had brought her here so he could have more control over when she left, and how. He had brought her here to tell her that he had already determined their future, without her input. And it bothered her.

"So that's it. No further discussion," she said.

He looked at her, no emotion readable on his face. "As I said, I did not need to even tell you about this."

"No. You didn't. But you chose to. Why?"

"It was important to me that you heard it from me. I didn't want you to feel like I was deceiving you if you were to find out later that the conditions of the will had been met after one year. I was concerned that if you found out about this through some other means, it would upset you."

"And you don't think this is upsetting?" she asked, incredulously.

He looked at her as if she'd grown wings. "I honestly don't see why, Emma. Nothing has changed for you."

No, she thought. Nothing had changed. She was still trapped in a marriage with a man who thought very little of her - certainly not enough to consider her feelings. She was still tied to him for two more years, living a lie that nobody but her grandmother and her sister was aware of. She had to live for two more years under his roof, two more years of getting to know the man under the icy exterior, but having him throw up barricades and firewalls whenever she got too close. So no, nothing had changed. Except the knowledge that this would remain a three year deal for him. No more, no less. A business transaction. A way to keep his own social world intact. And for reasons that Emma couldn't explain, his lack of consideration of her own feelings hurt her to the core.

Quietly pushing back her chair, she gently laid her napkin on the table. "I need to go, Mason. And if you don't want the scene you were trying to prevent by bringing me here, you need to let me."

He started to stand, but Emma shook her head quickly. "I mean it. I'm on the edge here, and you do not want to push me over it. I'll get a cab. Thank you for the wine."

"Emma, I don't understand why you're upset," he said, and for a moment, Emma felt sorry for him. Because he really *didn't* get it. She sighed, and reached out briefly to gently lay her hand on his.

Then, clutching her purse, Emma walked quickly to where she had checked her coat not long before, and then left the restaurant, breathing hard as she did so. Pulling the coat on as she walked, she headed to the corner and hailed a cab. She'd go home, she decided. She'd pick up Chaos, check on Max, and then go out for a while. She needed time to think.

Mason watched her go. Once again, she had reacted in a way that he didn't expect. True, he'd brought her to the restaurant so that they would discuss this quietly, he could explain his thinking, and they could have a nice meal before they went home that evening. He didn't understand her response. He thought that she'd be relieved that he'd taken the long-term out of the picture. It wasn't that he didn't think about that sometimes, but that he didn't want money to ever truly be a deciding factor in his personal life. Not now that his personal life included Emma.

But now, Mason realized that she was truly upset, though he had no idea why. Because she wanted out of the marriage? Maybe, he mused, but he wasn't about to let that happen. Not yet. And the contract that they had together was three years, nothing contingent upon the stocks being in his hands.

Raising his hand discreetly for the bill, Mason wondered if he'd done the right thing by telling her about the codicil. He didn't like the idea of keeping something so big from her, and wondered about it. He'd never felt the need to share anything like this with anyone before, so why did he need to tell Emma about this? Had that been a mistake?

Emma was still reeling with shock. There was no longer any reason for them to be married. The original rationale for the union was no longer in place, and there was absolutely no reason for them to stay together. She understood that it might look bad for Mason to suddenly divorce his wife after one year, but surely they could work out some sort of compromise - perhaps they could start to live apart again. But what irritated her, frustrated her, and made her want to pull her hair out was that he didn't even consult her. She thought they'd been close enough to a friendship for him to at least do that. He could have asked her if she were happy, and asked what she wanted. He could have agreed to a shorter time period if she expressed unhappiness. But he didn't even ask. And the fact that he just told her what he was planning, without even being willing to discuss it, told her a lot about his lack of feelings and respect for her.

She tried to picture what she might have wanted Mason to say. 'Thanks very much, but I no longer need you so goodbye?'

Or better yet, 'want to stay married to me and have kids so I can collect a few more million that I don't need?' No, both those choices were unlikely. Circling around again to his decision, she asked herself if divorce was what she wanted. If she were honest with herself, she'd say no. So what *did* she really want?

The answer came to her as she watched Chaos sniff around the bushes by the fence. She wanted Mason. Not as a pretend husband. Not as a friend. Not as a colleague. Not even just as a lover. She wanted him. For real. Because, God help her, she loved him. *Damn him*, she thought. She loved him, even though he was the coldest man she'd ever met. Even though he didn't give a damn about her or her feelings. Even though he never ever could love her in return. Even though he would divorce her in two more years without a second thought. She loved him. And that was going to be a problem. Because two more years of this would not only spoil her forever for all other men, it would kill her soul.

FIFTEEN

Emma and Mason spent the next two weeks steeped in politeness. Emma avoided Mason whenever he was in the house, and Mason took some care to be away from home as much as he could, knowing instinctively that Emma needed some space. He didn't intend for this relationship to go on like this for much longer, however. This new dynamic was stressful for all of them, and it was not what Mason wished to come home to each night. No, he needed the carefree and happy life they had been building before the codicil to the will had been revealed.

Surprising himself, he called his sister one evening and asked her to join him for dinner. Amanda and Emma got along well, but Mason knew that Amanda understood his own thinking and his own reasons for behaving as he did. So he'd just lay all of this out for her, he thought. Amanda might be able to give him some good advice.

Emma was hunched over her desk, reading the latest psychological assessment of one of the children that she represented when she heard a light knock on her door. Looking up, she was pleased to see her sister-in-law standing in the doorway, both hands wrapped tightly around the straps of her purse.

She jumped up and circled around her desk, smiling warmly. "Amanda! What a wonderful surprise! Come in! How's Greg?"

But Amanda didn't look happy to be there. In fact, she looked incredibly stressed. Emma looked at her in concern. "Amanda?"

Amanda sighed. "Look. Emma. You're my friend. But my brother just told me about the will, and about what he said to you, and I needed to come over and talk to you. Emma..."

"Amanda," Emma interrupted gently. "It's OK. Come in, please. You look exhausted."

"I haven't slept much lately, Emma. Look, if Mason were married to your sister, to Jen, I would mind my own business and look the other way and to hell with it all. But he's married to you, and I happen to think of you as one of my very best friends, not just my brother's wife."

Emma took a deep breath. "Have a seat, Amanda," she said as she led her friend to the couch. "Let me tell my secretary to clear out the next hour or so, and we'll close my door and talk. Is that OK, or do you want to go someplace else?"

"No. Here. It should be here."

Emma took a long look at Amanda, and then nodded. "OK. Be back in a sec."

After telling Rhoda that a family emergency seemed to be brewing, and to do what she could to reschedule her afternoon, she walked back into her office and closed the door behind her. Moving over onto the couch next to Amanda, she sat down, curling one leg up underneath her and leaning her other arm on the back of the couch.

"OK, Amanda. We have all the time in the world."

Amanda didn't seem to know where to begin, now that she was here.

"I know about my uncle's will. And the codicil," she added, turning toward Emma and looking directly into her eyes.

Emma took that in, then nodded. "OK."

"How much did Mason tell you?" she continued.

"That the codicil gives him permission to divorce me without losing his voting rights. And that there is a promise of significantly more money down the road if he stays with me and we have children."

Amanda nodded. "That's it in a nutshell. Look, Emma. I think Mason is falling in love with you. All of his life, he's been closed off from all emotion. I was the same for a long time, until I stopped caring what my father thought of me and started going my own way. Mason has stayed in the same business as our father and uncle – over time, he got harder and harder. More like my father. I think my uncle saw that, and that's why he wrote his will the way he did. He didn't see it as manipulative so much as caring.'

Emma opened her mouth to speak, but she had no words. She shook her head and stayed silent.

"If he chooses to divorce you out of some misguided sense of duty to you, he will be giving up on the best thing that ever happened to him, and doing it because he feels guilty for pulling you into this in the first place. And if he were to stay with you, without telling you about the will, that would be a secret that he'd have to carry, and I think he knew that it would drive a wedge between you. Particularly if you did end up staying together and having a family – if the conditions of the will ever got out, you'd always wonder if it was because he loved you, or because he wanted the money. So I think that's why he took that off the table right away."

Emma sighed. It was nice to talk about this with someone, she realized. Someone who really understood the situation that she and Mason found themselves in.

"Amanda, who else knows about our marriage? About the original will?"

"Just me, Mason, Mason's lawyer, and my uncle's lawyer."

"Not your mother?"

"Good heavens no."

"I didn't think *you* knew, to be honest."

"Neither did Mason. But Uncle Frank had talked to me about it before he wrote the will. I discouraged him from tying any of his fortune to Mason's marital situation, but the old man never listened to me."

"He didn't care if you married?" Emma asked.

"He knew that no amount of money would force me to marry anyone I didn't love," Amanda laughed. "And since I wasn't in the business, he had nothing to hold over me."

"Wow."

"Yeah."

"So that's why you weren't taken aback by our having separate bedrooms," Emma said, recalling the night Amanda had come over to see Max.

"I was hoping that you might have gotten together, but I wasn't completely surprised, no. Emma, Mason is who he is. He's not an easy man to live with or an easy man to love. But he has a heart of gold, and I have never seen him so happy or so engaged in life since you met. I'll admit that when I first met you, I was skeptical. I knew about the will, but I couldn't figure out how someone as nice as you would agree to marry Mason. You didn't fit the picture of someone who was in it for the money. Mason told me later about Jen, and about pushing you to honor the contract he'd signed with her, and I let him have it."

Emma leaned back on the couch, putting her feet up on the coffee table. Turning her head to face her sister-in-law, she asked, "So now what?"

"Have you talked to him?"

"I tried. He just said that we were staying together, and that was that. End of discussion. Here's the thing, Amanda. The will might be letting Mason out of his end of the bargain, but it doesn't let me out of anything, unless Mason wants to let me out. The contract between us states three years. It doesn't have any contingencies related to the will."

"Oh."

"I'm screwed no matter what, Amanda," she said softly. "I'm falling for your brother, and that's the God's honest truth. But he doesn't feel the same way. If he did, he'd consider how I felt, rather than just pushing me into something just because he can."

"Have you considered the fact that he may not want to let you go?"

Emma laughed then, actually seeing humor in the situation for the first time. "No, Amanda, I haven't considered that. Believe me, your brother is not interested in a relationship with me."

But Amanda just looked at her questioningly. "What would Mason be able to do to convince you that he really cared for you?"

Emma thought about it for a moment. "I think I'd know. If he let down his guard. If he showed me real honest emotion and real truth, I think I'd be able to believe that. Amanda, you know what I'm talking about. You have it with Greg. I can see it when you look at him, and when he looks at you. And you know that Mason and I don't have that."

"I've seen him look at you," Amanda pointed out.

Emma smiled sadly. "With curiosity, I think. He doesn't know what to make of me."

"It's more."

"Not yet. Amanda, I wish it were. But I need to be realistic."

Amanda reached over and gave Emma a hug. "My brother is a moron. But I don't think he's cold-hearted. I just think he's buried his heart behind a wall. And I like to think that you're breaking that down."

Emma laughed without humor. "Sure. Just call me sledgehammer." She glanced at her watch. "Do you have plans this afternoon, or do you want to go get margaritas with me?"

"Seriously?"

"Yup."

"I'm in," she said. "Let me just call my office and tell them that I'm not coming back. Oh, and I probably should call Greg to come get us later so we're not driving. Leave your car here. We'll take a cab to the best Mexican place I know."

Three margaritas, two baskets of tortilla chips and a bowl of salsa later, Emma was feeling slightly more tipsy than she could remember being in a while. She was grateful that Amanda had insisted that she leave her car at work, since driving home was so clearly not an option. At least, not for a few hours and after a few cups of coffee. Amanda was as much of a lightweight as Emma was, so the two were equally sloshed as they paid the bill and went out to the front of the restaurant to wait for Greg. He had texted moments earlier to let them know that he was close by.

"This was exactly what I needed tonight," Emma said to Amanda, hugging her shoulder as the stood outside in the fresh air. "Exactly. Thank you."

"It was what I needed too. Oh, there's Greg!" Amanda pointed out, taking hold of Emma's elbow as the two walked carefully over to the curb.

He leaned over and opened the door for them. "Holy cow. You two weren't kidding about being blotto tonight. Geez, how much did you drink?"

Amanda opened up the back door and helped Emma in before climbing in next to Greg. "Believe it or not, only three margaritas each."

"Three?"

"Over about three hours. We're cheap dates," Emma chimed in from the back seat.

"Apparently so. I think you two are going to need a keeper next time you decide to go out for drinks. Emma, you're headed home, I hope?"

"I am," she admitted. "There's no way I'm working tonight, and there's no way I'm driving tonight, so home it is."

Fifteen minutes later, Greg was pulling up in front of Mason's home, and Emma stepped out, leaning down to talk with Greg and Amanda through the window.

"Thanks for the ride. And Amanda, thank you for talking to me today. You're a good friend."

"Right back at you," Amanda said, reaching out and squeezing her hand. "Call me tomorrow and let me know you're all right?"

"I will. Goodnight," she said softly, watching as they drove away. Turning, she took a deep breath and headed toward the door. The lights were on, so Mason was home. This ought to be interesting, she thought.

"Hi honey, I'm home," she called sarcastically as she walked in the door. "Not that you give a crap, of course."

Mason appeared in the doorway of the living room and looked over at her. He walked over toward her, peering at her closely. "You're drunk," he finally said accusingly.

Emma protested. "Not entirely. I think I was drunk about an hour ago. Now I'm just pleasantly tanked up."

Mason's eyes narrowed. "Who brought you home?"

"Some guy I met at the bar."

Emma watched in fascination as his hands made fists. "Emma," he grated.

"Oh relax," she said with a giggle. "Greg drove me home. I went out for drinks with Amanda, and she was smart enough to arrange for transportation beforehand."

"Amanda?" he asked incredulously.

"Your sister?"

"I know who Amanda is. Why did you go out with her?"

"Because I like her. I need more of a reason than that?"

"What did you talk about?"

"Girl stuff."

"Like what?"

"Lipstick, dress colors, the boy sitting behind me in homeroom. You know. Girl stuff."

"Emma," he said again.

She sighed and looked up at him wearily. "You're uptight tonight."

"You're a bit less than uptight," he returned.

"True. But sobering up rapidly. I'm going to go walk Chaos and then go to bed. Is he out back?"

"Yes. But you can't walk him in your condition."

"I have no condition. And I want to go for a walk. So I'm going."

"Then I'm going with you."

"Suit yourself."

They walked along silently, Chaos sniffing everything worth sniffing along the road. Mason walked with his hands in his pockets, waiting for Emma to chat with him as she normally did. But Emma, despite still being a little tipsy, wasn't feeling especially chatty. She was in no mood to just pretend that nothing was wrong. So she watched Chaos, tugged him away from anything that he showed interest in eating, and could find no reason to speak to the man next to her.

"Emma!"

"Mal, what's up?" Emma greeted Malcolm happily as he ran toward them.

"I saw you and Chaos, and... oh, hello Mr. Parker."

"Hi Malcolm," Mason returned with a smile.

"Do you want to join us?" Emma asked. "You can even hold Chaos."

"Has he pooped yet?" the boy asked suspiciously.

Emma looked innocently down at the young boy. "I'm sure he must have before we started walking."

Malcolm shook his head vehemently. "Nice try, Emma. But heck no. I know your rules. You keep the dog."

"What rules?" Mason interjected, a puzzled look on his face.

"Whoever has the leash when the dog poops has to clean up," Malcolm explained.

Emma grinned. "You're too smart for me, Mal. But you need to get used to all of these smells and things if you're gonna be a vet someday."

"Yeah. Again, nice try. I'll take him after he does his business. Where are you going?"

"Just walking around. What are you doing up so late?"

"My parents are having a party. It's kind of noisy, so I sneaked out the back when I saw you."

Emma stopped and looked down at the boy, appalled. "Mal, you can't do that. Your parents might look for you, and they'll be freaked out if you're not in your room."

The boy looked up at her with knowing eyes. "They won't look for me, Em."

"Oh for heaven's...." Emma stopped at the look on the boy's face. Sighing, she reached out and hugged his shoulders. "OK. Come on along. We're not going to be out for long, though. Promise you'll sneak right back in and up to your room?"

"Emma..." Mason started to say, but Emma shot him a warning glance.

"I promise," Malcolm said.

"OK. But I still think you should learn to tolerate stinky stuff."

Malcolm rolled his eyes. "You need a new strategy, Em. That's not gonna work. Ever."

She laughed. "Hey, Mason's sister is dating a vet. You wanna come over some time and meet him and talk to him?"

Malcolm looked up at her, and then over at Mason, a look of excitement in his eyes. "Seriously?"

"Yup."

"When?"

"I'll ask. You need to come over anyhow. Max misses you."

"My parents are headed to Europe on Friday night. Can I come over this weekend?"

"You bet. I've got a few errands to run on Saturday morning, but come over in the afternoon. And I'll see if Amanda and Greg can come over too. Sound good?"

"Ahem," Mason cleared his throat, wondering if Emma would remember that a) he was standing there, and b) it was his house.

"Oops," Emma said, winking down at Malcolm. "Mason, do you have plans this weekend? Would you like to join us?"

Malcolm looked a bit worried by Mason's reaction. "Are you sure it's OK, Em?"

"Of course it's OK. Unless Mason already made plans that he didn't tell me about. Did you?" she asked him.

He sighed. Outnumbered and outmaneuvered. "No."

"Then let me check with Amanda and Greg. But you come over anyway. And bring Michelle if she wants to come."

"She won't. I think she likes having a break from me." At a glance from Emma, Malcolm sighed. "But I'll ask her anyway."

"Good man."

As they circled back toward Malcolm's home, Mason wondered why he felt like the odd man out. He listened to the easy rapport that Emma and Malcolm shared, and felt... like a third wheel. They loved each other, that was clear. They made plans easily, they teased each other, they laughed without restraint. And when they got back to Malcolm's driveway, Emma gave him a quick hug, then watched as the boy ran up the road and headed for the back door of the brightly lit house. Emma waited until she saw a small figure wave from a window on the second floor, and then turned toward Mason's home. Her conversation had ceased. Her laughter had faded. And that's when it hit Mason. He was jealous. Jealous of a small boy. What in the world? But Emma was different with him, and it bothered him. As they walked quietly up the driveway leading to his house, he realized that he needed to talk to Emma. He needed to see her smile at him again.

Emma circled around back and let Chaos off his leash to explore the backyard for a bit longer in his never-ending search for squirrels. After closing the gate behind him, she turned to head back to the house, and was surprised to find Mason still standing beside her. She had expected that he would go inside as soon as they approached his house.

"Emma," he said softly, stepping toward her and reaching out gently to touch her shoulder.

But Emma pulled away, deftly circling around him to head back toward the house. She stopped when she felt his strong fingers encircle her arm, preventing her from going any further. Turning, she looked up at him, her eyes narrowed slightly in suspicion and confusion.

"It's getting late, Mason," she said quietly, her gaze pointedly falling on where his fingers gripped her arm.

"Why are you avoiding me, Emma?"

"I'm not avoiding you."

"Emma."

"OK, I am. But you know why." She looked up at him then and sighed. "I'm tired, Mason. I'd like to go inside."

With his free hand, Mason reached up and gently brushed the hair back from her face.

She reached up and swatted him away.

"Stop it," she snapped. "Just stop it."

He looked surprised. "Emma, what's the matter? Why are you being so..."

"So what?" she challenged.

"Short-tempered."

She let out a snort of laughter, moving away from him, though her arm was still caught in his grip.

"Emma."

"*What?*"

"What's wrong?"

"Why do you even need to ask that?" she countered.

"I can't read minds," he pointed out.

She shook her head, taking a deep breath as she did. "You don't need to read my mind. I told you the other night why I'm upset. It doesn't take a mind reader to know that I'm still dealing with all of that."

His hand fell to his side.

"You're upset because I want to stay married to you?" he asked.

"Oh for heaven's sake," Emma sputtered, turning toward the house.

"Then why?"

His words stopped her. She turned back around, her temper flaring, and stepped up to him until they were nearly touching. Lifting her face to his, she fought to keep her anger from causing her voice to tremor. "I'm upset because you never talked to me about it. You made your own mind up without even thinking about me. You only thought about you, and about what you wanted. Did you ever once stop to think about me? About what I wanted? No," she said, putting up her hands in front of her. "Never mind. Don't answer that. It would hurt too much. I'm going inside, Mason. Let me be."

Spinning, she walked away from him. Once in the house, she made her way to her bedroom, letting Chaos in through the sliding glass doors, and getting him settled in his crate for the night. She was just closing the door of the crate when she heard her own bedroom door open. Spinning around, she saw Mason standing in the doorway.

"What the...? Mason, what the hell are you doing? You can't just barge in here like this..."

He stopped, leaning in the doorjamb, and shrugged his shoulders. "It's my house."

"That does not give you the right to just open my door and walk in on me. I could have been getting undressed."

As soon as she said that, she realized it wasn't the right thing to voice. Mason's eyes grew darker, and he just stared intently at her.

"What do you want, Mason?" she asked, her teeth clenched.

"You."

"Excuse me?"

He pushed himself away from the frame and stepped inside her room.

"We weren't done, Emma."

"Yes. We were. I have nothing else to say to you."

"I have a few more things to say to you, and then I'll leave you alone."

She stood in the middle of room, her eyes flashing, her hands on her hips.

"Go ahead then."

"I did think about you, Emma. I turned down my uncle's estate so that you never needed to worry about that. I offered to stay married to you, so it wouldn't hurt your reputation for us to divorce so soon after getting married."

"Offered?" Emma picked up on his wording, and repeated the offending statement incredulously. "You 'offered' nothing. You simply told me what you had decided."

He advanced toward her, stopping a few feet away from her.

"I decided based on what was best for you."

Her eyes narrowed. "And how would you know what's best for me?"

He crossed his arms in front of him and looked down at Emma, the coolness in his expression fueling her frustration.

"Tell me what you would want, Emma. How exactly would you like me to handle this?"

"By *talking* to me."

"I'm talking to you now," he pointed out mildly.

She sighed. He was right.

"Fine," she said at last, sinking into a chair in the corner of her room. She watched as he simply leaned against a wall, his arms still crossed, looking down at her.

"Don't glower," she said crossly.

A small twinge of a smile curled up the corner of his lip.

"Do you want a divorce, Emma?" His voice was low and his tone was mild, but Emma saw the storm in his eyes.

"Of course I do," she responded. "Yes. That's been what this marriage was headed for since the day we married. It's almost contractually obligated," she added sarcastically.

But Mason's response was gentle. "Do you want a divorce right away?"

Emma allowed herself to look over at the man, saw the closed expression on his face and wondered, for the first time, if the coldness was a protective mechanism. Her heart softened slightly.

"I don't know," she answered quietly. "I understand your need to protect your reputation, Mason."

"Your reputation too," he reminded her.

"Mine is mine to worry about." She hesitated. "What if we were to start spending more time apart? Maybe I could stay at my house for a few nights a week? And spend the weekends here?"

Mason was surprised at the wave of anger that rolled over him, but didn't take the time to analyze it.

"No."

"What do you mean 'no'?" Emma asked, fairly shocked both at his sudden response and the vehemence behind it.

"No. You live with me."

"Then what's the point of talking to me about this if you won't compromise?" Her eyes sought his. Hers were troubled and his were stubborn.

"You're my wife, Emma. As long as we are married, you live with me."

"And how long will that be?"

"That's the question, isn't it?" he asked mildly.

"How long, Mason?"

When there was no answer from Mason, Emma looked back down at her fingers, clasped tightly in her lap. When she looked up again, her eyes met his, and his gaze bored into her.

"Until I'm ready to let you go," he finally said, his expression blank, his voice cold.

She shook her head. "I don't understand," she said at last.

Mason pushed away from the wall.

"The contract is for three years, Emma."

She looked at him with doubt. "But Mason, surely, now that you know that the reason for the marriage is void..."

"Three years."

"Mason..."

With a sense of disbelief, Emma watched as Mason moved toward her, stopped in front of her, leaned down and placed his hands on the arms of her chair, trapping her in place.

"Why are you doing this?" she asked, close to tears.

"Because you're my wife, Emma. And I'm simply not interested in letting you go."

He realized when he said it that it was true. Grasping Emma's arms, he slowly lifted her from the chair and into his arms.

She had let him, but as soon as he pulled her to him, she came back to her senses and started to push at his chest. "Mason, what are you doing? This isn't part of the deal..."

"No. No, it's not," he agreed, his voice taut with tension.

"Mason," she tried again to push away, but he was strong. With his arms wrapped around her, she had no hope of moving away until he let her go. And he seemed to show no signs that he intended to do that. Instead, he just tugged her closer and said firmly, "Enough, Emma."

"Let go of me," she said through clenched teeth.

"No."

"Mason, this isn't fair."

"I'm done with fair, Emma. Particularly where you're concerned."

Lowering his mouth, he kissed her. It was not a loving, kind-hearted kiss, this one. It was a kiss of hard passion. A kiss of frustration. A kiss of ownership. But it still touched something in Emma. She remembered why she had told this man to stay away from her. Because when she was in his arms, there was no way she could resist him. But she needed to, she reminded herself, even as she kissed him back.

Behind them, Chaos whined in his crate, wanting to be out with his two favorite people. The noise gave Emma the distraction she needed to pull away from Mason. Breathing deeply, she managed to walk over to Chaos' crate and open the door. The happy dog bounded out, his tail wagging at high speed, moving from Mason to Emma and back again.

But Mason and Emma just stared at each other. Mason's cold and slightly predatory look was back, and Emma was sure that she just looked hunted. "What now?" she asked quietly, annoyed that her voice shook noticeably.

He stepped forward, stopping only when he saw the look of trepidation on her face.

"You don't need to be afraid of me, Emma," he said with a touch of anger in his voice.

But she nodded vigorously. "I do. I really do."

At this, his voice gentled. "I won't hurt you, sweetheart."

To herself, Emma thought, *you will. You won't mean to, but you will. If I let you.*

As Mason stood in her bedroom, his eyes fixed on hers, Emma's mind drifted back to something Jen had said earlier that month, about how Mason could have found another way to get his uncle's stock. About how he could have found someone else when Jen changed her mind.

Sinking onto her bed, she thought back to when she had first met Mason. His first reaction hadn't been to look at finding someone else to take Jen's place, or even to find Jen and bring her back - it had been to push her into taking her sister's place. Her. Emma. She had offered to find someone else. He had time before his 40th birthday to look around, and to offer the same deal to someone else. Even Jen had suspected that Mason could have found a way to get the stock, without it completely changing his life.

But Mason had changed his life. Completely. He had a wife, a dog, a kitten. He wasn't dating anyone, and he wasn't sleeping with anyone, even her. Well, except for that one time, of course. And he had done all of this to fulfill the terms of his uncle's will. But Emma still couldn't figure out why. Why her?

She felt Mason sit down next to her. Felt it as he reached out and gently brushed her hair back from her face. Felt it as he settled his arm around her shoulder.

"Why?" The word slipped out, and Emma didn't recognize her own voice. It was filled with haunted anguish, and she flinched even as she said it.

He turned her to face him, his hand caressing her cheek and her chin, his thumb lightly tracing the outline of her lower lip.

"Why what, Emma?" he asked gently.

"Why did you marry me?"

He hesitated, his hand stilling for a moment, falling to rest on her shoulder.

"Why are you asking me this?"

She looked up at him with a troubled expression that caught at Mason's heart. "Because I don't think it was for the stock, at least not completely," she continued. "You have other people in your life that you could have called on to help you with this. You could have challenged your uncle's will. You could have done any number of things. But there was no reason to push me into fulfilling Jen's contract, and no real reason to stay together now. Unless there was some other contingency that you haven't told me about. So why? Tell me, Mason," she begged. "If I am going to make it through two more years of an empty marriage, at least tell me why."

She felt his flinch before his hands dropped and he stood up.

"Mason?"

"You're right, Emma. It's late."

She watched in disbelief as he left the room. True, he bent down to pat Chaos on the head as he left, and he did look back at her once with something resembling tenderness on his face, but he still left. And Emma just sat there, trying very hard not to cry.

🐾 SIXTEEN

Back in his own room, Mason paced. He needed to figure out what he was doing with Emma, and what he wanted from her. Because she was right about one thing - the marriage had not been about stock, or his uncle's will, or anything but the fact that he'd seen her and immediately made up his mind to have her. And in Mason's world, he got what he wanted. So he'd coerced her into the marriage, kept her by his side, and had even slept with her, but he'd done it all on his terms. And for the first time, his conscience was beginning to bother him. Because Emma wasn't Jen.

His marriage to Jen would have been one of convenience only. They might have slept together, or he might have found satisfaction outside of the marriage, knowing that she was doing the same. But he'd promised Emma from the start that he wouldn't sleep around, and he was holding to that. Not just because he wanted to be a man of his word, but he truly, honestly, absolutely did not want to sleep with anyone else. He wanted Emma. His wife.

He had her once, he thought ruefully. He'd seduced her, taken her to bed, and then he had fled from her room before the night was half over. He had taken her trust in him and trampled it into the ground. And she had seemingly forgiven him for it. He'd spent the last year with her, getting to know her, laughing with her, learning to know her as he knew no one else. And he had been a better man because of it.

She had called their marriage empty, and while the words had hurt, he understood why she had chosen that term. Because while they lived together, dined together, and entertained together, theirs was a marriage of words, not love. A marriage of convenience, not choice. And for the first time in his life, Mason wanted more.

Emma sighed, standing up from the bed and wiping her tear-stained eyes. It had been an incredibly long day, and she was worn out. From her long conversation with Amanda, to the confrontation with Mason, there hadn't been a moment today where she had felt relaxed and... normal. Even her banter with Malcolm felt more tense than usual, knowing that he'd sneaked out the back door of his house to come and see her.

She needed sleep, but she was sure sleep wouldn't come. Not yet. So maybe a cup of tea first. And hydrating was a good idea after three margaritas earlier in the day anyway. She didn't want to wake up hung-over tomorrow - the last thing she wanted was to have a headache AND to have to deal with Mason.

Still in her work clothes, she changed into a pair of comfortable pajamas - long dark blue waffle fabric on the bottom stretching to her ankles, and a navy blue long-sleeved t-shirt on top. She washed her face with cold water to combat the puffiness around her eyes, then checked the mirror quickly to be sure she looked decent in case anyone glanced in one of their kitchen windows. Stepping quietly into the hallway, she was careful to close the door behind her so Chaos didn't follow her down and awaken Mason. No, scratch that, she thought as she eased out into the hallway. Mason was still awake - a light shone brightly through the crack under his door. Opening her door again, she left it ajar so Chaos could follow if he chose to. Max was nowhere in sight - perhaps he was in with Mason.

In the kitchen, she turned on a soft light over the stove, and proceeded to make herself a cup of tea. Chaos appeared next to her, and just leaned against her, as if somehow knowing that she was upset. With the water heating on the cooktop and a bag of tea in a teacup ready to be steeped, she knelt down to rub her dog's ears.

"It's going to be ok, Chaos. Really. We'll figure this out."

Chaos looked up at her with a look on his face, as if to say, *of course we will.*

Standing up, she poured hot water into her cup and allowed the teabag to sit for a few minutes while she stared out the back window into the darkness. Wow, she thought. Not good. Standing in the dark staring at nothing. Shaking her head at her own foolishness, she turned back toward the counter to pick up her tea. And nearly had a heart attack.

"For the love of God, Mason. Give a girl a warning if you're going to sneak up on her."

He shook his head. "I wasn't sneaking. You were lost in thought."

"Then clear your throat or trip over the cat or something. Geez. I think I lost five years of my life."

Mason was still in his trouser bottoms and his long-sleeve shirt, but he'd removed the tie and his shoes and socks and was standing barefoot in the kitchen. Emma's heart tripped over itself as she watched him lean back against the counter, his arms crossed.

"Why are you still up?" she asked.

But Mason gave no sign that he'd heard her. He just stood and looked at her, his gaze falling to her hair, draped loosely over her shoulders, down to her pajama bottoms and her feet, sticking out bare at the bottom. When his gaze returned to hers, there was fire in his eyes.

Emma recognized the look. Moving quickly around the kitchen island, she grabbed her tea as she did so, and stood defensively off to the side. She held her cup of tea in front of her in both hands, and looked at him cautiously over the rim.

"Emma," he said quietly, the fire in his eyes still burning as he moved around the island and stood in front of her, close, but not touching.

She closed her eyes. She honestly didn't know if she could take any more of this.

"Emma," he said softly. "I'll give you a divorce."

Her eyes flew open to meet his, which were still burning down into hers. She had a moment of pure relief, followed by the most searing, horrible emotional pain that she'd ever felt. She placed her tea, now forgotten, on the counter next to her, and clenched her arms around her waist.

"Why?" she managed to ask, kicking herself internally as she did so. She should be just accepting and running away from this conversation to go pack her bags. Why did it matter if he'd allow her to leave? But when she started to tell him that she'd be gone in the morning, she found herself again asking, "Why?" She needed to know. Needed to know if there was any hope here at all for her, or if she should run as far and as fast as she could.

"Does it matter?" he asked softly. "It's what you wanted."

"Yes. It matters. Is it because of the codicil?"

"No. You were right. This was never about the will, or the amended version."

"Then why?"

He turned away, but not before Emma saw the same pain she felt, reflected in his eyes. Reaching out, she grasped his arm and waited until he turned to face her. "Why, Mason?"

He sighed deeply. "Because if I don't let you go now, I won't be able to ever let you go," he admitted.

Dropping her arm, Emma just stared at him, confusion all over her face, but a tiny spark of hope igniting in her heart.

"I don't understand," she said at last. "You..."

"What is there to understand?" he asked, interrupting her with a harsh tone in his voice. "Just take it and go."

But Emma had seen the emotion in his eyes, before he'd shuttered them. Before he'd retreated behind his wall again.

"No," she said. Firmly this time. With no hesitation.

"Emma..."

"No. Not just no, but hell no." She stomped her bare foot in frustration. "Mason, for God's sake, talk to me. I need to know what you're thinking and feeling, because Lord knows I've never seen you feel real emotion before. But if you're feeling anything now, anything at all, you need to tell me. Or we might both turn our backs on the best damn thing that ever happened to either of us. So you tell me, Mason Parker, and don't you dare lie. Why did you change your mind, and why are you now in such a hurry to kick me out the door, when an hour ago you were holding to three years?"

"Empty years, Emma," he said with bitterness.

She looked at him as if he were crazy, but then her words to him kicked in, and she realized what he was talking about. Gently, she reached out and stroked his cheek with the back of her hand. "Not empty years, Mason," she said softly. "Empty marriage. The two are different. My last year with you hasn't been empty. It's been..."

She stopped, unsure how much she should reveal. This man could trample on her heart so easily...

Mason was looking at her intently.

She sighed. "Mason. Please. Tell me why you changed your mind."

His face, usually so devoid of emotion, showed doubt and fear and anguish, and Mason let her see it. He looked her in the eyes, reached up to smooth the hair away from her face, and said quietly, "You deserve more than me."

She stood, in her bare feet and her pajamas, her hair loose around her face, and waited for him to explain.

"Come," he said at last, his voice low and even, as he held out his hand for her. She looked up at him, completely unsure what was happening, but wanting to know, once and for all, what he was thinking. She placed her hand in his.

He led her into his study, and over to his couch, gently drawing her down next to him.

"Jen was right," he said quietly, looking her directly in the eye, still holding her hand in his. "The only reason I entered into an agreement with her was for my uncle's stock. I liked Jen, and figured that we could survive for a few years without killing each other. She'd get money, I'd get the stock, and we'd be done. And we'd probably be fairly good friends, by the end of it. If she had said no, I would have found another way to get it. But she said yes, and it simply made my life easier."

"But that doesn't make sense," Emma said, shaking her head. "Why the contract?"

"Two reasons. One, I was giving her a lot of money. I wanted the reason for it on paper so if she reneged on the deal, I'd get it back, and so there'd be no question, ever, as to why. Two, I wanted her to think twice about the arrangement - and to back out before she signed on, if she was going to. Once I put things in motion, I didn't want her pulling out of it."

"But she did."

"She did."

"So why..."

"Didn't I just ask for the money back and let it go?"

"Yes."

"You showed up at my door."

Emma nodded, expecting him to elaborate with some story about needing revenge or taking advantage of an opportunity, or...

But Mason knew she hadn't understood. "Emma, YOU showed up at my door."

She looked puzzled, and just shook her head slowly, her eyes still on his face. "Mason, I don't know what you mean."

"I took one look at you and knew I needed to have you. The contract was a perfect excuse."

Emma's eyes narrowed and she pulled her hand back from his touch. Turning on the couch to face him, she curled her feet up and wrapped her arms around her legs. She glared over the top of her knees at him. "You didn't think of just asking me out?"

"No."

She looked at him, her eyes steadily holding his. "Why not?"

"I don't have a great track record with women, Emma."

"Your mother and sister would say that you date the wrong women."

"I didn't want to take a chance that you'd say no. Or that I'd scare you away within the first week."

"Why did you think you would do that?"

"You said it often yourself - I don't show emotion."

She sighed, resting her chin on her right kneecap. "Well, you're right about that. But..."

"Emma, I needed time to show you who I am. And the only way I knew to do that was to bring you into my home."

She sat silently, watching him carefully, digesting his words. She still didn't know what they meant for her future, but she knew that opening up about his feelings was incredibly hard for him, and she would do whatever she could to help, even if it meant that he was telling her goodbye. She loved him. She could do no less. Telling herself to be careful, she sighed.

"OK. I almost get that," she said at last.

The corner of his mouth curved up slightly in a rueful half-smile. "Yeah. I figured you might."

Knowing that she might regret asking, but needing to know the truth, Emma said quietly, "What I don't get is why you slept with me. Once. And regretted it so completely that it never even came close to happening again."

She watched as his eyes darkened, and his hand reached out to thread his fingers into her hair, his thumb lightly stroking her cheek.

"That was a mistake," he said softly, curling his hand around her head to prevent her from pulling away at his words. "No, Emma," he continued, his thumb circling round to her lower lip. "Not that kind of a mistake. I don't regret making love to you. I've thought of nothing else for months. I've wanted nothing else for months."

"Then why?" she asked, her eyes filling.

He moved his hand to gently brush the tears from her eyes. "Because I'm a moron. Emma, I left in the night because I felt something I'd never felt before. With anyone. I've had sex with other women before, Emma, but this was different. I made love to you that night. And it was more intense, more amazing, more phenomenal than anything I'd ever felt before. With anyone. I felt a connection, Emma. And it scared the crap out of me."

"So why didn't you just talk to me about it the next day?"

"Like I said, I'm a moron. And I had no idea what to say to you. If I told you what I was feeling, I was afraid you'd run the other way."

Emma sighed. "How about, 'sorry for leaving, I'm a moron'?" she asked.

He chuckled, his thumb gently tracing the contours of her cheekbone.

She smiled slightly.

"Emma, I still want you. I want you every day, every time I'm with you. I see you with Chaos, or Max, or Malcolm or my mother, God help me, and I see this amazing woman. A woman who deals with life as it comes, and enjoys it. A woman who helps me be someone I want to be. And a woman that I promised I wouldn't touch again, unless I meant it. Emma, I mean it."

She closed her eyes then, feeling her tears trickle out and run down her cheek. Mason reached over then and pulled her onto his lap, his hand tenderly wiping the wetness away.

"Why are you crying?" he asked softly.

"You're divorcing me," she reminded him.

"No," Mason responded gently. "I'm offering to give you a divorce. There's a difference."

Her eyes flew open and locked on his.

His look was intense as he cupped her cheek in his hand and spoke quietly but firmly. "Listen to me, sweetheart. I do not want a divorce. If it were up to me, I'd tear up the damn contract and start from scratch. I want to stay married to you, Emma Jameson Parker. I want to have you in my bed every night. I want to have children with you. I want to walk the dog with you every night. I want to fight over who gets to have Max on our lap. I want to make sure that Malcolm has the chance to be a vet, if that's what he wants to be. I want to eat your cooking, roll my eyes at the mess you make in the kitchen, and laugh when my mother eats more of what you make than even I do."

He spun around then and deposited Emma back on the couch, kneeling down in front of her and grasping her hands in his. "Emma, I love you. I fought it for what seems like forever, because I didn't want to be the kind of husband to you that my father was to my mother. But I love you. Marry me. For real this time. Be my wife. Stay with me, Emma. Please."

She was still crying. He had blown it. She was going to say no, in a nice way of course, but she was going to walk out on him. Oh God, he thought. He didn't think his heart could take it. He felt Emma join him on the floor, her bare feet against his knees as she squatted down in front of him, holding her hands tightly wrapped around his.

"Mason, you idiot," she said softly, tears flowing down her face. "I love you. I've loved you since the day you ordered a t-bone steak at dinner, just so you could bribe my dog. I don't want a divorce from you."

Mason's heart filled, and relief overflowed into every bone in his body, but he was still unsure. "Then why were you so upset when I refused to give you one?"

"Because I didn't want us to stay together for business reasons. Or because it looked right to the rest of society. And, if you didn't love me and couldn't love me, I wanted out," she admitted. "I was getting in too deep, and I didn't think I'd survive if we stayed together for two more years and then divorced."

Standing up, Mason reached down and gently lifted Emma up into his arms. Encircling her in his embrace, he stood, his head resting on hers, his hands stroking her back as he caught his breath. After a moment, he pulled back, his hand reaching around to carefully wipe the remaining tears from her face.

"Then you'll marry me?" he asked.

"I'm already married to you," she hiccupped.

"Then you'll stay married to me?" he grinned.

"Yes. Yes, Mason," she said, holding him tightly and sobbing out her relief.

"Do you want a real wedding, Emma?" Mason asked tenderly. "I know I deprived you of that, and I'm sorry."

But Emma shook her head. "I had a real wedding, Mason. Complete with a ring that I love. I don't need more than that. A wedding now would seem strange to me."

"Then how about a honeymoon?" he asked with a smile.

"Now you're talking!" she smiled through her tears. "Can we take Chaos?"

Mason laughed. "No, we cannot take Chaos. He would feel neglected since I plan on focusing all my attention, every day, on you."

As if he knew he was being talked about, Chaos strolled into the room, his tail wagging as he looked at his two favorite people holding on to each other. He walked up to them, looked up, and barked.

Mason laughed as he reached down and scritched the dog behind the ears.

"Emma, you have changed me," he said softly as he looked her in the eyes from his kind of awkward position. "I never would have allowed a dog in the house. Or a cat."

"Or a wife?" she added.

He grinned. "That I asked for when I coerced you into marrying me. But I never expected anything other than someone to sleep with. I never expected to fall in love."

His expression turned serious. "Are you sure, Emma? I'm not an easy man."

"I'm sure. If you can bend enough to accept this motley crew, you can bend enough to deal with whatever life throws at us."

"I love you, Emma."

"And I love you. With all my heart."

EPILOGUE

"**Chaos**! Get back here! Oh for the love of God...." Emma traipsed after Chaos, who was scampering after a small furball on the back porch.

"Malcolm, what in the name of all that is holy is that crazy wife of mine doing?"

Malcolm looked up with a grin at the exasperated man standing next to him, watching his wife meander around the back yard. "I think she's trying to keep the dog from chasing the cat," he said, laughing.

"How can she chase anything? She's nine months pregnant, and moving about as fast as a turtle."

"I heard that!" came a response from behind one of the nearby bushes.

Mason grinned. "Emma, get your pretty little butt and your pretty super-sized belly back over here. I'll deal with Chaos."

Emma sighed and moved back over to the porch, lowering herself carefully onto one of the chairs and reaching for a glass of lemonade.

"It's your fault," she proclaimed wryly as she pushed a glass and the pitcher of cold lemonade toward Malcolm.

"Now what?" he asked.

"You brought home the new kitten. Where do you keep finding these animals, anyway? And don't tell me under a bush. I don't think we have this many bushes in the neighborhood."

He grinned, pouring himself a glass.

Emma looked over at him, her eyes narrowing in suspicion. "You're not gonna answer me, are you?"

Malcolm just laughed and changed the subject. "I just signed up for my classes for the fall," he told Emma.

"Oh yeah? What did you decide? Are you doing the business track or the science track?"

Mal shrugged. "I'm hedging my bets. Dad will freak if all I'm taking is math and science. So I've got a couple of other courses in there too to make him happy. And we'll see. I'm still a kid. Maybe I'll choose to do something completely different."

"Yeah? Like what?"

"I don't know. Maybe I'll run a hotel or something."

Emma rolled her eyes. "Oh, great idea. You can put a stray cat in every room. You can call it Animal Fur Inn. Just warn your guests beforehand in case any of them are allergic."

Malcolm looked over at Emma and rolled his eyes right back at her. "Oh ha," he said.

Emma leaned back, watching Mason and Chaos playing together in the yard while the now-abandoned cat was sitting on the back porch, grooming herself. Her hand rested lightly on her swollen belly as she contemplated her life. It was good, she thought. Since she was no longer able to do much cooking, Dorothy had insisted on joining them for dinner frequently, bringing with her a fridge-full of catered meals for her son and daughter-in-law to enjoy. Malcolm's parents were out of town, so he and Michelle were frequent guests, and Emma laughed watching Dorothy and Malcolm forming a friendship. Even Amanda and Greg joined them when they could, and Emma was waiting patiently for them to announce their engagement. She hoped they weren't waiting until the baby was born - this family could deal with more than one joyful event at a time.

Her own family was ecstatic with the news of Emma's pregnancy. Her grandmother was going to craft fairs and buying knitted booties, telling Emma that she didn't have the patience to knit, but she wanted her great-grandchild to have homemade stuff. Emma responded by telling her that her great-grandchild needed homemade STUFFING some day, but the old lady just shrugged and sipped her martini. Her parents had long forgiven Mason for eloping with their daughter, and had welcomed him whole-heartedly to the family. And Jen...

"I told you so," she said with a grin.

"I know you did. I just didn't believe you."

"That's because you didn't believe that anyone could fall in love with you at first sight."

"I still don't. It took more than sight. It took me standing up for you, you idiot."

"Yeah, so you have me to thank," Jen shrugged good-naturedly.

Emma laughed. "Yeah, I guess I do."

"So you'll name your kid after me?"

"Oh, hell no. But you can babysit. Occasionally. If Malcolm is around to keep tabs on you."

Jen grinned. "I love you, Em."

"I love you too."

"Still mad?"

"Nah. I'm finally over it."

Mason looked over at his wife and smiled a smile of contentment. His father no longer played any part in his thinking - Emma had shown him how different their marriage could be, and how different Mason himself was from his father. And he knew that he was, deep in his heart. He was happy. He wasn't sure his father had ever been happy.

Leaving Chaos chewing on a stick, Mason walked over and leaned over to kiss his wife. As he did so, he watched her pull away from him with a grimace.

"What? Did I forget to brush my teeth?" he asked.

But the look on Emma's face was unlike anything he'd seen before - a mixture of wonder, fear, and a lot of love. "Mason... I think..."

"What?"

"I think our baby is about ready to join the world," she said softly.

"Whoa, I'm out of here!" Malcolm stood up suddenly, knocking his chair over.

"Oh come on," Emma teased. "If you're gonna be a vet, you're gonna need to learn all about delivering little ones."

"Oh no I don't," Malcolm said. "I'm gone." Stopping, he fixed Mason with a stern glance. "You call me when you know anything," he ordered.

"Yes sir," Mason laughed. "But I think it will be a while yet. She just started."

"No she didn't. She's been having those things all afternoon. Ask her."

"Emma?"

"Well, a few," she admitted.

"How far apart?" Mason demanded.

"Oh, about every ten minutes or so."

"What???"

"Relax. The hospital is right down the street."

"Yeah, but you need to build in time for me to run around in a panic, for heaven's sake. Come on. We need to call your doctor, get you to the hospital, get your suitcase, call our families..."

Emma laughed. "Mason, I'm fine. The suitcase is in the car, I called the doctor earlier, and we've got time to call our families once we get to the hospital."

"Then what are you waiting for?"

She grinned up at him. "I'm going to sit here for ten more minutes until the next contraction has passed. Can you crate Chaos and make sure that the animals are all inside?"

"I'll do that," Malcolm said seriously. "You guys go."

"You sure?"

"OH yeah. I do not want to see this baby born. I'm happy to deal with the animals. Go."

Laughing, Emma started to stand, and Mason rushed over to help her. "You ready for this?" she asked.

"More than ready," he responded. "I love you, Emma Parker. And I'm going to love that kid of ours. How about you? You ready?"

"Yeah, I'm ready. Ignore what I scream at you in the delivery room, OK? I love you. And I will forever."

"OK. Let's go usher our little one into the world. You get first dibs on counting fingers and toes."

"Well, I should hope so," she groused. "Since I'm the one who is doing all the work."

Mason laughed. "Emma, you are amazing. In case I forget to tell you later."

She grinned. "You won't forget."

And he didn't.

ABOUT THE AUTHOR

Elizabeth Powers has been writing since she was a child, mostly because she couldn't imagine *not* writing. She models the animals in her stories after her own furry household members, and she and her husband live with their own version of Chaos, as well as another dog (watch for her next book!), and two cats in upstate New York.

Printed in Great Britain
by Amazon.co.uk, Ltd.,
Marston Gate.